TONY TUCCI

First Edition – August 2017

Library of Congress Control Number: 2016910758
© John Granville Leonard III

ISBN: 978-0692438213
ISBN-10: 0692438211

Available from Amazon.com and other bookstores
Available on Kindle and affiliated online stores

Misc. Photos via iStock.com

See the complete
Cast of Characters
at back of book.

"In thy face, I see
the map of honor,
truth and loyalty."

– William Shakespeare

MONDAY

1

Beneath a moonlit sky, a beat-up Econovan, retrofitted with a jacked-up suspension and all-terrain tires, roared north along an ancient riverbed towards the Texas border.

Inside the dusty cab, Carlos and Mateo, two soldiers from Mexico's infamous Juárez Cartel, peered intently through the dusty windshield at the Chihuahua Desert. Gang tattoos covered their thick arms and beefy necks. Machine guns rested on their laps. Extra gun magazines and a half-empty six-pack of bottled beer lay on the floor between them.

Mateo, in the passenger's seat, grabbed a brew, popped off the top with his stainless-steel-capped front teeth and drained it in a single swig. He tossed the bottle out the window, smirking at the sound of shattering glass.

In the back of the windowless van, ten men huddled in the blackness, bumping and banging against each other as the van lurched along the rocky road. They had each paid a small fortune to the cartel to smuggle them into America, the promised land of hope, prosperity, and free shit. They were close to the

1

end of their long journey, and God willing, new lives awaited them.

The bouncing headlights revealed a scorched and unforgiving landscape. Scrawny patches of creosote and prickly pear poked up around the boulders lining the rough road. A few mangy pronghorn bucks scampered up a rocky slope to avoid the fishtailing van as it careened down a dry ravine toward the transfer spot a few miles away—just on the other side of the U.S. border.

The tepid beer did little to calm the smugglers' nerves. Over the last several months, U.S. border security had increased substantially, complicating their every move. There were more random patrols, motion sensors, and video cameras hidden along the most-traveled coyote routes—and unmanned drones hovered above.

As Carlos negotiated a particularly nasty stretch of the cratered, rock-strewn road, Mateo stuck his head out the window to scan the sky. High above, he thought he saw a blinking light moving through the thin clouds in the late November sky. He quickly ducked back inside the cab.

"Fuck!"

"What?" asked Carlos in Spanish.

"I saw a flashing light! There's a drone up there!"

"Idiot! Drones are too small to be seen at night. Just relax!"

After a few minutes, the nervous Mateo looked out his window again in search of the UFO, but saw nothing. He reached for another beer, but Carlos knocked his hand away.

"Not now! Check in the back."

Mateo grabbed a flashlight and slid open the small window on the back-wall panel. The light played across the drawn, desperate faces shimmering in the darkness. He closed the window.

"Everything is okay."

Undetected by U.S. surveillance, the van continued its trek until Carlos spotted a large barrel cactus that marked the side road up to the plateau. The van raced up the embankment and ripped across the arid plain. About two hundred yards ahead, half-hidden in a thick bramble of decaying cholla, a pick-up truck flashed its headlights twice. Carlos cut off the van's lights and rolled to a stop about ten yards from the truck. Dust kicked up by the van swirled like smoke in the pick-up's halogen headlights. Carlos and Mateo grabbed their weapons, jumped out of the van, and walked toward the truck.

"Hello, my friends!" Mateo said, shouldering his AK-47.

Squinting, Carlos raised his hand to block the glare of the bright lights. He saw the silhouettes of two men step out of the camouflaged truck, both wearing headscarves to partially cover their faces. The men raised semi-automatic handguns equipped with silencers and shot twice.

Thump-thump. Thump-thump.

Carlos and Mateo crumpled to the desert floor, clutching at gaping chest wounds. With their guns still pointed at their victims, the assassins slowly walked over to the bodies and delivered two *coup de grâce* headshots into the writhing cartel members.

Blood ran black in the moonlight.

Silently, the assassins went to work. One grabbed a gas can and rag from the pick-up. The other produced a flashlight and walked to the rear of the van. He pulled open the doors, releasing the stench of human sweat and body odor into the cool night air. Recoiling at the smell, he swept the beam of the flashlight around the inside of the van. The stowaways were a rather eclectic bunch. Some wore filthy t-shirts, jeans, and baseball caps; others were cloaked in drab serapes. They all looked frightened, parched, and weary.

"Allahu," the assassin said.

No one said a word…

"Allahu!" he repeated loudly.

Two men with hoods over their heads stirred in the back. Each one whispered, "Akbar."

The assassin carefully studied their faces with the flashlight. In Arabic, he said, "You two. Get out!"

The men crawled past the others and exited the van.

A young Mexican sitting near the open doors asked in broken English, "What's happening?"

The assassin responded by slamming the van doors closed in his face. Next, he wrapped a metal chain around the door handles and locked it tight with a padlock. The other assassin was busy dousing gasoline over the hood, inside the cab, and on both sides of the vehicle. Then he soaked the rag and shoved it into the gas tank. He lit the rag on fire and tossed the burning matchbook onto the front seat. Flames quickly spread across the dashboard, upholstery, and surface of the van, licking into every nook and cranny. The men trapped in the van started to choke and gag as smoke filled the rear compartment. There was a panicked chorus of muffled yelling as hands pounded and feet kicked against the walls and doors of the quaking van.

The assassins and smuggled men hustled past the bodies of Carlos and Mateo. Thirty yards further on, they passed two other cartel members who lay gagged and bound in a ditch. Both had been executed with pistol shots to the backs of their heads.

The four men ran down a small bluff and climbed into a waiting SUV—just as the van's gas tank exploded into a huge fireball.

As the SUV vanished into a large swath of scrub brush, screams from the burning van echoed into the night

TUESDAY

2

Gold Coast
Long Island, New York
5:00 p.m.

Tony Tucci turned the new black Mercedes limo onto the main road in North Hampstead, one of the wealthiest and most historic enclaves in the world. The coastal community in Nassau County, on the North Shore of Long Island Sound, was once the playground of America's high society. In the early 1900s, the Vanderbilts, Cornwells, and Guggenheims built lavish, castle-like mansions with spectacular gardens along this hallowed stretch, which was also the backdrop for F. Scott Fitzgerald's *The Great Gatsby*.

Over the years, the area attracted legendary publishers, composers, entertainers, and a handful of infamous Mafia families, but now its residents were mostly "the nouveau riche": Wall Street hedge-fund managers, high-tech entrepreneurs, and professional athletes. The area was saturated with multi-million-dollar McMansions and quaint commercial enterprises, but it still carried its old patina of grand opulence and wealth. The limo would have seemed pretentious on most streets in America, but along the storied Gold Coast, no one noticed.

Tony, a world-weary man in his early sixties, was heading to the northern tip of Sands Point after running a few errands. Driving safely under the speed limit, he turned up the volume on the satellite radio to listen to a report about precious metals. He smiled when he heard some financial "experts" were predicting another drop in the price of gold.

"Time to buy," Tony told himself.

As the limo headed north through town, the setting sun cast a golden glow on the hamlet's buildings and lush foliage. Tony had lived in the relaxed ambience of Sands Point for almost two decades. He always went out of his way to be friendly to others in the upscale community; however, like all men with a dark past, Tony maintained a certain distance from most people.

The limo eased up to a four-way intersection. Across the street was a weed-covered lot with a dense copse of oaks. The trees had lost their leaves, revealing a large dilapidated billboard farther back in the woods—which stirred in Tony a half-forgotten memory. For a fleeting moment, he imagined the enormous eyes of Dr. T.J. Eckleburg from Fitzgerald's classic novel staring down at him. He remembered his high school English teacher saying the depiction of the optometrist represented "the eyes of God."

Now, over fifty years later, that divine symbolism was not lost on Tony. Legions of corrupt and treacherous men had traveled along this very same route to pay tribute to, and take their orders from, the man who lived at the end of the road—Don Mario Conti.

Tony was one of them.

He felt the doctor's eyes pierce and probe into his soul until his past was laid bare. A cold wave of repressed shame and guilt washed over him. Grimacing at the dull, throbbing pain in his crippled right leg, he willed the light to change. When it did, he floored the accelerator.

After a series of turns down quiet, well-manicured roads, the limo arrived at a dead end. Tony drove onto the expansive, private cobblestone driveway and up to the gatehouse beside the wrought iron gate. "Conti" was inscribed over the towering ivy-covered archway, flanked by ten-foot-tall rock walls that stretched around the sprawling property, eventually disappearing into Long Island Sound.

Enzo Colombo, the portly old guard, leaned out of the gatehouse window just as the limo pulled to a stop.

The driver's window lowered slowly. Dressed in a dark gabardine wool suit with a red silk tie and U.S. flag pin in his lapel, Tony had silver-tinged black hair and warm but penetrating blue eyes.

"Hey, Tony," Enzo said, his words slightly slurred. "What are you up to?"

"Not much."

Tony held up a small pharmacy bag. "Just picked up some meds for Mr. Conti."

"How's the old man doing? He hasn't left the house in weeks."

Tony measured his words carefully. "He's tired a lot, but still in good spirits."

Although they were not particularly close, Tony and Enzo had known each other for a long time.

Back in the 1980s, Enzo suffered a fractured skull during a robbery at one of the family's strip joints when two punks tried to steal a large stash of cocaine from the back office. A vicious blow from a tire iron reduced Enzo's already borderline IQ by another ten points. Acknowledging the man's sacrifice, Don Mario made Enzo the estate gatekeeper for life.

Wearing a thick cardigan sweater and tweed golf hat, Enzo came across as an affable chap—notwithstanding the loaded Beretta shotgun resting right under the window.

The scent of freshly brewed coffee drifted out of the stone gatehouse. Tony knew Enzo had an espresso machine and jars of chocolate-coated biscotti inside.

When he wasn't manning the front gate, Enzo was at Belmont Park or Aqueduct playing the horses. He spent his work hours reading the racing form, smoking cheap cigars, and muttering to himself. Despite his diminished mental capacity, he took great pride in his betting system, which against all odds often provided some decent paydays.

To stroke Enzo's rather fragile ego, Tony always made a point of asking him about his luck at the track to let him gloat about his latest big score.

"How are the ponies treating you these days, Enzo?"

Enzo beamed. "I made two grand last week at Aqueduct on a twenty-to-one filly."

"Excellent! But don't forget to pay your taxes."

"Yeah, right." Enzo snickered as he peered down onto the front seat of the limo. In addition to Tony's elegant cane, he saw an iPad and the *Wall Street Journal* on the passenger seat.

"Are you still playing the stock market, Tony?"

"Keeps me busy."

Enzo lowered his voice to a whisper. "My wife's cousin, some Wall Street jamook, handles our savings. I don't know shit about investing, but I'm pretty sure that he's fucking us over with a bunch of extra fees. Would you mind taking a look at our stuff some time?"

"Of course. Just get your paperwork together and we'll sit down."

"Thanks, Tony. I really appreciate it."

Enzo pressed the button to open the heavy gate and the limo glided along the winding driveway toward the main house.

The Conti Estate covered more than thirty acres of sculptured gardens and groves of pine and fir. Rock bridges spanned man-made streams. Walking paths meandered through secluded meadows and along the half-mile private beach. Some of the other amenities included a tennis court, stables, croquet field, swimming pool, and cottages. The imposing Conti mansion was a 15,000-square-foot red-brick edifice with ten bedrooms, twelve baths, plus a detached eight-car garage.

After passing a huge fountain imported from Italy in the circular driveway, Tony parked the limo by the front porch, behind a red Ferrari Italia and a black Escalade.

Stiff and in pain, both constant companions most days, Tony emerged from the limo with his cane in hand and limped around the house to the servant's entrance in the rear.

3

The rich aroma of Italian cooking engulfed Tony as he entered the bustling kitchen. The room was filled with gleaming stainless steel cabinets and counter tops, commercial-size gas stoves and ovens, and a cadre of busy cooks. Garlic and olive oil simmered in frying pans. Organic vegetables drained in multiple sinks. Fresh-baked bread was pulled from ovens. And ribbons of homemade pasta were meticulously laid out on cutting boards next to boiling pots of water.

The gregarious head chef, Ciro Manza, dismembered a plump chicken with a meat cleaver. When he saw Tony, he bellowed, "Buonasera, Mr. Tucci!"

"Good evening, everyone," Tony said. The staff nodded and smiled without missing a beat.

Ciro had been the Conti chef for about five years. He was a partner at a prestigious culinary academy in the City, wrote articles about Italian cuisine, and had published a best-selling cookbook. Beneath a mop of curly black hair and red jowls, his spotless white chef's coat bulged like a overstuffed cannoli, straining to contain his 300-pound girth. For a man of immense size, he moved delicately around the kitchen, barking instructions at his assistants as they chopped, diced, and stirred.

With a large walk-in refrigerator and well-stocked pantry, Ciro could whip up practically any five-star entree in a matter of minutes.

"We're having a feast! Want something to eat?" the merry chef's voice boomed as he hoisted a goblet of red wine.

"No thanks, Ciro," Tony said, "but it sure smells good."

Chef Ciro tore off a piece of Italian flatbread, dabbing it into a frying pan. "Pane e aglio, vita mia!"

Tony's Italian was a little rusty, but he recognized the old proverb, which translated to: "Bread and garlic, my life!"

Tony walked over to a maid fussing with a vase of long-stem roses and handed her the pharmacy bag. "This is for Mr. Conti."

She took it and quickly left the kitchen.

Tony glanced into the employee dining room and saw three men eating. He knew Gino "The Juice" Marino and Al "The Frog" Franchetti, who both worked for Dante, the Don's eldest son, but the third man, younger than his dining companions, was a stranger.

As Tony entered, Gino looked up. "How ya doin', Tony? Gonna join us?"

"Not tonight, guys." He hadn't had a meal with Gino or Al in years—nor did he want to.

Gino sucked up a noodle from a heaping bowl of linguine and steamed clams. "Sure? This pasta is fuckin' delicious."

"Yeah," Al said as he dumped salt over his food. "You oughta grab a bowl."

Both Gino and Al were long-time soldiers and "made" men in the Conti family. The two were inseparable and Dante's most trusted associates.

Heavily muscled, with a shaved head and acne scars, Gino was the most intimidating member of Dante's current crew. His long-term abuse of anabolic steroids contributed to his legendary mood swings and insane fits of rage. There were many stories about Gino's disturbing out-of-control behavior. From bar brawls to random incidents of road rage and petty acts of revenge, "The Juice" always seemed to be on the edge, ready to snap. He had spent a year in Kings County jail for head-butting an off-duty cop who made the mistake of looking at him sideways, and almost decapitated a prostitute with his bare hands after she made fun of his drug-shriveled package. Anger management was not his strongest suit, but Gino was street smart, brutally efficient in his duties, and unflinchingly loyal—the perfect Mafia capo.

Al was about five years younger and almost as scary. He never questioned an order from his boss and relished the required wet work of a true enforcer. With a fat gut hanging over his belt like a fleshy glacier, slicked-back black hair, and bulging eyes, Al looked like a bullfrog. After a few drinks, he was famous for making his eyes move in different directions at the same time. "The Frog" brought down the house with that creepy trick every time.

"I appreciate the offer, guys," Tony said, "but I have to drive Angela to the City. Then I'm going to Mancini's for a late dinner. I've been craving their veal scaloppini."

Gino and Al exchanged an odd look and then quickly turned back to their food.

"Mancini is a good guy," Al croaked.

"Yeah, give him our best," Gino added coldly.

"Sure" Tony said, now sizing up the stranger—a chiseled young stud with a crew cut and thousand-yard stare. "Who's the new guy?"

Gesturing with his meaty paw, Gino said, "This is Frank Salvadore, a friend of ours from Philly. He's helping us with a little project."

Tony offered his hand, and they shook. "Tony Tucci. Nice to meet you."

Frank had an awed look on his face. "You're *the* Tony 'Two Triggers' Tucci?"

"That was a long time ago." Tony shrugged and turned back to Gino. "So—what's the project?"

Suddenly, the air in the room grew frosty.

Gino shoved a hunk of bread into his mouth. "You'll have to ask Dante."

That wouldn't happen. Tony was not, and never would be, part of Dante's inner circle. There was too much bad blood between the two. Besides, Tony was not a made man in the Conti family, meaning he had never carried out a contract killing. Although he was a close confidant of the Don and a former major player in his gambling empire, Tony never really fit in with the other guys because he was regarded as too softhearted and cerebral, and never carried a gun.

In the early years, Tony had witnessed numerous beatings doled out to degenerate gamblers who refused to cover their bets. Those "tune-ups" always turned Tony's stomach, but at the time, he rationalized the actions based upon the unwritten code of the streets: *If you gambled and lost, you paid—one way or another.*

Regardless, before some poor schmuck got the crap beaten out of him, Tony often tried to intercede to buy more time or arrange for a payment plan. It rarely made a difference and the deadbeat gambler usually got a vicious ass-kicking from Conti family thugs like Gino and Al, who actually enjoyed using a ball-peen hammer on the loser's kneecaps.

"By the way, I hear the old man wants to see ya," Gino said.

"Well, enjoy your dinner, gentlemen," Tony replied and hobbled out of the room.

The three men continued to eat until Frank asked, "So what's the real story behind the 'Two Triggers' legend?"

Gino wiped his mouth with a white cloth napkin.

"About twenty years ago, the Conti family controlled a big hunk of the gambling in the City until some other wise guys decided to muscle in on the action. They sent three hitmen to whack Don Mario down in Little Italy—but Tony screwed up the whole thing. Somehow, he grabbed two pistols and charged right at the assassins—firing both guns like a mad man. Bullets were flying everywhere!"

Gino took a gulp of wine. "Tony was able to kill all of them, but he got nailed four fuckin' times and his right leg was almost blown off by a shotgun blast. Some dumb pedestrian also got cut down in the crossfire... It was a blood bath."

"Fuckin' A," Frank said.

"Tony spent over a year in the hospital. He lost a kidney, got toxic shock from all the lead in his body, and had a bunch of operations to repair his leg. Then he had to learn to walk again. He was really messed up for a long time."

"And can you believe it?" said Al. "The Don didn't even get a scratch."

They ate in silence for a while.

"Before the assassination attempt, Tony handled the finances for the family's gambling operation. I guess he's some kind of math whiz," Gino said, finishing his pasta. "But by the time he was able to come back to work, the old man, who was pretty shaken up about the whole thing, decided to move all his eggs into construction. Tony helped build the business, but when Dante took over about seven years ago, Tony was put out to pasture."

"And now, he's just the family driver," Al said, licking sauce off his huge lips.

Gino leaned close to Frank and whispered, "By the way, no one calls him 'Two Triggers' anymore. Now, he's just known as 'The Gimp.'"

Gino punched Frank in the arm, and they all roared with laughter.

4

Tony walked through the formal dining room and into the palatial foyer. With its tall dome ceiling, stained glass windows, and marble floor, it had the feel of a mini-cathedral. Several large oil paintings hung on the walls, framing the sweeping staircase leading to the second floor.

Tony went directly to the closed library door on the west side of the foyer. As he raised his hand to knock, he overheard a heated exchange between Mario and Dante raging inside. He paused momentarily to listen.

"Forget it!" Mario snapped in a hoarse voice.

"But I'm telling you, we can make millions on this deal," Dante bragged.

"I don't care! It could backfire and bring a lot of heat!"

At that moment, Tony sensed the presence of someone and turned to see Carla Conti, the Don's beautiful wife, standing in the doorway of the living room. Holding a tumbler of scotch, she asked, "Can I speak with you, Tony?"

"Of course, Carla."

Tony followed her through an arched doorway that opened into the spacious living room with a wall of floor-to-ceiling windows overlooking the Sound. The tastefully decorated room was filled with elegant antique furniture and oriental rugs.

Carla stood beside a white grand piano with her arms folded. Two decades younger than the Don, she was a striking woman in her late fifties, with tinted auburn hair and an attractive figure. With an unlimited wardrobe budget, Carla always dressed exquisitely. Tonight, she wore an elegant burgundy Dior pantsuit accented with a canary yellow scarf.

"Mario and Dante are fighting again, aren't they?" she said flatly. It was more of a statement than a question.

"Sounds like it."

Carla shook her head. "I guess things never change. Dante has always been so damn defiant and headstrong. Did you know he was a breech baby?"

"Obstinate since 'Day One,'" Tony replied.

They both smiled knowingly.

"Did you hear?" Carla asked. "Maria just had Dante served with divorce papers. She wants a big hunk of money, their house in West Islip, and full custody of the kids. He's furious about it… Frankly, I think it's enough to push him over the edge."

Tony was adamant. "He should never have hit her."

"Especially in front of my grandchildren, for Christ's sake," Carla said, unable to hide her disgust.

She took a hearty drink. "Well, onto more pleasant things… I understand you're driving Angela into the City to see her mysterious new boyfriend."

"That's the plan."

"Have you met him yet?"

Tony shook his head.

"I'm curious about him, but Angela won't tell me a thing. She said they met about two months ago. All I know is he's a surgical resident at Manhattan Medical Center."

"Must be smart."

"We'll find out on Thursday. I insisted she bring him to Thanksgiving Dinner."

She finished her drink. "You know, Angela is no slouch either. Yesterday she got her acceptance into that Master's program in child psychology at Cornell. She starts in January."

"That's fantastic! She earned it."

His smartphone buzzed in his pocket, and he checked the screen.

"Looks like you have a call," Carla said.

"No, it's just a stock alert."

"Isn't the exchange closed?"

"Ours is, but the Asian exchanges open in a few hours and that Middle East crisis is affecting all the world markets," Tony said matter-of-factly. "Like they say: money never sleeps. What happens in Hong Kong and Japan can have a substantial impact here. And I don't like surprises."

Carla moved closer. "You really are serious about this day trading, aren't you?"

"Drivers have a lot of free time."

"And how's the market treating you?"

"Not bad," he said sheepishly. "It's been a little dicey this year, but I'm up over twenty percent year-to-date."

Carla laid her hand on his arm and flirted playfully. "Tell me, Mr. Buffett, what's your secret?"

"Nothing special. I just do my homework. You know, study the financial statements and charts, watch the insider trading lists, and use a little common sense."

"But you have to have a little luck too, right?"

"I don't believe in luck."

"Maybe Mario should let you handle *our* finances."

Tony let out a nervous laugh. "I'll stick with my day job."

Carla turned serious. "How's everything else going, Tony? You doing okay?"

"No complaints," Tony said, even though his bad leg was on fire.

She patted his arm gently. "Just take care of yourself. I don't know what we would do without you."

He looked into her eyes. They had a special relationship based on a long history and mutual respect. Carla was only in her early twenties when she met and fell in love with the handsome young Mario, who at the age of forty, was already a powerful player in the New York families. Over their long marriage, she had been a devoted and caring wife, bearing the Don three children: Dante, Giovanni, and Angela. Until the time of the failed hit on Mario, Tony and Carla were mere acquaintances. Since then, they had become close friends, but it ended there. Despite a certain light-hearted sexual attraction between them, they both loved Mario and would never cross that dangerous line.

Carla pulled away, shaking the ice cubes in her empty glass. "Well, I need a refill."

As he watched Carla sashay across the room towards the bar, he worried about her. She was a strong woman, but over the last several years she had turned into somewhat of a lush. Maybe it was all the difficult years of being a Mafia wife and mother. Dante alone was enough to drive anyone to drink. His reckless behavior and barbaric acts had damaged everyone in the family. Her second son Giovanni, known as Johnnie, was doing five years at a federal penitentiary in Kentucky for drug trafficking—another Dante scheme gone awry. And now Mario was in failing health. Carla was shouldering a heavy load, but she still managed to project a positive and upbeat attitude.

She refilled her glass and turned to face Tony. "If you meet Angela's boyfriend, I want a full report."

"Of course."

She playfully wagged her finger at him. "And I'll see you at Thanksgiving dinner too. Seven o'clock sharp. Okay?"

"Looking forward to it," he said, watching her exit the room.

5

A moment later, Tony stood before the library door again, preparing to knock. The heated conversation between Mario and Dante raged on.

"For the last time, no!" Mario yelled.

"Well, I'm still gonna take the meeting."

"The hell you are!"

Tony knocked.

"Come in," Mario said.

Tony entered the warmly lit room. Like the rest of the mansion, it featured traditional architecture with a high ceiling, mahogany bookcases filled with old tomes, and dark hardwood floors. Across from the bay windows, an entire wall was covered with an antique gun collection.

The focal point of the room was a large marble-faced fireplace. Above the mantle, cluttered with family photos and other memorabilia, were crossed swords dating back to the Crusades. Two throne-like armchairs faced the fireplace. Don Mario Conti, a feeble-looking man in his late seventies wearing a silk robe, pajamas, and slippers, leaned out of his chair to greet his guest.

"Tony! Good to see you."

Dante Conti came straight from Central Casting for a low-budget mob flick. Wearing a double-breasted suit, white shirt with an open collar, and large gold cross on a chain around his neck, the thirty-six-year-old Conti heir stood beside the fireplace smoking a cigarette. Like an active volcano, Dante was always on the verge of a violent eruption, ready to spew obscenities, racial slurs, and sarcastic comments.

Still flushed with anger from his argument with his father, Dante glared at Tony as if he was the problem. He took a long drag and flicked the butt into the fire.

"I gotta run," he said, brushing by Tony without another look.

The door slammed shut behind him.

Mario pointed to the rolling table bar topped with amber-colored bottles and a silver ice bucket. "Want a cognac?"

"No thanks," Tony replied. "I have to drive Angela to the City."

"I respect that." Mario said, raising his glass. "So… did you overhear our little disagreement?"

"It was hard to miss."

Tony bent down to pet Buddy, the wolfhound at Mario's feet. Buddy's tail wagged at his touch.

"I just don't get it," Mario said. "Our construction business is completely legit. And booming! All Dante has to do is oversee the day-to-day operations and collect our kickbacks from the subcontractors. We're living on Easy Street, but he's still not satisfied!"

Tony walked over to the bar. "What's the problem now?" he asked, pouring a club soda over ice.

"My son still wants to be a mobster. That's what!"

The old man was flustered. Tony could see from Mario's patchy red face that his blood pressure was rising.

"When he's not out carousing and gambling, he's planning his next big scheme. Last year it was that money laundering thing and then the mortgage scam. I thought his new nightclub project was going to keep him occupied, but now he wants to sell missiles or some shit to a fuckin' Mexican drug cartel. Can you believe it?"

"What kind of missiles?" asked Tony as he refilled Mario's glass with Hennessey XO.

"I don't know, but it could put us in jeopardy with the Feds." Mario took a long pull on his drink. "That's one of the reasons I wanted to see you, Tony. I know you're not part of Dante's crew and you guys have a lousy relationship, but I need you to keep your eyes and ears open to find out what's going on. Come to me with any information. Okay?"

Tony shrugged. "Dante won't have it. He freezes me out of everything. And Gino and Al know to keep me at a distance."

"Just do the best you can, Tony. Okay?"

Tony took a sip of his soda water and nodded reluctantly.

Through the library's windows he saw the taillights of two vehicles—Dante's Ferrari, followed by the Escalade with Gino and the boys—weaving through the estate toward the main road. The night was young and they were just going to work.

Tony guessed they were heading to the old Meat-Packing District on the west side of Manhattan, where Dante was putting the final touches on another one of his projects: a swanky, new nightclub called Inferno. Mario knew his son was involved with some kind of trendy bar in the City, but he had no idea of the enormous scope of the project.

Tony had made it his business to learn—quietly— as much about Dante's activities as possible. From the sporadic drug deals and cruel extortions to the luxury car hijackings and routine robberies, Dante and his crew were always looking to make a fast buck. If the ailing Mario knew all the details about his son's on-going illegal activities, he would have a coronary.

Mario turned his attention to the fire. "For once, I wish Dante would listen to me. After seventy-eight years on this planet, I've learned a few things."

Tony said, "Like the old saying goes: Growing old is inevitable; growing up is optional."

Mario's laughter erupted into a coughing fit.

"Need some water?"

"No, no," Mario said as he tried to clear the persistent phlegm in his throat. "It'll pass."

Waiting for Mario to regain his composure, Tony glanced around the library. Always warm and comfortable, it was Tony's favorite room in the house. In the wake of the assassination attempt, he and Mario had spent many hours there, discussing life, business, and books.

Maybe it was their advancing age and life experience, but both men were drawn to history. Sipping cognac in front of the fire, they engaged in deep discussions on the nature of good and evil, power and politics. They read the works of great Greek philosophers and the biographies of the visionaries and villains who had changed the course of mankind: Alexander, Jesus, Genghis Khan, Muhammad, Churchill, Hitler, Stalin, and Mao.

Regrettably, over the last few years, their frank and in-depth talks had waned in the face of Mario's deteriorating health and Dante's escalating criminal activities. Instead of debating man's motivations for power and conquest or the great battles that shaped world history, they spent their time together trying to figure out ways to save Dante from himself.

Tony cared deeply for the Don, but he was tired of Dante's antics and secretly wished he would be convicted of something and sent away for a long time.

"There's something else," Mario said.

He pulled a piece of folded paper from the pocket of his robe and stared at it. "Yesterday I got a call from Enrico Ferro. Remember him?"

"He was with the Bruno Brothers, right?"

Mario nodded. "I always suspected Nicky and Benny Bruno were behind that hit on me, but I couldn't prove it. Now, Ferro is dying of cancer and he wants to confess all his sins. He swore to me the Bruno brothers planned the hit, hired those killers, and provided the guns and getaway car."

Tony slowly sat down in the other armchair facing the fireplace and leaned his cane against the armrest.

"Benny's dead," Mario said, "but Nicky 'The Runt' still lives in the City."

For the next minute, they both stared at the flames.

Finally, Mario said, "If I had known about this years ago, I would have whacked both of them, but now I'm too old to want revenge—just for myself."

He leaned closer to Tony. "But that little bastard Nicky is responsible for crippling you. You lost everything trying to protect me. Your young wife, your mobility, your ..."

As his voice trailed off, his eyes turned icy cold.

"Just say the word and that animal will disappear. A couple trash bags in the Hudson. Gino and Al can take care of it." Mario took another gulp and added, "Or you can kill Nicky yourself if it makes you feel better. Either way, you have my blessing."

Tony said nothing. Immediately after the shooting, he had an intense curiosity about who was responsible for the attempted murder, but there was so little to go on and he was in too much pain to dwell on it.

Ironically, in that fateful hail of gunfire, Tony himself snuffed out any chance to learn more details about who was behind the attack. The three dead men were freelance hired guns imported from Miami. They all had long rap sheets for aggravated assault, robbery, and murder.

At the time, thanks to Tony's creative management skills, the Conti's gambling empire was the biggest and most profitable in the City—a very juicy target, ripe for the taking. It was obvious someone in the New York underworld hired the assassins and there were plenty of suspects.

As Tony's horrific wounds healed and the years wore on, his personal desire to expose the perpetrators of the plot and exact revenge began to fade.

The assassination attempt had shaken Mario to his very core. With a beautiful wife and three children, his priorities suddenly changed. Since Tony faced a long and challenging recovery, Mario didn't have anyone else in his organization smart and loyal enough to oversee the daily gambling operations, so he agreed to sell his assets to two other families in exchange for a lump-sum payment of $50 million, plus a ten percent piece of the action over the next decade. He used the substantial proceeds to dramatically expand the family's fledgling construction business.

Tony helped Mario transform the company from a mid-sized concrete contractor into a multi-faceted regional enterprise encompassing road construction, freeway landscaping, and building demolition. Leonardo Scarpia, a tough, no-nonsense construction manager, supervised the day-to-day operations.

Over the next ten years, Tony and Leo had the perfect marriage: Leo ran the crews and equipment while Tony played the political games and crunched the numbers. Conti Construction won many lucrative contracts based on Tony's ability to carefully craft bids to undercut the competition using volume buying and a lean, flexible group of subcontractors.

It was understood each subcontractor would kick back five percent of their profit to the Conti family—a reasonable amount that still left them with a good profit and the desire to keep working for the company. Tony, who hated the strong-arm tactics of most mob-related businesses, never had to resort to physical violence to collect money or win contracts because he had a reputation for fairness and civility.

But that all changed when Dante decided to get involved in the business. Backed by his knuckle-dragging crew, the cocaine-fueled Dante started to use intimidation and extortion to land major contracts from unscrupulous politicians and bureaucrats. In the great mob tradition, he demanded bigger kickbacks from their loyal, hard-working subcontractors. Tony and Dante repeatedly butted heads over those tactics.

Given their strained relationship, which dated back to Dante's teenage years—something had to give. Mario stepped in and tried to make peace, but Dante insisted Tony resign from Conti Construction, once and for all. If not, Dante threatened to go off on his own to "deal drugs, and maybe get into human trafficking and prostitution."

When Carla heard about his dire ultimatum, she freaked out. Mario balked too. He knew how valuable Tony was to the operation, but he was fearful his treacherous eldest son would follow through on his threat. Plus, Mario figured he could keep a closer eye on Dante if he were working directly under him.

Mario wept when he broke the news to Tony. He confessed his shame for being forced into such a decision, but he felt he had no choice. With his typical aplomb, Tony agreed to gracefully step down.

Although he remained a close confidant to Mario on other issues, Tony kept a distance from Conti Construction, Inc.; however, other people within the organization secretly came to him with concerns and complaints about Dante's notorious management style. Tony listened, advised, and never betrayed their trust.

The last time Tony and Dante had a heated argument was three years ago when Dante dragged Mario's younger son Johnnie into a dangerous drug deal that led to his five-year conviction.

Mario handed Tony the slip of paper. "That's Nicky Bruno's address on the Upper East side. Apparently, he visits a pond in Central Park every morning around ten o'clock to play with his toy motorboat… Pathetic."

As Tony stared at the note, his cane slid off the armrest and clattered loudly onto the hardwood floor—startling both men. They looked down at the antique walking stick with its polished black shaft and carved ivory handle sculpted into the head of an eagle.

Mario had given the cane to Tony as a gift when he was learning to walk again. It once belonged to a diplomat murdered during the Franco-Prussian War in 1870. The cane cost a fortune, but Mario didn't care. It was a small token of thanks for Tony's selfless, heroic act to save his life and a symbol of their enduring friendship.

Slowly, Tony rose, put the paper in his pocket and picked up the cane. "I should be going. Angela is waiting."

Mario asked, "What do you want to do about that filthy little man?"

"I'll think about it."

Mario sipped his cognac. "And keep an eye on Dante."

As Tony left the library, Mario turned back to face the fire.

6

Outskirts of El Paso
3:00 p.m.

Jake Crowley, Special Agent with Homeland Security Investigations, crouched over the bloated bodies of two Mexican cartel members laying in a ditch on the U.S. border east of El Paso, Texas.

The air was heavy and putrid with the smell of burnt flesh. Hundreds of flies buzzed around.

"These boys are getting ripe," he said.

Standing behind him, Sheriff Rex Royal, an old-school country lawman with chrome-plated sunglasses and a leathery face, squinted up at the late November sun. "What'd you expect? They've been baking in the sun waiting for you."

A ruggedly handsome man in his early forties, Crowley wore pressed Levis, ostrich cowboy boots, and a white dress shirt with rolled-up sleeves. At 6'2," he had the lean, hard physique of a former athlete and the quiet confidence of a black belt in Taekwondo. Prior to joining the elite unit at the U.S. Department of Homeland Security, he had spent ten years with the Dallas Police Department, including a five-year stint as a homicide detective.

Crowley stood and surveyed the busy crime scene.

Police SUVs were parked around the perimeter, joined by coroner and forensic vans. Several deputy sheriffs combed the brushy terrain for additional evidence as techs photographed and fingerprinted the inside of the abandoned pick-up truck, made footprint castings, and bagged shell casings. The incinerated van still smoldered, releasing small wisps of smoke from its blackened carcass.

"So, let me guess," Crowley said, gesturing at the two bodies with huge holes in the back of their skulls. "These two hombres were waiting in that pick-up truck for their buddies to arrive with the latest batch of smuggled illegal aliens, but some other dudes showed up and spoiled their little rendezvous."

He pointed at a rocky bluff about fifty yards away. "To avoid detection, our mysterious interlopers parked their vehicle back there where we found those tire tracks. They snuck up on the pick-up, smoked these two losers, and took their places to wait for the van."

Crowley and Sheriff Royal walked over to the bullet-riddled bodies of Carlos and Mateo, still sprawled in front of the pick-up truck. "When the van showed up, the interlopers shot these guys and took control of the van."

"You federal boys are a lot sharper than I thought," the Sheriff replied, removing his white Stetson to wipe the sweat from his brow with the back of his hand. "Yeah, that's pretty much how we figured it, but we still don't know why they torched the van."

The intense heat from the fire had melted the windows, tires, and everything else, reducing the van to a charred heap of twisted metal. The rear doors had been pried open with a crowbar to reveal the hideous carnage within. Disfigured beyond recognition, the scorched bodies were piled high near the rear of the van, where they had futilely sought to escape through the chain-locked doors. The horror of what must have happened inside the van during the fire was unfathomable.

As Crowley and the Sheriff approached the hellish cavity, a young Asian female forensic technician scraped a DNA sample from one of the grotesquely burned victims.

"We're pretty sure there are eight bodies inside," Sheriff Royal said.

The stench was overwhelming. Crowley removed a small tin of vapor rub from his pocket, dabbed some above his upper lip, then offered it to the Sheriff.

"No thanks," the grim-faced lawman said. "After being here all day, I'm getting used to the smell."

Apparently, the forensic tech wasn't. Suddenly, she leapt out of the van, ran to the nearest patch of fishhook weed, and puked loudly.

"You okay, sweetheart?" Sheriff Royal asked, reaching out to her.

Embarrassed, the young woman replied, "I'll be fine, sir."

It took a moment for her to compose herself before she teetered over to one of the forensic stations. Crowley could tell the old sheriff was an honorable lawman who cared deeply for his staff and the good, decent folks in his crime-ridden county.

He took a closer look inside the van. "Have you seen anything like this before, Sheriff?"

"Hell no. This is goddamn sick," he replied. "And what about you, Crowley? Have *you* ever seen anything like this?"

The Sheriff was a wily old coot who knew how to play the interrogation game: *Always answer a question with a question.*

As a matter of fact, Crowley had witnessed four very similar scenes over the last two months; however, since it was an active investigation his boss deemed "a possible matter of national security," he had to be careful about what he divulged to anyone.

Crowley met the Sheriff's eyes. "I've seen worse."

The Sheriff sensed the Fed was holding back information, but dropped it.

Crowley said, "Maybe we're dealing with some local vigilantes. Could they be trying to scare off the cartels?"

"I doubt it. No one from around here is this depraved."

"Speaking of cartels, those four dead dudes all have Juarez gang tattoos. Are you aware of any other Mexican gangs running drugs or illegal aliens through this area?"

"We've also had to deal with the Sinaloa and Los Zetas cartels from time to time," the Sheriff said. "It's a basket of snakes. Except for their tattoos, you can't tell them apart."

"Tell me about it," Crowley said. "For the last few years, I've chased plenty of those assholes all over the country. Seems like there's an endless supply of them—and it's getting worse."

Sheriff Royal took a hard look at Crowley. "I heard through the grapevine you tracked some big-time meth dealer all the way down to the Florida Everglades. And when you finally caught up with him, you fed him to a big gator… Any truth to that story?"

Crowley knew he had a reputation across the Southwest for being a loose cannon who used unorthodox tactics to get information and mete out justice. Exaggerated tales of how he dealt with hardcore criminals bordered on the absurd, but he didn't go out of his way to discourage them. Being known as a psycho with a badge was a handy tool when dealing with dangerous men.

The lanky Federal agent stepped away from the van. "Meth is the worst drug on the planet. My niece got strung out on it over in San Antonio, so it got personal for me. Bottom line: I love animals and that gator was hungry."

Sheriff Royal chuckled, but Crowley could tell he didn't believe him. Like most experienced lawmen, he had a good nose for detecting bullshit.

Crowley looked the Sheriff in the eye. "Of course, I would never intentionally kill anyone in custody. That would be stupid, illegal and frankly, my boss would be pissed. But I think you'll agree some criminals are so evil and unrepentant that they need to be straightened out the old-fashioned way, right?"

The Sheriff nodded.

"So—here's the real deal... I had to transport that meth dealer all the way back to Arizona to be arraigned in a federal court. The idea of sitting next to him on a five-hour flight from Florida made my skin crawl so I decided to drive. I rented a small moving van and put that low life in the back of the pitch-black cargo space, along with food and water, a big batch of his own vile product—and a twelve-foot long Burmese python some yahoo had pulled out of the swamp."

Crowley paused to let the visual sink in. "Well, it took three long days to drive the two thousand miles back to Phoenix. I guess he consumed all the meth to stay awake to avoid the snake. Anyway, by the time we arrived, he had some nasty bites but was still alive.

He had also gone completely mad. Last I heard, he was in some nuthouse."

The Sheriff smirked. "Man, that's bad ass."

It was also a lie, but Crowley was tired of that old gator story and figured this new twist on it would spread across the Southwest like a prairie fire. He subscribed to the old adage: *Never let the truth get in the way of a good story.*

They turned their attention back to the carnage. A flatbed truck with a crane unit arrived to transport the corpse-filled van to the morgue.

Over his long career in law enforcement, Crowley had seen his fair share of human misery and acts of senseless cruelty, but these latest atrocities along the border set an appalling new standard for cold-blooded murder.

Despite the almost identical *modus operandi* at each of those recent crime scenes, Crowley still found it impossible to get used to the gruesome images of death and degradation. The medical examiners, who had to untangle that glutinous mass of melted flesh and bone in the van, would surely have nightmares for the rest of their lives.

Crowley knew he would too.

They looked out across the shimmering landscape.

"I sure could use a cold beer right about now," Royal said, wiping more sweat away.

"Me too," Crowley said, "but I've got to get to Tucson for a meeting. No rest for the wicked."

Crowley couldn't get into specifics, but later that evening he was scheduled to interview a Mexican national who had survived a similar BBQ outside Nogales. The half-broiled hombre was blown out the back doors of another van when it exploded two weeks earlier. Since then, he had been in a drug-induced coma with second- and third-degree burns over most of his body. His doctor had finally agreed to let Crowley spend a few minutes with the dying man.

"We'll need all these field and forensic reports emailed to the Homeland Security offices in Phoenix no later than 9:00 a.m. tomorrow," Crowley said.

"We'll take care of it," the Sheriff replied.

They shook hands. The Sheriff pointed over to an idling SUV. "That deputy will drive you back to the airport."

"Thanks. And keep up the good work."

"And keep those reptiles well fed."

With a wink, Crowley imagined the next dose of justice.

7

The Conti family limo sped across the Triborough Bridge toward the Upper East Side. Seated in the back, Angela Conti stared down the East River at the sparkling New York City skyline.

A pretty college student with raven black hair, full red lips, and designer eyeglasses, Angela was smart with a good heart. Tony adjusted his rearview mirror to see her in the soft light of the luxurious rear seating area.

"You sure are quiet tonight, Angela. What's bothering you?"

"I'm worried about Papa. He doesn't look good."

"He's tough," Tony said reassuringly. "He'll be okay."

The sleek limo turned off the bridge and onto the first of a series of streets that led to the prestigious Manhattan Medical Center on the eastern edge of Central Park.

"I don't know. His doctor said he's very weak. Mom is putting on a happy face, but she's really worried too."

"I've known your father for over forty years. He has always had the heart of a lion."

"Even lions get old and frail," Angela said, dabbing a tear.

Sensing a need to change topics, Tony asked, "So who's the lucky guy?"

Angela sighed. "You know, the last time you asked me that question, you were taking me to my senior prom."

"Yeah, I remember your date. He was a nerd in a pale blue tuxedo."

"I heard he just got an MBA from Wharton. He'll be filthy rich in a few years."

"But he'll still be a nerd," Tony said.

Angela reached for a bottle of Evian water from the built-in bar. She took a sip and then checked her make-up in a small cosmetic mirror. "My boyfriend's name is Hal. Mutual friends introduced us at a reception at the Museum of Modern Art a few months ago. It was one of his few days off."

"Sounds like an interesting guy."

"All I'll say is… he's tall, dark, and handsome. And he treats me like a queen."

"He better!"

Angela smiled at Tony's protectiveness. He had been that way since she was a little girl.

"I think I'm in love."

"That's good enough for me."

As she typed in a text message, the limo turned left onto Park Ave.

Tony kept prying. "What kind of doctor is he?"

"He's training to be a heart surgeon."

"Maybe he should consult with Mario's doctor."

"Hal has offered to help in any way, but I haven't said anything yet to either Mom or Dad." Angela paused. "Let's just see how things go at Thanksgiving dinner."

"Yes, Carla said he was coming."

"Unfortunately, she insisted."

"And the problem is?"

Angela shrugged. "He's nervous about meeting 'the family,' if you know what I mean."

Tony nodded in silent understanding. "Well, try to have a little faith."

The limo pulled up in front of the entrance to the medical center on Fifth Ave.

Angela's phone beeped, and she checked it.

"That's a text from Hal. He's going to meet me right inside."

Tony grabbed his cane and walked around the back of the limo to let Angela out onto the sidewalk.

After kissing him on the cheek, she said, "Thanks for the ride, Uncle Tony. We'll see you Thursday evening."

"Looking forward to it."

Just inside the lobby, he saw Dr. Hali Dia, a tall, black African dressed in surgical scrubs, embrace and passionately kiss Angela.

"Here comes trouble," Tony said to himself.

8

After dropping Angela off, Tony drove to his old neighborhood. Italian Harlem, now known as East Harlem, lies northeast of Central Park roughly between 96th and 125th streets from Lexington and Madison Avenues to the East River.

Starting in 1878, huge waves of immigrants from Sicily and the Italian peninsula began to pour into the country. Until the 1930s, Italian Harlem was home to tens of thousands of first- and second-generation Italian residents, open-air produce markets, butcher and pastry shops, over-crowded apartment buildings—and legendary organized Italian crime syndicates.

When Antonio Maximo Tucci arrived into the world in 1950, his family lived on the third floor of a non-descript four-story tenement house on East 116th Street. At that time, many Italians still resided in the area and there was a strong sense of community and shared values.

Growing up, Tony was baptized and served as an altar boy at Our Lady of Mt. Carmel Church, the first Italian parish in New York. He attended public schools, played at the local parks, and frolicked under gushing fire hydrants on hot, humid summer afternoons.

Tony and his buddies knew every inch of the neighborhood—each business, building, alley, rooftop, and pigeon aviary. Shopkeepers called him by name and gave him shaved lemon ice in exchange for running small errands.

By the time Tony's childhood days were over, more than half the district's Italian residents were long gone and the old neighborhood was changing rapidly as the nearby African-American and Puerto Rican enclaves of Harlem began to press in around it.

Many Italian-Americans migrated north to the Belmont neighborhood in the Bronx, clustered around Arthur Avenue and East 187th Street, or relocated to Staten Island. But the Tucci family stayed and thrived in Italian Harlem until Tony was a freshman in high school—a when a devastating series of events changed the course of their lives.

Tony pulled the limo into the loading zone in front of Mancini's Trattoria a venerable family-owned Italian restaurant on East 118th Street. As he reached for a copy of *Barron's* and his cane, the parking attendant opened his door.

"Good evening, Mr. Tucci," the thin, young Puerto Rican said eagerly. "How are you?"

"Fine, Ramon. And you?"

"Very good, sir."

Armed with a quick smile and smooth, dance-like moves, Ramon was a college student who had parked cars at the restaurant since he got his driver's license.

Ramon couldn't help but drool over the shiny Mercedes limo. "Man, what a sweet ride! This must be the S550 Pullman Premiere Edition you told me about, right?"

"Spoken like a true automotive aficionado." Tony knew Ramon's dream was to become an automotive engineer. He had graduated with honors from high school and was currently taking prerequisite classes at City College.

"Yeah, I researched it online. Mind if I look inside, Mr. Tucci?"

"Be my guest."

They walked around the back of the limo. Ramon opened the rear door and peered inside. "Wow!"

"Go ahead. Get in."

Ramon grinned and climbed inside. He sat in one of the soft white leather seats in the far back, running his hand over the polished wood siding while looking up at the flat screen TV mounted above. "Man, I could get used to this."

"Keep up your studies, and one day you will. In the meantime, help yourself to a drink."

Ramon grabbed a soft drink from the bar and scooted out. Tony handed him the keys and said, "Don't let it out of your sight."

"Of course not, Mr. Tucci. I'll leave it right where it is. Should attract business!"

Ramon jogged over to the restaurant's massive, etched-glass front door and opened it for Tony. As he entered, Tony shoved a $100 bill into Ramon's shirt pocket. "For the college fund."

9

Over the years, Mancini's Trattoria had lost most of its luster, quietly slipping onto the precipice of obscurity.

When it first opened for business in the early 1920s, the Italian-American neighborhood was flourishing, and there were many competing restaurants offering traditional old-country cuisine. For decades, Mancini's was one of the most popular eating establishments and served as a hangout for wise guys from Pleasant Avenue and other parts of the city.

Given the huge shift in demographics to a heavily Hispanic population, there were now only about a thousand Italians left in the vicinity, most of them clustered around the old Catholic church several blocks to the east. Tourists in search of the neighborhood's great Italian heritage found only a barbershop, bakery, famous pizzeria, and an exclusive Neapolitan bistro. As a result, Mancini's catered to a few local residents and those old-timers like Tony, who ventured back to the neighborhood for an authentic Italian meal.

With a certain historical charm that transcended its general run-down condition, Mancini's was an Italian time capsule floating in the sea of Spanish Harlem. Except for a few mandated additions to the kitchen to meet the evolving standards of the Department of Health, no capital improvements had been made in years. In the empty foyer, oil paintings of sunny Sicilian landscapes hung above hardwood benches that had once held waiting throngs of hungry patrons. The impressive Cherrywood bar featured big mirrors and white marble backsplashes. The centerpiece was an Italian flag that had waved in the stadium in Rome when Italy won the World Cup in 1934.

Every square inch of wall space above the marred wainscoting was covered with framed sepia-tone and faded color photos of groups and individuals, caricatures of famous visitors and local celebrities, and other memorabilia spanning the eatery's long history. In the comfortable dining room, the tables were draped in white tablecloths and the walls were wrapped with hand-painted murals. There was also a private dining room in the rear, where it was rumored a mobster was garroted in the early 1970s.

The smells of garlic, marinara sauce, and fresh Italian bread had seeped into the walls and furniture, giving the place the timeless scent of an Italian family kitchen. Tony had been coming here since he was a kid. It was home.

As Tony entered the bar, Paolo Mancini warmly greeted him. "Tony! What a pleasure to see you!"

"Paolo! Always the perfect host!"

Paolo was the son of the original owner and looked just like him. With a bushy gray mustache that framed a toothy smile, he wore a baggy black suit and gravy-stained tie.

Constantly in motion, Paolo wore every hat in the place. He manned the bar, ran back and forth from the kitchen to sample the food and yell orders at his two forlorn chefs, checked on each table to make sure everyone was happy with the food and service, and even bussed tables when things got really busy—a rather rare occurrence.

Paolo removed a "reserved" sign from a table in the corner against a wall surrounded by racks of wine bottles and Tony sat down. The perch provided a safe, panoramic view of most of the establishment. It was Tony's table. No one else ever sat there unless he invited them.

Paolo reached behind the bar and extracted a wine bottle and burgundy goblet. With great flair, Paolo poured a half glass and placed it before Tony. "You have to try this Sangiovese from the old country. It's superb!"

"Okay, but only if you twist my arm."

Tony swirled the glass around a few times to aerate the rich red vintage, breathed in its bouquet, and then sampled it. "Very nice."

"It's 'the blood of Jove,' my friend. Enjoy!" Paolo set the bottle in front of Tony. "Listen, we'll have to catch up later. I've got a party in the back room I need to check on. Do you want me to put in your regular order?'

Tony nodded as he took another draw on his wine glass.

"Great! I'll be back soon," Paolo said as he hustled off.

Enjoying the moment, Tony began to read his newspaper when Connie Ricci, a waitress who had worked at Mancini's for many years, approached him.

"Excuse me, Mr. Tucci."

"Good evening, Connie. How are you this evening?"

A hard-working single mother, who was also a part-time hairdresser, Connie nervously clutched her order book. "I'm sorry to bother you, but..."

Tony could see she was agitated. The warm, friendly smile that usually greeted guests was gone. She looked like she carried the weight of the world on her shoulders. Tony stood and pulled out a chair for her. "No problem. Please have a seat."

She sat, staring down at the table until Tony asked, "What's wrong?"

"It's my daughter, Gina. She's a senior at Saint Carmen High School... Gina is a very sweet and sensitive girl, but she's overweight and has some self-esteem issues." Connie wiped away a tear from her cheek. "I'm sorry."

"Take your time," Tony said reassuringly.

Wringing her hands together, she continued. "The problem is... there are three girls who constantly bully her. They send her nasty, hateful emails and text messages, and ridicule her on those social media sites. For months, she's been very depressed and..."

She started to sob.

Tony gently put his hand on her shoulder. "Go on, Connie."

She pulled a damp tissue from her pocket. "Gina tried to kill herself a week ago. She took some old pain pills from my medicine cabinet. They had to pump her stomach at the hospital. She almost died."

"Tell me, who are these girls?"

"The queen bitches of the senior class!" Connie cried angrily.

"Did you talk to their parents?"

"Yes, I tried, but they refuse to believe their pretty, perfect daughters can be that mean."

"And what about the school administration?"

"They did nothing, claiming there are privacy issues. And now, my little Gina is afraid to go back to classes. She cries all day long and is still threatening to kill herself."

Connie tried to compose herself, but the tears still flowed. "I'm so afraid for her. I don't know what to do."

"I'm not sure if I can help, Connie, but please write down those girls' names."

She pulled a page from her order book, quickly jotted down the three names and handed it to Tony.

He shrugged. Dealing with high school bullies was hardly his thing, but his heart was touched by Gina's problem. "Let me give it some thought."

"You're so kind, Mr. Tucci," she said, pushing back more tears as she quickly exited the bar.

10

As a Puccini aria played over the sound system, Tony glanced around. It was a typical weekday evening at Mancini's. The restaurant was empty except for a few couples chatting quietly over candlelit tables, a large Hispanic family celebrating a kid's birthday, and two loud, obnoxious businessmen drinking and playing dice at the bar.

Tony stared at the note from Connie. Ever since he'd foiled the hit on Don Mario, desperate people had come to him with their problems. The fact that he not only survived the bloody massacre but also triumphed over incredible odds, created the mystique that he could do the impossible.

He became a celebrity in the old neighborhood, a man of honor and power who took the time to listen to each and every person who approached him. People from all races and classes of society—the rich and poor, the young and the old—told him gut-wrenching stories about their victimizations, their destroyed lives, their desires for justice and revenge.

In most cases, Tony offered common-sense advice, encouraging people to peacefully resolve their dilemmas through dialog or the legal system. For more contentious situations, he often acted as a mediator between the aggrieved parties. Inevitably, Tony's interventions resulted in positive outcomes, because he could be very persuasive; however, certain recalcitrant individuals required special treatment.

Over the years, he had successfully dealt with thieves, extortionists, sexual deviates—even killers, who preyed on the innocent and weak. Using a combination of shrewd intellect, the strength of his reputation, and a dash of intimidation, Tony had convinced many dark souls to change their ways.

Although he was committed to nonviolence, Tony let the guilty think he was capable of the most extreme measures. His threats, both real and implied, were always taken seriously. After all, he had killed three cold-blooded assassins in short order. Surely, he could easily spill blood again—or dispatch others to deliver retribution as needed.

Tony knew bullies came in all shapes and sizes. If their predatory behaviors were not thwarted at an early age, they became more emboldened, aggressive, and dangerous in their later years.

Recently, Tony had dealt with two such individuals: an attorney who was ripping off widows by grossly overcharging for legal services and a bad cop extorting money from small neighborhood businesses. After a brief face-to-face meeting with Tony, the blood-sucking barrister agreed to refund all his fees to the spinsters before he left town—never to return. And the police officer was busted after a series of incriminating videotapes of his shakedowns were delivered to NYPD Internal Affairs.

Tony knew victims came in all shapes and sizes too—like Darrell, a fourteen-year old boy, filled with a murderous rage. Unable to control his anger after his father was killed in a savage street mugging, Darrell got in a series of vicious fistfights with kids at his junior high school and was expelled. Worried about his downward spiral into alienation and violence,

Darrell's uncle asked Tony to talk with the boy. Although he had limited experience in dealing with kids in crisis, Tony saw a little of himself in the troubled teen. While he pondered how to get the kid back on track before he killed someone, Tony heard about another teenager named Jamie who was going blind due to a rare eye disease. Jamie was also angry and frustrated about his new plight in life. Tony had a hunch the two boys might get along and arranged for a meeting. Once Darrell saw how helpless and frightened Jamie was, his tough guy persona melted away. The boys spent two hours alone and soon became fast friends. Darrell vowed to help his new friend cope with his disability. Tony derived a special satisfaction knowing both boys would be okay.

Sipping his wine, Tony decided how to handle the cruel high school girls and made a cell phone call to put his plan into motion.

Paolo arrived with a basket of fresh bread and a small Caesar salad. "I'm so sorry to keep you waiting, Tony, but that party in the back is very demanding," he said as he ground fresh pepper over the salad.

"I'm in no hurry. Take your time."

Paolo sat down on a bar seat beside the table. Tony noticed that he seemed exhausted and distracted, not his typically upbeat self. Tony's eyes wandered over to a framed wall photo of Tommy Mancini, Paolo's only son, who was in the National Guard. It showed Tommy in full combat gear, cradling an M16 at some remote outpost in the Middle East.

"I haven't seen Tommy since he got back from Afghanistan. How's he doing?"

"Didn't Gino and Al tell you? They took him out to celebrate about a month ago."

"No," said Tony. He knew Gino and Al had known Tommy since he was a kid because everyone in the Conti clan loved to eat at Mancini's, but their generosity seemed surprising.

Paolo sighed. "To tell you the truth, Tommy's having a tough time readjusting to being back here in the States."

"That's typical. I was a mess too when I got back from Vietnam. In hindsight, I was suffering from post-traumatic stress. Now it's an epidemic."

"It's more than that, Tony. I think he's using drugs. He's still on active duty with the Guard, but he seems to be stoned all the time."

"It's probably just a phase, but he should talk to a professional."

"I suggested that he go to the V.A. for some counseling, but he said they could kick him out of the Guard if he admits to any psychological problems," said Paolo.

"I'm not sure that's true, but I've got someone he can trust outside the system. Remember Dr. Rose, that psychiatrist I brought here for dinner a while back?"

Paolo nodded. "Yeah, he seemed like a decent guy. Do you really think he can help?"

"Absolutely. He's worked with lots of vets."

Tony and Hunter Rose had been friends for over forty years, dating back to his second tour in Vietnam. Rose had served as a medic in his platoon and treated him for minor wounds. Tony had saved his life several times during firefights in the bush. After leaving the Marines, Rose attended medical school and eventually became a psychiatrist. He was one of Tony's closest confidants and a trusted resource.

"Can you get Tommy here this Sunday at seven p.m.?"

"Probably."

Tony removed a small notebook from his breast pocket and made a note. "Good, I'll set it up with Dr. Rose."

Paolo stood up, looking relieved. "I really appreciate it, Tony."

He poured a glass of wine for both of them. "I saw Connie talking with you earlier. You must feel like 'The Godfather' on his daughter's wedding day. Everyone has a special request—a plea for help."

Paolo tipped his glass to Tony. "Cheers to the 'Godfather of East 118th Street.'"

Slightly embarrassed, Tony smiled. "It's my pleasure."

* * * *

As Tony dined on a perfectly prepared dish of veal scaloppini, he casually read the newspaper, making notes about some stocks and start-up companies to follow-up on.

After enjoying some chocolate gelato and an espresso, he made a few phone calls, including one to "The Kid" who lived a few blocks away. As usual, the price of admission to see his brilliant young friend was a double order of Mancini's spaghetti and meatballs. Tony ordered it to go, paid his bill, and left a generous tip.

11

Jake Crowley entered the University Burn Center to interview the only witness to survive one of the van burnings on the border. For two weeks, the patient, a Mexican national, had been in a drug-induced coma due to his extensive burns.

Crowley took the stairs to the second floor and approached the nurse's station. Flashing his Homeland Security badge to a female nurse, he said, "Good evening, ma'am. I'm Jake Crowley, here to see Dr. Jorge Gonzalez."

After a cursory glance, she replied, "He's waiting for you in Room 203, two doors down on the right."

"Much obliged."

Crowley entered the bright, antiseptic room. Dr. Gonzalez, a short, middle-aged man in a white coat with reading glasses perched on the end of his nose, stood beside the plastic-shrouded bed making notations on the patient's computer chart. Another nurse was inside the tent adjusting an IV line.

The patient was wrapped in white gauze and connected to numerous medical devices. His arms and legs were spread out on swing supports to allow for air circulation around his wounds. The man's red, scarred face flashed in vivid contrast to the sterile white linens around him. His eyes were shut and his breathing labored and loud.

"How's our patient, Doc?" Crowley asked as he walked over to Gonzalez.

"He remains in very critical condition. I backed off the morphine to keep him as lucid as possible for your interview, but he's in intense pain. You only have about five minutes to speak with him."

"Do we know his name yet?"

"Jose Medina. Claims he's from Mexico City. He only speaks Spanish."

The nurse exited the oxygen tent and Crowley moved closer.

"I speak Spanish, but I need a witness." Crowley turned to the doctor. "Would you mind?"

"No problema," Dr. Gonzalez said as they stepped inside the plastic shroud.

Crowley removed a small digital recorder from his sports jacket, turned it on, and placed it on the metal tray stand beside the bed. He leaned in close. "Hello, Jose. I'm investigating what happened to you the night the van exploded out in the desert. Is that okay?"

Jose opened his bloodshot, blurry eyes and nodded ever so slightly.

"What happened before the van was set on fire?"

Jose swallowed hard. "A man wearing a scarf around his face opened the back doors and... said something."

"What?"

"Uh... I think he said 'Allah.'"

"You mean like the religious name?"

"Yes... Then he said it again and two men in the back answered."

"What did they say?"

"Ak... Akbar or something ..."

Crowley and Dr. Gonzalez made eye contact.

"They said, 'Allahu Akbar'?"

Jose nodded, his eyes distant.

"Then what happened?"

"The two men got out... The masked man chained the door shut and... the van was set on fire."

"What did those two men look like?"

"I couldn't see... It was too dark."

Jose shuddered with pain. Dr. Gonzalez moved over to the IV and picked up a syringe. "He needs more morphine."

Crowley waved him off. "Just one more question. Do you remember anything else?"

Jose turned his eyes away. "Just the flames... and the screams."

Crowley picked up the recorder and turned it off. "Thank you, Jose. Go with God."

Dr. Gonzalez injected more morphine into the IV drip, and they exited the tent.

"What's the prognosis, Doc?"

"Massive infection has set in. He'll be dead within forty-eight hours."

Crowley glanced back at Jose, who had drifted off. "Poor guy."

"Allahu Akbar. That's what those crazy jihadis are always yelling, right?"

"Yes. It means 'God is great.' It's a very common saying in peaceful Muslim cultures, but it's also a battle cry for Islamic extremists."

Dr. Gonzalez frowned. "So terrorists are coming across the border?"

Crowley looked him in the eye. "What you just heard is classified. Please don't discuss it with anyone."

They walked out of the room.

Crowley said, "You know, my boss is a Muslim too and he loves this country. I promise you, we'll find out who did this and justice will be served."

Dr. Gonzalez shook his head. "Too bad Jose won't be here to see it."

12

Inferno, Dante's new nightclub, was in the old Meat-Packing District on the west side of Manhattan. Situated on a busy corner near 14th Street, the renovated, two-story, 25,000-square-foot space was a former commercial storage facility.

Back in June, hiding behind a sham corporation, Dante had negotiated a three-year lease-to-own contract with the building's owner to secure a low monthly rent. Of course, Dante had no intention of sticking around after the first six months—the life expectancy of most New York nightclubs. He would make a quick boatload of cash and then bust the place out.

He hired a flamboyant interior designer named Nigel Peach, who had decorated other trendy nightclubs in the City and Vegas. Within minutes of touring the venue, Nigel announced the design theme should play off Inferno—the first part of Dante Alighieri's 14th-century epic poem Divine Comedy.

"I see a fiery palette of red, yellow, and black! Lots of mirrors and throbbing strobe lights will make this place burn with erotic excitement and raw energy," the designer squealed as he pranced around the empty club. "We'll have nine different VIP areas patterned after the 'Nine Circles of Hell,' flaming cocktails and more! It will be fantastic!"

Whether it was a stroke of creative brilliance or just a way to massage his new boss's huge ego, Nigel's concept for Inferno pushed Dante's buttons big time. With visions of riches dancing in his head, Dante green-lighted a budget of $1,000,000 for the renovation, interior decorating, and furnishings. He also invested another $500,000 to hire an experienced club manager to oversee daily operations, a social media director, promoters to pre-sell the expensive VIP tables, several bodybuilders as bouncers, dozens of waitresses and bartenders, as well as a public relations firm and ad agency to develop the club's logo, website, advertising campaign, and slogan: "Inferno. It's hotter than Hell!"

To finance his swanky nightclub, Dante embezzled a big hunk of the start-up money from Conti Construction, which he planned to pay back before the company books were audited in January. He borrowed the rest from a mob family in Philadelphia, which came with a hefty "vig," or interest rate, that cost Dante an additional $10,000 per week.

Unfortunately, Dante's estimated budgets were woefully inadequate for the escalating costs and unforeseen expenses. In October, in a desperate attempt to generate some much-needed income, he placed $250,000 in bets on World Series games with a connected sports bookie in Boston—and lost his shirt. Faced with mounting debt, interest payments, and last-minute expenses, Dante arranged for another risky loan from a Jersey hood named "Chainsaw Eddie" Giordano, who would be stopping by the club soon.

Inferno's grand premiere was scheduled for Saturday night and the social media sites were already buzzing about: "the newest bridge-and-tunnel nightspot that will set the City on fire!" A bevy of high-profile celebrities, Wall Street power brokers, trust fund brats with black Amex cards, a Saudi prince and his entourage, and some of Dante's mob associates had promised to attend the exclusive opening night gala.

Expensive cars and limos will be showcased out front as parking valets snatch huge tips and palm drugs to the social elite heading to the inner sanctums. The waiting line will stretch for blocks; however, with the exception of some fashion models and buxom bling queens, every other wannabe party animal will be rudely turned away. Those lucky enough to get past Dante's douchebag doormen and the red velvet ropes will pay a hefty cover charge and obscene sums for overpriced alcohol and mediocre service. Inside, parched patrons will drop $25 for a tap beer at the overcrowded bars while $1,000 bottles of Dom Pérignon will pop at the VIP tables. A famous DJ will play a deafening mix of electronic dance music as every drug imaginable is snorted and swallowed. Intoxicated lovers will perform salacious sexual acts in bathroom stalls and the small rooms that rent by the minute. And reporters from the leading entertainment tabloids and blogs will be given free booze to guarantee glowing reviews.

By catering to the hedonistic appetites of its affluent clientele, Inferno was destined to become one of the City's most decadent destinations for endless boozing, dancing, and drugging—creating the illusion that it really was the "hottest" spot on the planet.

Sitting in his private suite on the second floor by a window that overlooked the main dance floor, Dante dropped his cigarette into an empty highball glass and pushed it aside.

Down on the lower level, Danny Demarco, the young hyped-up club manager, was lecturing the newly hired staff. Every employee, dressed in a red vest and yellow shirt, was expected to attend the pre-opening rehearsals to learn each club procedure, including how to operate the digital, hand-held credit-card readers as well as techniques for dealing with demanding, inebriated customers. Knowing they would share in the automatic 20-percent gratuity added to every liquor and food sale, the staff could hardly wait for the big Saturday night kick-off.

Dante had already dealt with a plethora of problems, payments, and personalities—and the night was still young. He spent an hour with a Madam named Alexandra Dufrane, who ran a stable of high-priced call girls. Dante proposed a mutually beneficial partnership in which Ms. Dufrane's "escorts" would be allowed full access to Inferno to troll for wealthy men in exchange for a hefty cut of the prostitution profits.

Next, he had a meeting with a drug dealer, Dino "Dimebag" Scarfetti, who was connected to another well-known New York family. Scarfetti had solid connections for crystal meth, heroin, and cocaine, as well as a pipeline to some offshore drug lab that churned out millions of tabs of high-quality Ecstasy, Ketamine and LSD. Dante told Scarfetti he could work the nightclub with only his most discreet dealers, and he should report to Gino with the nightly take.

Dante figured the drug sales and prostitution profits would bring in an enormous and unreported extra income—the real gravy.

As he lit another cigarette, there was a knock on the door. Al stuck his head in and said, "Eddie Giordano just got here, and he's got two of his goons with him."

For Al to call anyone a "goon" was so comical, Dante had to suppress a chuckle. "Tell Eddie to come in, but his friends can wait outside."

"Sure, boss. And after they leave, Gino and I are going to take care of that thing."

That "thing" was a problem with another nightclub owner named Raul Garcia, who operated The Palace—a glitzy, retro-themed venue that played the biggest disco hits from the '70s and '80s—located only a block away.

Dante was obsessed with controlling the very lucrative area adjacent to the wealthy enclaves of lower, westside Manhattan. Two other smaller clubs in the vicinity had already shuttered their operations after Gino and Al paid them "friendly" visits, but Garcia refused to bow to their demands to close his doors. Only the feisty Cuban entrepreneur, with a reputation for hardheaded confrontation, stood in Dante's way to untold riches and fame.

Dante took a drag. "Get rid of that little prick. I'm tired of fuckin' around with him."

Al winked. "It'll get handled tonight."

A moment later, the most notorious loan shark in New Jersey strolled into the room like he owned the joint.

Giordano was a cold, heartless character. Short and stocky with a ridiculous jet-black pompadour and pencil-thin mustache, he'd earned his nickname by carrying around a chainsaw, which he used on deadbeat clients. He had worked as an enforcer for the

Teamsters and a bagman for the Mafia family who ran the garbage business in Jersey. Basically, he was a freelance psychopath who would do pretty much anything if the price were right.

Giordano dropped a satchel on the table and sat down across from Dante.

"Tell me that bag is full of cash and not your famous chainsaw," Dante said with a nervous laugh.

"Both!" Eddie said, pulling out a small chainsaw and placing it on the table.

Dante stared at the scary tool, looking for any residual blood or chunks of flesh—and was pleased when he saw none.

Eddie dumped out the remaining contents in the bag: twenty-five $10,000 packets of hundred dollar bills wrapped in rubber bands.

"Is it all there, Eddie?" Dante asked, taking a long drag on his smoke.

"Two-hundred-fifty large. Want to count it?"

"Fuck no," Dante replied as he walked over to the well-stocked bar on the back wall. "Want a drink?"

"Johnnie Walker Black. Neat."

Dante poured them two fingers each as Eddie peered down at the glowing red dance floor.

"Good job on the decorations, Dante. This place really does look like Hell," Eddie said, lifting his glass as a toast. "No wonder I feel right at home!"

They enjoyed a good laugh over that as Dante sat back down. "What are the terms again?"

"There's an upfront fee of $25,000 that's due next Wednesday, and after that I'll go with three points per week. That's only $7,500 a week. Very fair."

Eddie made strong eye contact with Dante. "But I want to be paid back in full within sixty days. I'm not the fucking BofA, capiche?"

Dante shrugged, knowing he had no choice in the matter. The final pre-opening expenses were staggering. He needed at least $150,000 just to stock the refrigerators and bars with booze and food. The balance would go to cover the back-due interest on his other street loans. But Dante wasn't worried. He figured the first week's profit would be at least $300,000, and his pending arms deal would generate millions more.

The first floor below them went dark. Flashing strobes and colorful wall motifs that looked like dancing flames flickered on. The sound system began to throb with a techno beat as the new staff got used to the working conditions in the club.

Dante slid the soundproof office window shut to drown out the music, but the floor and walls still reverberated with the pulsating bass line.

"I've heard on the street that you've got a few other loans out there," Eddie said, slamming back the rest of his drink. "Frankly, I don't give a shit about who else you owe. Just remember I'm the first to get paid."

"Sure, Eddie."

Dante was surprised a low-level hood like Giordano knew so much about his shaky finances. Just like the dead-eyed predators they were named after, most loan sharks usually swam in their own turbid waters looking for new victims. They didn't exactly hold an annual Loan Shark Convention to exchange information about various clients, debate "vig" rates, or watch demonstrations about the newest trends in torture.

What really concerned Dante was that rumors of his escalating debts would get back to his father before he could pay them all off. The last thing he needed now was suffering the wrath of the old man.

Eddie held up his glass. "How about a refill?"

Dante grabbed the bottle, topped-off Eddie's drink, and said, "Listen, we're booked solid for this opening weekend, but I'd like to set you up with a VIP table anytime you want. I'll cover everything, except for the women and drugs."

"Thanks for the offer, Dante, but this place probably won't get swingin' until midnight, which is way past my bedtime," the stone-cold killer smirked. "After all, I need my beauty sleep."

Dante wanted to make a wisecrack, but he kept his mouth shut.

13

East Harlem
9:30 p.m.

Exiting the Mancini's Trattoria, Tony told Ramon he was going to visit a friend in the neighborhood and would probably need to be picked up later. Ramon was thrilled at the prospect of driving the new Mercedes and eagerly agreed to wait for Tony's call.

Cloaked in his trademark black fedora, overcoat, and red scarf, Tony walked east through the old neighborhood. Every block was shrouded with memories, both good and bad.

Most of the old retail outlets and food shops were under new ownership, but the rows of apartment buildings and small homes with their classic brick and mortar, concrete stoops, and metal railings remained the same. Tony had lost touch with most of his childhood friends, but he saw them now in the shadows, darting in and out of time, playing 'Hide and Seek' and 'Kick the Can.'

Tony continued his arduous walk until he reached the corner of Pleasant Avenue. The old wise-guy social clubs and hangouts along the infamous six-block stretch had been replaced with retail stores, legitimate small businesses, the Manhattan Center for Science and Math, and the nearby East River Plaza with a Costco and Target.

He shrugged, knowing that change was bittersweet but inevitable. Life goes on…

Tony hobbled around the corner to Jefferson Park and down the quiet residential street to the "The Kid's" home.

Like many of the buildings in the City, the front door was up a half-flight of stairs while the basement was accessed via descending stairs on the side. Tony opened the wrought iron gate and went down the steps to the landing outside the basement door. He referred to this level of the house as "The Bunker" because the lower-level exterior windows were all bricked in, and the place looked impenetrable.

Beneath the watchful gaze of a surveillance camera, Tony pressed the buzzer on the intercom. The red eye of the camera bore in on him, and the outer door popped open. He entered under the staircase and shut the first door securely behind him. He stood before yet another imposing steel door. As two more cameras swept over him, the mouth-watering smell from the warm bag of spaghetti and meatballs filled the small compartment.

A younger man's voice came over the intercom. "Those meatballs better still be hot, Tony!"

"My balls are always hot," Tony deadpanned into the camera.

"Well then, come on in, you dirty old man!"

The door beeped open and Tony entered.

Jeremy Allen, a good-looking thirty-year-old in a wheelchair, with a shock of black, wavy hair and well-developed upper body, rolled up to Tony. "Great to see you, T!"

They hugged, and Tony handed him the to-go package from Mancini's.

Jeremy quickly opened the bag and took a big whiff. "Smells fantastic! Want some?"

Tony patted his stomach, "No thanks, but go ahead."

With a quick flick of his wrists, Jeremy spun the wheelchair around on its back wheels and rocketed over to the mini kitchen on the side of the spacious room.

As Jeremy removed one of the cartons from the bag and grabbed a fork, Tony looked around.

The main room was built around Jeremy's custom work station—a U-shaped desk topped with three large monitors connected to a temperature-controlled computer cabinet. Besides the kitchen, there was a small sitting area with a couch and chairs, a well-equipped workout space stocked with several exercise machines and racks of free weights, and an elevator that could access all three floors in the house above. In the rear, there was a windowless bedroom with an unmade king-size bed and a handicapped-accessible bathroom with all the amenities.

The brick walls were covered with neon art, painting the subterranean setting with a colorful luminescence. Tony couldn't help but notice a new addition to the room: a huge 90-inch flat-screen ultra HD TV mounted on the wall in front of Jeremy's desk. The incredibly realistic picture looked like the north shore of Oahu, where daring surfers glided down the face of massive waves in the late afternoon sun.

"That's impressive." Tony said.

Jeremy rolled up beside him with a huge meatball perched on the end of his fork. "Pretty cool, huh! It's a gift from my boss in D.C.—kind of a 'bonus.'"

"What for?"

"You know I can't talk about my work," Jeremy said, "but have you ever heard of Stuxnet?"

"Sure. I read about it in the Times. It was some kind of computer virus created by the Israelis and the U.S. to knock out Iran's nuclear facilities about ten years ago. It set back their program for years."

Jeremy patted himself on the back with his free hand and took a big bite out of the meatball. "That was child's play. Wait 'til they meet Stuxnet 2.0. It's a doozy!"

"So—that's what you've been working so hard on for the last few months?"

"Sorry, T, but I can't confirm or deny such a vicious rumor. 'Cause if I tell ya, I'll have to'—well, you know."

"Very funny."

"Anyway, my boss knows I don't get out much so he wanted to bring the world to me. Just got that unit installed last week," Jeremy said, sucking down some spaghetti.

"Is that a DVD you're playing?"

"Hell no! That's a live feed from a government camera over in Hawaii."

"A live feed?"

Jeremy scarfed another juicy meatball, dripping a glob of sauce onto his Foo Fighters t-shirt. "Yeah, I got access to a huge data bank with the links and codes to practically every major city, state, and federal camera system in the country. But I wanted to see more so I snooped around a little and was able to tap into the surveillance cameras on some of our NASA and military satellites, and some other stuff that would blow your mind."

"You hacked into all those systems?"

"Like I always say: 'Firewalls are meant to be burned down and I'm fuckin' Fire Marshall Bill!'"

Jeremy cruised over to his large desk. "Go ahead. Pick any place on the planet."

Tony thought for a moment. "Okay. How about Paris?"

"In a jif," Jeremy replied as his fingers flew across the keyboard. He slashed through numerous pages at lightning speed until he finally hit the return button. "Okay. Check it out!"

A spectacular video feed of the Arc de Triomphe in Paris appeared on the giant screen. Using a joystick, Jeremy swiveled the camera 180 degrees and zoomed in and out. Given that it was a few hours before dawn, the streets were virtually empty, but the panoramic views were breathtaking.

Jeremy quickly flashed through a few other famous destinations around the city: outside The Louvre, the Eiffel Tower, along the Champs-Élysées.

"Amazing," Tony said.

"It's my special window on the world."

As Jeremy plunged deeper into the spaghetti, Tony sat down to watch the quiet streets of Paris on the huge screen. His right leg throbbed after walking the eight blocks from Mancini's.

With his cane resting across his lap, Tony slowly and methodically massaged his right thigh with both hands. Every time he went through this painful ritual, he reflected on the deadly gun battle that had ripped his leg apart twenty years earlier. The assassination attempt on Mario Conti may have lasted only a few seconds, but Tony's recollection of the bloody event was still a long, slow motion nightmare…

* * * *

It was a cold, gray day in lower Manhattan... Riding around the City in the back of a limo, Tony was accompanying Don Mario on his typical Monday rounds.

Despite Tony's repeated warnings about the dangers of establishing predictable travel patterns and daily routines where he could be susceptible to foul play, Mario adamantly refused to change his schedule. "Relax, my friend. No one wants to kill me. I get along fine with all the families." Still, Tony was always on edge whenever Mario asked him to come along.

After buying fresh flowers and Italian anisette cookies, they visited Mario's aging mother at an upscale nursing home. While Mario sat at her bedside for an hour, praying and holding her hand, Tony met with their key Capos at a coffee shop next door to review the past week's receipts from the Conti gambling empire.

Later, on their way to Mario's favorite lunch place, they discussed the weekly take. Thanks in large part to Tony's clever expansion of the sports book and a growing network of private high-stakes floating card games, business was booming.

Vinnie Talia, Mario's trusted driver and bodyguard, pulled up to the curb in front of the small neighborhood restaurant in Little Italy. As Vinnie bent down to open the back door for Mario, an assassin walked up behind him and pumped two .38 slugs into his head. The burly bodyguard fell forward into the limo, splattering blood and brains all over the interior.

Instinctively, Tony pushed Mario down to protect him and grabbed the pistol from Vinnie's shoulder holster. Taking deadly aim, he shot the assassin twice through the heart.

Standing in the shadows about fifteen yards away, two other hitmen tore open their trench coats to reveal some intimidating hardware: an Uzi submachine gun and a sawed-off 12-gauge shotgun. As they rushed over to finish the job, Tony picked up the assassin's pistol, leapt from the limo, and ran toward the startled killers with both of the handguns blazing.

The first blast of buckshot from the shotgun slammed into an unwitting pedestrian, who was caught in the crossfire on the sidewalk, killing him instantly.

As Tony continued to charge straight ahead, the other contract killer sprayed bullets from the machine gun. Although Tony was hit four times, his adrenaline rush propelled him forward.

Luckily, the Uzi jammed, allowing Tony to get within pointblank range. He emptied his weapons into the hitmen who crumpled to the pavement.

In his death throes, the shotgun-wielding assassin pulled the trigger one last time. The errant blast hit Tony's right leg, shredding his knee and lower thigh...

It was a miracle his leg wasn't completely blown off.

During a heroic series of surgeries in which the leg was rebuilt with titanium rods and screws, tissue from all over his body, and cadaver parts—his leg was saved.

Beneath the frightening patchwork of Frankenstein-like stitches and multi-colored skin grafts, his frayed nerves and shredded muscles still screamed out in pain.

He dry-swallowed several aspirin and continued to knead his leg in vain. It throbbed and convulsed with internal tremors. Despite the on-going chronic pain and disturbing memories of that fateful day, seeing his young friend in a wheelchair made Tony eternally grateful for what remained of his limited mobility.

* * * *

Tony had known "The Kid" for almost twenty years. Jeremy's mother, Sarah, was one of the nurses who took care of him in the difficult months after the shooting. Originally from Israel, she was a beautiful woman and avid reader. They spent many late nights at the hospital talking about books, old movies, and life in general.

As their friendship blossomed, Sarah confided in him that she was a widow with a young son, who was brilliant but beset with psychological and physical problems.

Their lives had been shattered on Jeremy's eighth birthday. Sarah's husband, a successful African-American businessman, and Jeremy were on their way to see a Knicks' game at Madison Square Garden. As they were getting into their car, a cab driver lost control of his speeding vehicle and slammed into them. Her husband died instantly and Jeremy's legs were crushed, leaving him in a wheelchair for the rest of his life. Jeremy also became agoraphobic—deathly afraid of leaving the house, his safe zone.

Shortly after Tony left the hospital, Sarah invited him over for dinner. Almost immediately, he and Jeremy bonded over their handicaps, love of Italian food, and competitive games of chess. For the next few years, Tony and Sarah enjoyed a romantic relationship while young Jeremy toiled over a hot keyboard. He was a computer savant who wrote code and engaged in many extraordinary feats of amateur hacking.

Eventually, Tony and Sarah drifted apart, but they remained good friends. Tony and Jeremy kept in close contact.

Jeremy was a real prankster with a wicked sense of humor. When he was just sixteen years old, juiced to the gills on Cherry Coke and Skittles, he'd hacked into the deepest regions of the Pentagon's computer system. Using a pirated offshore banking account in Bermuda, Jeremy tried to purchase a refurbished Blackhawk helicopter on behalf of a mythical country in Central Asia he called 'Ujerkistan.'

Eventually, the prank unraveled and FBI agents busted him. When the Feds tried to forcibly remove Jeremy from his house, he completely freaked out— he had not been outside for eight years. His panic attack was so severe he had to be strapped down and heavily sedated.

For the next two weeks, he resided in a clandestine hospital run by the government. After an extensive battery of IQ tests and psychiatric interviews, the Feds realized young Jeremy could be a very powerful asset for the National Security Agency (NSA), where teams of elite American hackers waged cyber warfare against international terrorists and rogue states.

A plea deal was arranged, and all pending charges against Jeremy were dropped. In exchange for his full-time servitude to the U.S. government, his mother insisted Jeremy be allowed to pursue a college education and be protected from any possible outside dangers. Special arrangements were made with MIT so he could study from home. Further, the government "hardened" their house, installing a sophisticated security system and completely remodeling the basement to create a highly functional, comfortable work and living space for the exceptional teenager.

During the exhaustive government background check of Jeremy and his mother, their connection with Tony Tucci came to light. Even though he was a decorated veteran, the Feds were highly suspicious of Tony's ties to the Conti family and insisted Jeremy end their friendship. Without hesitation, "The Kid" told his handlers Tony was like a father to him, and there was no way he was going to terminate their relationship. It was "a deal breaker." Ultimately, the Feds relented. Thereafter, Tony continued to visit Jeremy a couple times a month, and their friendship grew even stronger.

By the time Jeremy was 23, he had earned a Ph.D. in Electrical Engineering and Computer Science, becoming a confident and highly regarded hacker with the NSA's "Tailored Access Operations," which specialized in breaking into foreign governments' computer systems, among other nefarious activities.

Only Tony and his mother knew what he really did for a living. The few others who were allowed to enter Jeremy's residence thought he wrote code for a big video game company based in Silicon Valley.

Jeremy finished off the spaghetti and yelled, "Incoming!" And then belched loudly.

"Very nice," Tony said, used to Jeremy's erratic behavior.

Jeremy was half adult, half child. He was a computer genius who could disassemble the most complex, encrypted networking and operating systems, but he could also act like an immature teenager.

After tossing the empty food carton into the trash, Jeremy rolled over to one of the weight machines and knocked out a quick set of pull-ups. "It burns, baby! It burns!"

Jeremy's upper body was well developed, thanks to the relentless toning and lifting he did throughout the day during short breaks away from his computer, but his legs were shriveled and useless.

"I think I'll do some leg presses next," Jeremy said with a straight face and then burst out laughing.

Tony laughed too. "Man, you're really in a good mood today."

"No shit, Sherlock!" he exclaimed, popping a wheelie across the room.

It was refreshing to see Jeremy feeling so good. Over the years, Tony had watched Jeremy experience many dark times as he tried to come to terms with his disabilities. Being wheelchair-bound was a difficult but surmountable issue; but the added psychological problems associated with a deep-seated anxiety disorder like agoraphobia was a double whammy.

When he first met Jeremy, Tony arranged for Dr. Rose to come to the house to treat him. By the standards of the widely used "Panic and Agoraphobia Scale" test, young Jeremy was off the charts. Still, Dr. Rose worked with him for a solid year, during which Jeremy made slow and steady progress. One warm spring day, Dr. Rose managed to get Jeremy to venture out onto the front porch, but a random screech of tires down the block sent him rushing back inside in a panic—never to leave again—until the Feds blundered in.

Of course, Jeremy was acutely aware he was damaged in more ways than one. When he felt an anxiety attack coming on, he threw himself into his work, sometimes coding for 72 hours straight, then crashing for a day or two. During these manic sessions, he perfected his "rootkit," a hacker term for stealthy software that can be hidden on computer systems. Undetected, he could break into computers all over the world and install his own spyware, bots, spiders, and destructive viruses.

His work became his salvation.

Jeremy grabbed a book from the corner of his desk, spun around, and rolled back over to Tony. "Here. Check it out."

It was a thick tome of Chinese text with a cover photograph of the famous terracotta warriors from ancient China.

Tony asked. "What? You're studying Chinese now?"

"That's right, T. Like they say, 'Know thy enemy.' The Chinese are fucking with us, hacking into everything and stealing our secrets. Well, what goes around—comes around."

Tony fanned through the book and shook his head. "I thought code was a universal language."

"It is, but by understanding Chinese history and culture, I'll learn how they think. My goal is to be fluent in Mandarin within a year. It's no big deal. Uncle Sam even hired a special tutor for me. Her name is Lei and she visits me three times a week."

Jeremy nodded at the unmade bed in the back bedroom and winked. "Lei means 'thunder' in Chinese. And I can confirm she's definitely 'thunder' in the sack. Our study sessions are very hot."

Jeremy was also a sex addict. Since he never left The Bunker, he relied on high-priced call girls to visit him. Tony had set him up with an escort service in the City and he was a very popular client with the girls.

"Careful, Lei could be a spy for China," Tony said.

"God forbid! She could suck my best hacker secrets right out of me!"

That got a big laugh.

Jeremy was Tony's dear friend and surrogate son, but also an invaluable resource. Shortly after his 21st birthday, Tony and Jeremy had a long conversation about being a moral man. Tony confessed some, but not all of his sins, to Jeremy—and how he had evolved physically, emotionally, and spiritually.

Tony recalled that he was a gifted student in his younger years, but never finished high school. Instead, Tony completed his education in the jungles of Vietnam and the streets of Manhattan and Brooklyn, where he learned hard realities about his fellow man.

He had come to understand a sad, universal truth: Most people were motivated by self-interest and greed. Of course, there were many different shades of selfishness and gradations of greed, but they all quickly faded away in the face of the greatest motivator of all: basic survival. The desire for self-preservation trumped all.

Tony told Jeremy that, based on his reputation as a problem solver and fixer, many people came to him with pleas for help. These unfortunate souls needed someone to deal with the predators ruining their lives. Most of the time, Tony could resolve these matters on his own with a short face-to-face meeting, but there were special cases when he needed in-depth personal information about the perpetrators.

He asked Jeremy to be his partner, using his awesome online hacking skills to investigate finances and backgrounds. Subsequently, Tony would meet with those individuals to convince them to change their behavior and make amends for their cruelty to others. If they did not, Tony unleashed Jeremy to secretly steal their assets, and destroy their credit and reputations.

Tony and Jeremy never profited personally from their covert activities. Any "appropriated" monies were dispersed to various charities through non-traceable, third-party offshore bank accounts. Meanwhile, their targets faced years of legal hassles and sometimes even financial ruin.

Jeremy enjoyed the work, claiming it was "fun to fuck with the evildoers." He called Tony and himself "The White Hats"—another popular hacker term.

Tony and Jeremy had dealt with all kinds of malevolent people who needed to be morally realigned and, in some cases, severely punished. One of their more memorable cases was a man named Omar Karga, aka "The Turk," who was preying on a good man named Clarence Johnson...

14

About a year ago, Tony stopped by Mancini's for a late evening meal. He noticed an older black man sitting alone at the end of the bar, working on a stiff bourbon. A few years older than Tony, he had sad brown eyes and a fringe of short, white curly hair.

Tony could tell the man was upset about something. After a while, he walked over to the bar and sat down beside the pensive gentleman. The TV mounted on the wall above them was broadcasting a Yankees' game. Tony wasn't a rabid sports fan anymore, but he knew the hometown team would never make the playoffs.

"Looks like the 'Bronx Bombers' are out of it again," Tony said in an attempt to launch a conversation.

The man shifted on his barstool. "Yeah, but unlike some businesses, they'll be around forever."

Tony sipped his wine. "I assume you're a businessman and things aren't going well," he said, trying to penetrate the man's stony facade.

The man frowned. "What's it to you?"

"Sorry, I didn't mean to pry. At least, let me buy you a drink."

As Paolo freshened the man's glass, Tony extended his hand and said, "My name is Tony Tucci. It's a pleasure to meet you."

They shook hands.

"Thanks. I'm Clarence Johnson… I rarely drink alcohol, but tonight I feel like getting plastered."

He took a hearty swig and told Tony his story…

* * * *

Clarence had a major dilemma. For the past thirty years, he had owned a small, neighborhood grocery store in Mott Haven, one of the poorest parts of the South Bronx. It was the only store within a half-mile radius where people could buy basic food items, including fresh vegetables and fruits.

He had endured every imaginable retail horror story: robberies, break-ins, serial shoplifting, attempted arsons, refusals by suppliers to service the store, and worse. He had been stabbed, shot twice, and was once locked in his walk-in freezer overnight where he almost froze to death. He survived everything fate and the mean streets could throw at him. But like the old Marine he was, Clarence stayed true to his mission to provide his neighbors with a reliable, well-stocked store where they could get good quality merchandise at a fair price. If anything happened to Clarence's store, the locals would have to travel a great distance to a large supermarket and haul their groceries home via the bus or subway.

Clarence was beloved around the neighborhood for his humble demeanor and compassionate deeds. He provided food and volunteered at the local soup kitchen, trying to help anyone in need. He was revered by virtually everyone—even the sadistic local street gangs respected Clarence and left him alone.

The problem was a Turkish slumlord named Omar Karga, who owned numerous retail properties and apartment buildings in greater Harlem and the South Bronx. He had purchased the empty corner lot right next to Clarence's grocery store and was in the process of building a fast-food franchise.

Originally, Clarence was pleased about the new addition to the neighborhood because it would create jobs; however, when Karga approached Clarence, saying he wanted to purchase his property because he "needed extra parking space," Clarence knew Karga's motives weren't honest.

The parking issue was a ruse. The City had required more than adequate parking before they approved Karga's building permits. Also, the neighborhood was so dangerous, most people would use the drive-through anyway. It was obvious Karga didn't want a competing enterprise near his new restaurant, especially one that sold frozen dinners, sandwiches, and other snacks.

Karga offered Clarence a paltry $125,000 for his property—a 3,000-square-foot, two-story red-brick structure. The store was on the first floor and Clarence's personal residence was upstairs, where he cared for his eighty-five-year-old invalid father. The offer was an insult and no sane person would have taken it seriously. When Clarence politely said "no," Karga grew indignant and threatened him with financial ruin if he didn't sell.

Using his contacts within various city and state regulatory agencies, Karga launched an aggressive campaign to bring Clarence to his knees. First, the state liquor authority launched an undercover sting operation busting Clarence's employees for not properly checking a few minors' IDs before selling them beer. That cost Clarence more than $10,000 in fines and placed his liquor license in jeopardy.

Next, the City Building Department conducted a surprise visit and found numerous minor code violations. After another $15,000 in penalties and improvements, Clarence's cash savings were wiped out.

Finally, earlier that day, he was notified that the state franchise tax board planned to audit every one of his sales receipts for the last three years. He kept adequate records and had paid all his taxes in full and on time, but now he would have to hire a high-priced accountant or tax attorney to represent him during a prolonged and expensive audit. With a personal annual income of only about $40,000, Clarence did not have the financial resources to carry on. The grocery store was his life and he saw it all slipping away.

Clarence snapped.

Barely controlling his anger, he told his clerk he needed some air and abruptly stormed out of his store. For the next few hours, he randomly walked southward in a haze of anger and frustration until he stumbled into Mancini's.

Tony was a good listener. People relaxed in his presence because they sensed he was genuinely interested in them as human beings. With hands folded and a welcoming smile, Tony carefully weighed their words and motivations. For two hours, he listened intently to the broken and depressed Clarence.

Tony learned many things about him, including that he was a fellow ex-Marine who had also served in Vietnam. During his sole tour, Clarence survived the Tet Offensive in Da Nang in 1968 and was later wounded in the Battle of Kham Duc before he was shipped home. Tony arrived a few months later in the fall of 1968, where he endured two tours with the 1st Marine Division. They bonded over a few war stories and shared experiences.

Clarence's predicament was a simple case of Omar Karga's extraordinary greed. Given his substantial real estate holdings, Karga already had plenty of money and power, but he wanted more.

Before the assassination attempt on Mario Conti, Tony had also been a slave to avarice. A shrewd handicapper and bookmaker, he made big bank for the big boss. Recognizing talent when he saw it, Mario had moved Tony up within the organization and paid him handsomely. But Tony still wanted more: a big house, fancy boat, fast car, and the ability to travel first class all the time.

The power was intoxicating, too.

Although Tony sought to keep a low profile, his close association with the Don and pivotal role in the family's gambling operations generated a deep respect among everyone in the Conti organization and the other New York families. For years, he reveled in the power, prestige, and money—but down deep he knew he was selling his soul and one day he would have to atone.

After dinner and a final round of drinks, Tony offered Clarence a ride home. Clarence was surprised when he saw the limo parked in front of the restaurant, but he was truly shocked when Tony slipped in behind the wheel.

"Man, from your clothes and cash, I thought you were some rich guy—not a chauffeur!"

"Why don't you sit in the back for the ride home? Go ahead. Make yourself comfortable."

Half-drunk, Clarence peered in at the limo's lavish interior but shook his head. "Nah, that's not my scene. I'd rather hang with you up front. After all, we Marines have got to stick together."

He settled into the passenger's seat.

In silence, they drove into the foreboding Mott's Haven neighborhood until Tony finally spoke.

"If you're okay with it, Clarence, I'd like to have a chat with Omar Karga. I think I may be able to resolve this situation and you'll be able to keep your store."

"You're a good man, Mr. Tucci, but I doubt a chauffeur is going to convince a ruthless dude like Karga to change his mind. He's one mean mofo."

Smiling to himself, Tony secretly relished the challenge. Karga was a rapacious pig who needed to have his priorities readjusted.

"First, call me Tony. And second, I think Karga will back off once he understands a few things."

"That would be a miracle!" said Clarence. "I guess I don't have anything to lose... Sure, go for it."

Before Clarence got out of the limo, he thanked Tony for dinner, the conversation, and the ride home.

"Semper fi," Tony said.

They shook hands and nodded goodnight.

15

A week later, after Jeremy did some online sleuthing into Karga's general finances and private life, Tony had enough ammo to have a candid chat with the predatory Turk.

Karga had just remodeled a spiffy new twelve-story office building on the East River. He moved his executive and managerial teams onto the top floor, keeping the premiere office for himself. The ninth floor, a 5,000-square-foot space, was available for rent. Posing as a prospective leasee, Tony set up a meeting to view the space with Karga's personal assistant.

In an effort to project a successful profile, Tony hired a friend's son, Casey Flynn, a struggling young actor, to play chauffeur for the sham visit.

The Mercedes limo rolled through the security gate into the small parking area in front of Karga's building at eleven o'clock in the morning. Casey, dressed in a suit and tie, got out and held the rear door open for Tony. Anyone looking down from the office building would see a well-dressed man with a cane emerge from the back of the limo and enter the foyer.

After being greeted by Karga's assistant, they took the elevator to the ninth floor. During the brief ten-minute tour of the office, she spoke non-stop about the benefits, amenities, and pricing associated with leasing the space. When Tony confirmed he was interested in pursuing a contract, she said the building's owner, Mr. Omar Karga, insisted on meeting any potential new renter.

Of course, Tony welcomed the invitation. As he was escorted to the waiting room outside Karga's private suite, numerous employees, all looking like unhappy bean counters, ran in and out of small offices, carrying files and reports. The assistant disappeared behind Karga's closed door. After a few minutes, she emerged and ushered Tony inside.

Karga's office was spacious, sparsely furnished, and flooded in warm sunlight. Tall windows revealed a spectacular view of the East River and Astoria beyond. Huge modern abstract paintings hung on the white walls and colorful Turkish rugs covered the painted concrete floor.

When Tony entered, Karga was on the phone, facing the river with his back turned. He was speaking loudly in his native language and gesturing wildly with his free hand. Finally, he ended the call and turned to meet Tony.

"I apologize for keeping you waiting, but I had to deal with a rather messy matter with one of my landlords," said Karga.

Yeah, the tenants probably wanted the hot water turned on, Tony thought.

The Turk extended his hand, "I'm Omar Karga."

They shook.

"And I'm Tony Tucci."

The Turk spoke English quite well, but his accent was as thick as hummus. He was a fat, balding, middle-aged man with bushy eyebrows and beady eyes magnified behind oversized red-tinted glasses on a gold chain. Wearing a white silk shirt, pleated slacks, and Gucci loafers, Karga tried to project a wealthy persona—but the garish, solid gold Rolex on his wrist made him look like a Middle-Eastern pimp.

Karga gestured at the wall of windows. "A spectacular sight, don't you think?"

Tony walked over to take in the view. "Yes, it's very impressive."

They marveled at the panorama until Tony pointed down at a small island in the middle of the river. "Have you ever been to Mill Rock Park?"

"No."

"When I was a kid, I used to sneak out there all the time with my friends. Depending upon the weather and the size of the boat, it can be a treacherous round trip, but well worth it."

"You're a local boy?" asked Karga, scrutinizing Tony more closely.

"Yes. I was born and raised here back when it was mostly an Italian-American neighborhood."

Karga stroked his perfectly coiffed beard. "Ah yes… I've heard that Pleasant Avenue was once a big Mafia stronghold. Is that true?"

"In the 1960s and '70s, it was the center of the heroin trade and money flowed like the East River. Pleasant Avenue was clogged with brand-new Cadillacs, wise guys wore shark-skin suits, and most of the cops were on the take." Looking out across the skyline, Tony smiled. "It was a wild scene."

Tony could feel Karga's eyes dissect him. No doubt about it, he was a ruthless businessman who was very wary of others. He also smelled like a French whorehouse, doused in cologne to mask the musky scent of his chronic sweating.

"Please have a seat," Karga said.

As Tony walked around the desk, he caught a glimpse of Karga's two computer screens. One was filled with emails and a spreadsheet while the other displayed a dozen surveillance cameras covering the inside and outside of the building.

Karga was definitely a control freak.

There were four uncomfortable-looking Scandinavian designer chairs positioned in front of his glass desk. Tony selected one near a window because it would make Karga face the harshest sunlight.

Squinting, Karga asked, "Tell me, what type of business are you in, Mr. Tucci?"

Tony removed a business card from his pocket and slid it across the desk. Many years ago, he was given a box of business cards when he worked for Conti Construction, but he rarely handed them out, thinking they were too pretentious. He'd found the cards that morning and brought some along as convenient props.

Karga studied the card. "Conti Construction... Yes, I think I've heard of it. You guys are big into concrete work, right?"

"Yes, we specialize in road construction—and concrete shoes," Tony said with a wry smile.

Karga didn't seem to get the joke. If he had heard any rumors about Conti's mob reputation, he didn't betray it.

"So, do you like the office space downstairs, Mr. Tucci?"

"It's very nice."

"And you understand the terms? The monthly rent is $25,000, but all utilities are included. If you want any remodeling, we'll have to work out the details. And we'll require a minimum two-year contract and a $50,000 deposit."

Tony shifted in his chair. "I have to confess, I came here under false pretenses. I no longer work for Conti Construction, although I'm still closely associated with the Conti family. We have no interest in renting your space. Actually, I'm here to discuss another matter."

Clearly irritated, Karga leaned back in his chair. "And what is that ?"

"Clarence Johnson."

Karga's gaze narrowed. "Never heard of him." He slowly rose to his feet. "And now, I think you should leave."

Tony didn't move. "I'm not going anywhere. You would be wise to hear me out."

"I'm a very busy man and—"

"Sit down and shut up!" Tony said coldly.

It was like someone slapped Karga across the face. He glared down at Tony with angry eyes. After years of building a financial empire on the backs of others, he was used to being in the power position.

Tony calmly gestured to Karga's chair. "Please, sit."

Reluctantly, The Turk sat back down.

"As I was saying, I'd like to talk about what you're doing to Clarence. Your relentless efforts to drive him out of business are taking a toll," Tony said, watching his prey closely. "You'll be happy to know his life savings have been wiped out to pay for the penalties, fees, and repairs you so cleverly orchestrated with those city and state agencies. And now, with the pending sales tax audit, Clarence has no choice but sell you his business and home for your ridiculously low offer."

Karga couldn't hide the tiny smirk that crossed his lips. "I really don't know what you're talking about."

"Let's drop the bullshit, Karga. I'm here to help."

"Help?"

"If I walk out that door, you'll lose your investment in that new fast food franchise next to Clarence's grocery store. I guarantee it."

"That's absurd. You can't possibly know—"

"I know all about you… You came to this country with a nice wad of family cash and purchased your first property in Harlem in 1992. Over the years, you've purchased fifteen old tenement hotels and converted all of them into low-cost, public housing units where you can double-dip, collecting rents and lucrative government subsidies. With all the cash you generated as a slumlord, you've also purchased eight strip malls, some office buildings, and warehouses."

"All that is public information," Karga replied. "You don't know anything about me and never will."

Tony pulled out his notebook and opened it.

"You have a personal net worth of over $40 million. Last year, your corporate profit was $10 million. You're currently in negotiations to purchase a big cinema complex in Flatbush, and three commercially zoned lots up in the Bronx. You have safe deposit boxes in Switzerland and the Cayman Islands, plus numerous bank accounts scattered over three states."

Tony locked eyes with Karga. "Want to know the balances?"

That finally wiped the smirk from Karga's fat face. A light sheen of perspiration gleamed across his forehead. "Where? Where did you get all that information?"

"In three short days, I've amassed a huge file on you. Trust me, it wasn't that hard. You just have to know how and where to look. In this digital age, there's really no such thing as 'personal privacy' anymore, and I happen to have some great resources that are always eager to help, especially when it's to right a terrible wrong. And you crossed the line with Clarence."

Karga leaned back in his chair and took a deep breath trying to control his temper. Sweat began to roll down the side of his jowly face, dripping onto his silk shirt.

Tony continued. "I know where you live, where you vacation, and shop. I even know who your hot young wife is screwing behind your back."

Tony made up the last part about his wife—he couldn't resist.

Again, anger flared in Karga's eyes. "Your visit has nothing to do with Clarence Johnson. This is a shakedown, right? What do you really want?"

"Like I said, I just want you to stop hassling Clarence. It's that simple."

"And if I don't?" snapped the surly Turk.

"Then your new fast food franchise is going to have problems."

"What problems?"

"I hear those joints throw off a lot of cash. With all the traffic on nearby 3rd Avenue, it could be a real gold mine."

"What problems, damn it!?"

Tony glanced down at his notebook. "Are you familiar with the B&B gang that runs the neighborhood in Mott Haven where you want to do business?"

"There are gangs everywhere. Why should I care?"

"It's a violent subset of the Bloods, who control most of the South Bronx. You've heard of the Bloods, haven't you?"

Karga sat there quietly fuming, his damp silk shirt stuck to his hairy chest. Tony was starting to enjoy himself and knew a few exaggerated facts would enhance his presentation.

"The leader of that gang is Crazy Clyde. Apparently, he prefers to use a machete on his enemies in the local drug trade. The cops have linked him with a half-dozen unsolved murders, but no witnesses will come forward... Anyway, Clyde also loves his momma, Roberta, who lives about two blocks from Clarence's grocery store. Roberta and Clarence go way back, and she shops there almost every day. From what Clarence told me, I think they have a romantic relationship."

Now, glowering like a trapped animal, Karga squirmed in his chair. "What does that have to do with me?"

"Well, I've been thinking. Your new restaurant would make a great clubhouse for Crazy Clyde and the B&B boys. You know, they could hang out there during the day, grab some food, sell some drugs, get high, invite over some of their fellow Bloods... Of course, it would probably wreak havoc on your bottom line since no customers will want to go anywhere near the place."

Karga leaned forward on his desk. "So—if I leave Clarence alone, you'll make sure this gang stays away from my business?"

"Hell no! I'm just speculating," laughed Tony. "But I'm sure if Clarence asked Crazy Clyde to play it

93

cool, he probably would, just to make his momma happy."

Karga reflected on his predicament. Finally, he said, "Tell me, why are you doing this? What does that black bastard mean to you?"

Tony scowled. He detested racial slurs of any kind. "Be careful, Karga. I consider Clarence to be a friend—even though we've only met once."

Karga was perplexed. "You've got to be kidding! You go to all this trouble for a man you hardly know?"

"We share a sacred bond."

"And what's that?"

"We both served as Marines in Vietnam."

The Turk sneered, "That war was an atrocity! It was American imperialism at its worse."

Tony's gaze narrowed as he carefully measured his words. "As a foreigner who has come to this great country and done extremely well, you should remember that men like Clarence fought to secure your rights and freedoms."

"And I pay plenty in taxes too!" scoffed Karga. "In America, it's always all about the money."

"If that's what you think, pal, you have no idea what makes this country tick." Using his cane to stabilize himself, Tony stood. "So—do we have a deal?"

Reluctantly, Karga nodded.

"And, as a gesture of goodwill, you need to cut a check to Clarence for $50,000."

Karga laughed indignantly. "Are you insane?"

"He's already out-of-pocket for $25,000 for all the shit you put him through. The rest is for his pain and suffering."

The Turk thought for a moment and said, "Okay, okay… I'll pay him back the $25,000, but not a penny more!"

"This isn't a negotiation, Karga. You'll pay $50,000 in full and kill the audit too," Tony said sternly.

"I will not!" Karga shouted, leaping to his feet. It looked like his head was about to explode.

Tony calmly replied. "Sure, you will."

Karga stomped around the side of his desk and got into Tony's face. "You're nothing more than an extortionist. A Mafia errand boy!"

So Karga had heard the stories about the Conti family's mob connections. Good.

"Come on, Karga, everyone knows there's no such thing as the Mafia."

Karga was now quaking with rage, looking like he wanted to punch Tony in the face. "Oh, that's rich! Especially coming from a little wop who grew up on Pleasant Avenue."

Still, Tony kept his cool. "Like you said, it's all about the money, and you have plenty of it."

"And if I don't pay, what are you going to do?"

Tony took a step back from the infuriated man. "You need to consider the consequences of your decisions. That's all."

As Tony exited the building and slipped into the back of the waiting limo, he knew Karga was watching his every move on the monitors in his office.

Just like the other morally bankrupt souls who preyed on the weak and had the misfortune to cross his path, Tony knew Karga would write that check—especially after he learned more about Tony's past and his deep ties to the legendary Conti family.

In retrospect, Karga realized calling Tony "a Mafia errand boy" had been a big mistake, one that haunted him through many sleepless nights. As a result, Karga decided to beef up his personal security, and he hired an expensive private detective to follow his wife around. Ironically, she really was cheating on him with a handsome young Wall Street attorney.

After a nasty divorce battle, which Karga had to bankroll, he was forced to liquidate $20 million of his real estate holdings to buy her off. It was a steep price to pay for messing with Clarence Johnson—and Tony Tucci.

Jeremy observed: "Karmic payback can be a real bitch."

16

A few weeks after Tony's encounter with Karga, Clarence dropped off a package at Mancini's for his new friend.

Sitting alone in the bar one evening, Tony unwrapped the package to find a book about the Vietnam War—*The Things They Carried* by Tim O'Brien. He smiled, knowing it was a profound study of men in combat.

Tucked in the back, he found a short note from Clarence that read:

Dear Tony,

I have no idea what you did or said to Karga, but his attorney just dropped off a check for $50,000 and the state cancelled the audit of my books. I'm in shock!

The attorney also said I am supposed to tell a local gangbanger named "Crazy Clyde" to stay away from Karga's new fast food joint. I played along, but I've never heard of that guy. What's up?

Anyway, I am forever in your debt.

Semper Fi, Clarence Johnson

P.S: Please stop by the store anytime. You're entitled to a lifetime supply of Slim Jims!

17

Back in The Bunker, Jeremy asked, "So who's our next project?"

Tony removed the slip of paper Mario had given him and handed it to Jeremy. "This one is personal for me. That's the address for an old mob guy named Nicky Bruno. He was responsible for the hit on Don Mario Conti."

"No shit?"

Tony nodded. "He probably has a lot of hidden assets. You'll have to dig deep."

"Piece of cake. This cretin probably thinks his stash is untouchable, but I'll bet his castle is crufty."

"Crufty?"

"It's hacker slang. Means 'poorly built.' Except for the Benjamins under his bed, I'll find everything he's got," Jeremy said confidently. "But I can't get to it for a few days. I'm crunching on a special project for my boss."

"That's fine. I've waited twenty years to confront him. A few more days won't matter," Tony said. "By the way, I'm curious about something. Aren't you worried your boss or some other NSA hacker is tracking our extracurricular activities?"

"Of course. I wouldn't expect anything less from my colleagues at the agency. I always run special software to check for bugs. My system is clean; however, for *our* special projects, I've taken some extra precautions. First, I don't use this computer," he said, gesturing at his expansive government-supplied system. "Instead, I have a secret encrypted laptop that's loaded with all my spyware. And second, I have tapped into the wireless router of a small company on the other side of the block so I can use *their* IP address for all our digital wet work. We're golden, baby!"

Tony stood. "Well, I better get going. Call me when you have something."

"I'm psyched about this new project, T. It'll be fun to burn that Bruno bitch!" Jeremy announced as he wheeled over to the door to open it for Tony. "And thanks again for dinner."

"You bet. And good luck with your Chinese lessons."

With a mischievous smirk, Jeremy replied, "Yeah, it's dark and lonely work, but somebody has to do it."

10:30 p.m.

Once outside, Tony buttoned up his overcoat, bracing against the late evening chill. His leg was aching too much to walk back to Mancini's, so he called Ramon to pick him up in the limo.

Snow began to swirl down, lightly covering his fedora and shoulders. Although he was basically at peace in his life, Tony felt an ineffable sense of dread and foreboding. There was something dangerous stirring in the periphery of his world like a hungry beast circling a campfire.

Tony couldn't quite comprehend what it was, but he knew his quiet existence was about to be shattered by forces far beyond his control.

18

New York City
10:45 p.m.

Gino and Al parked the black Escalade in a secluded dark alley behind The Palace, the popular discotheque near Inferno. Dante had made it clear he would not tolerate any competition in the immediate neighborhood and Raul Garcia's nightclub was the last holdout. Something had to be done about it before Inferno opened its doors in a few days.

For the last month, Gino and Al had shadowed the disco owner, tracking his daily schedule, watching his comings and goings. Garcia was a creature of habit. They could see the dim light on in Garcia's office in the back corner of the converted warehouse. He worked alone until 11:00 every night, Monday through Wednesday when the nightclub was closed, and then went directly to his flat in the West Village.

On two previous occasions Gino and Al had made a point of bumping into Garcia…

* * * *

The first time was two weeks earlier, while Garcia was sitting at a small sidewalk table in front of a nearby deli, eating a sandwich and reading the newspaper.

Garcia was a small man, maybe 5'6", with a well-manicured beard, razor-cut hair, slim-fit Nike sweat suit, and new Air Jordans. He looked like he worked out on a regular basis, projecting the cockiness and intensity of a streetwise nightclub owner.

Dante's goons strolled up, grabbed two chairs and sat down across from him.

"Man, that sandwich looks delish," said Gino.

"It is," mumbled Garcia. "Can I... help you?"

Gino reached over, grabbed half the sandwich and took a big bite. "Wow! That is good."

"Me too!" said Al, playfully wrestling the sandwich from Gino's meaty grip and taking an even bigger bite.

Garcia recoiled in his chair. "Hey, what is this?"

"Just getting to know our new neighbors," Gino replied. "Your name is Raul Garcia, right?"

The disco owner nodded skeptically.

Gino used Garcia's napkin to wipe his mouth. "You've probably heard that we're opening a new nightclub right down the street called Inferno."

"Yeah, so what?" he said indignantly, trying not to show any fear.

Of course, Garcia knew all about Inferno. He had heard rumors that a mobster named Dante Conti owned the new club and was spending a fortune to renovate it. And it didn't take a genius to figure out that these two assholes were his muscle.

"Well, as a businessman, you understand supply and demand, right? There's only a limited supply of rich fuckers who can party at a fancy nightclub every weekend," leered Gino. "And when there's too much competition for those customers in the same neighborhood, it's a lot harder to make a buck."

Al grabbed Garcia's mineral water off the table and toasted Gino. "Impressive! You oughta teach Economics at NYU!"

Smirking, Gino shoved a fresh toothpick into his mouth.

Garcia was getting pissed.

Al took a gulp as Gino continued, "So we think the neighborly thing for you to do is pack up The Palace and move on."

Garcia folded his arms across his chest in defiance and snapped, "You're threatening me?"

The ballsy little Cuban reminded Gino of a bantam rooster—tough and aggressive but also small and annoying.

"No one is threatening anyone, Raul. We're just talkin."

"Well, hear this, neighbor," Garcia said sarcastically. "I've spent the last three years working my ass off to make The Palace the top nightclub in the District. I'm not going anywhere."

Although he was clearly irritated, Gino kept his cool and leaned in closer to get in Garcia's face.

"Look, little man, you've had a good run here, but things change. Just cash in your chips and get out of Dodge. Or things could get real ugly and—"

He cut himself off when a couple of businessmen sat down at the table right next to them. Disgruntled at the sudden interruption, Gino nodded at Al and they both stood up.

"Well, thanks for lunch," said Gino, all friendly-like, and dropped Garcia's used napkin on the table. "We'll see you around."

Garcia was fuming as Dante's burly henchmen walked off down the block toward Inferno.

His first impulse was to run to the cops and tell them about the intimidation and veiled threats, but he quickly reconsidered. Dante could have some of the local police in his pocket who would tell him about the complaint. And how would the mobsters react if he raised a stink? It was a dangerous gamble to trust the authorities, Garcia thought. He decided to keep the conversation to himself—at least, for a while.

* * * *

The other shoe dropped the following Sunday night...

Sundays at The Palace were not as jammed-packed as Fridays and Saturdays, but there were still plenty of diehard disco fans to keep the party alive until the wee hours of Monday morning.

Known for its glitzy dance scene and dazzling lighting, The Palace was covered in mirrors from floor to ceiling. With the addition of hundreds of pulsating, multi-colored strobe lights and a giant twirling disco ball, the nightclub was awash in glittering reflections.

As the music throbbed, expensive champagne and vodka flowed at the VIP tables. Shapely waitresses in shimmering silver mini-skirts passed around trendy hors d'oeurves. During roundtrips between the dance floor and their bottle-strewn tables, patrons shared cocaine-packed snuff bullets and smoked weed in the bathrooms.

Business was brisk.

Raul Garcia was making one of his frequent sweeps through the club around midnight, checking on his employees and cajoling with customers, when he spotted Gino and Al sitting at a table near the busy dance floor.

As the waitress left to retrieve their drink order, Garcia made eye contact with Gino. He had been expecting another visit from these goons, but he was surprised they'd just stroll into his club and sit down.

Feeling more at ease and confidant on his own turf, Garcia walked over to the table and asked in a loud, sarcastic voice to be heard above the pounding music. "And what brings you here—neighbors? "

"We thought we'd check out your club, Raul," Gino mugged as he looked around. "Very swanky!"

"Yeah, I love what you've done with the place," said Al with a big shit-eating grin. "Got enough mirrors?"

Garcia forced a smile, glowering at the gangsters sprawled in front of him. Gino wore a shiny sports jacket and a ridiculous dress shirt unbuttoned down to his navel to showcase his hairy chest. The collars were the size of mud flaps. Thick gold chains hung around his neck like dog collars, and the omnipresent toothpick dangled from his mouth. Sporting tinted sunglasses and a garish pinstriped suit with a bulging vest to constrain his titanic gut, Al held a huge unlit cigar between his chubby, ring-laden fingers.

Just a couple of goombahs out for a night on the town.

Gino gestured at the giant, sparkling disco ball that hung down about twenty feet above the dance floor. "Wow! That thing is impressive!"

"It's the biggest disco ball east of Vegas," Garcia replied, quite proud of the centerpiece of his nightclub. "It's over ten feet wide and weighs almost half a ton."

"Sounds like my dick," smirked Al.

Laughing obnoxiously, Gino slapped his cretin sidekick on the arm. "Hey! That's a good one!"

As the DJ cued up another Bee Gees' song from the Saturday Night Fever soundtrack, the waitress arrived with a bottle of Cristal and two glasses. She deftly popped the cork, poured two full glasses for the mobsters and laid the bill on their table.

Gino pulled a wad of cash the size of a fist from his pocket, but Garcia picked up the check and handed it back to his employee.

"These gentlemen are my guests. Bring them whatever they want."

"Thanks!" Gino replied and emptied his champagne glass in one swig. "That's excellent."

Winking at the waitress, he added, "Since it's on the house, you better bring another bottle, honey."

Next, Gino grabbed a menu off the table, glanced at it and then stuffed it into his pocket. "Hope you don't mind, Raul. It's always good to see what the competition is charging."

Although he was quaking with rage on the inside, Garcia kept up his "friendly" façade. He didn't want to comp these clowns, and they probably thought he was a pussy for doing it, but he hoped his gesture of good will might help cool the tensions between them.

He was wrong.

Gino turned deadly serious. "Frankly, we thought you'd be throwing a big 'going-away' party tonight. Looks like you didn't get the message when we talked the other day."

Garcia nodded at two brawny bouncers standing beside the main bar. A moment later, the massive ex-NFL linemen loomed behind their boss, staring down at the two Italians.

"Hey, look! It's 'Dumb and Dumber'!" Al quipped, laughing at his own lame joke.

Gino was not amused. The little Cuban rooster is actually trying to intimidate me, Gino thought. Me! If I ever get the chance, I'm gonna wring his puny neck!

"Like I told you last week, I'm not going anywhere." Then, in a strained attempt to be diplomatic, Garcia added, "Look, there's no reason we can't peacefully co-exist. We won't even be competing for the same clientele. The Palace caters to an older demo that wants to relive the early disco years. And, from what I've heard, Inferno will be playing a contemporary mix of hot hits, hip-hop and trance that will appeal to a totally different crowd. Trust me, there are plenty of customers to go around. It'll all work out."

Dante would mock such an assertion. He would never leave the success of Inferno to chance. In all his business dealings, he demanded exclusivity and total dominance.

Gino was about to give Garcia a final dire ultimatum, but held his tongue. If he made any verbal threats and something bad happened to the little shit, the bouncers could serve as potential witnesses. Instead, he just rolled the toothpick around in his mouth, staring menacingly at Garcia. Sensing the vibe, Al lit up his cigar, tilted his head back, and blew a cloud of acrid smoke in to the air.

One of the bouncers, a Samoan with a short mohawk and monstrous tattooed biceps, stepped forward and warned, "Hey! There's no smoking inside the club, pal."

Garcia waved him off. "It's okay. Tonight, they're our guests."

There was an awkward moment as the two groups of men engaged in a final, silent face-off. Finally, Garcia turned and led his bodyguards away.

Laughing behind the back of their host, the mobsters popped the cork on the second bottle of champagne and quickly ordered another. While Al gawked at the hot women gyrating on the dance floor, Gino considered how to deal with the defiant nightclub owner.

Initially, they planned to torch the nightclub late one night; however, during their long hours casing the joint and talking about the options, Gino and Al decided Garcia needed to be silenced once and for all. After their threats and intimidation, they couldn't let Garcia run to the cops and press, claiming he was a victim of some mafia conspiracy to shut his disco down.

Dante agreed. Garcia was going to get whacked. The question was—how?

Gino and Al had killed plenty of people at Dante's behest. Usually, it was handled discreetly—you know, a few bullets in the head or a slit throat, quick dismemberment, and then a trip to the river or the nearest dumpster. Problem solved.

But there were certain instances when Dante demanded more "creative" ways to deal with those who fucked with him. Murders that sent a message— loud and clear.

Once, Dante agreed to purchase a large quantity of marijuana from the Golden Triangle in Northern California in order to sell it to a major drug dealer in the Bronx. They had agreed on fixed price for the risky shipment; however, at the last minute, the dealer refused delivery because had purchased some dope from another source. Stuck with two tons of the stinky herb and no other buyers, Dante flew into a rage and told his crew to make an example out of the double-crossing dealer.

Gino and Al kidnapped the man, tied him up, and wrapped him from head to foot in butcher paper. Ironically, he looked like a giant doobie lying on the floor in an empty garage in Hunt's Point. While Al videotaped the execution for Dante's later enjoyment, Gino drenched the end covering the dealer's head with lighter fluid and set it on fire.

Another memorable murder sent a clear message to Dante's new partners involved in stealing luxury cars off the streets of Manhattan. For two straight years, Dante had regularly sent oversea containers filled with expensive autos like Ferraris, Porsches and Mercedes to brokers in the Middle East. It was a very lucrative gig that brought in plenty of extra cash for the entire Conti crew. Unfortunately, the NYPD caught one of his car thieves in the act. Before being released on bail, the thief agreed to testify against Dante in exchange for a lighter sentence.

A week later, the cops found the car thief, stripped naked with his hands chained to the steering wheel of stolen Porsche convertible, in shallow waters under a pier in Newark Bay. His bloated body was covered with ravenous blue claw crabs.

All charges against Dante were dropped.

And now Dante expected his boys to devise a clever way to dispatch the pint-sized, pain-in-the-ass Cuban.

As he popped a fresh toothpick between his lips, Gino glanced up at the slow-spinning mirrored disco ball. Up in the shadows of the high ceiling, he noticed a network of small catwalks that serviced the sound speakers and extensive lighting system—including the disco ball, which was suspended by a single cable.

Looks a little dicey, Gino thought.

A few hours later, Gino and Al left the nightclub with a fresh bottle of Grey Goose and two drunken cougars who still wanted to party. The waitress wasn't surprised that the loud, rude thugs stiffed her on the tip.

* * * *

11:00 p.m.

Back in the Escalade, two days after their visit to The Palace, Gino and Al kept their eyes on the light in Garcia's office.

Tonight, they had an extra passenger in the back seat. Manny Rizzo was a forty-five year old ex-con with a lengthy rap sheet for burglary and grand theft. A master locksmith and security-system expert, Manny was on the Conti Construction payroll as an electrician, but he basically worked for Gino on special projects like jacking safes from lucrative cash businesses and the occasional arson. Chugging a Red Bull, the ex-alcoholic was anxious to get to work. A backpack filled with the tools of his trade lay on the seat beside him.

Everything had been carefully planned out. As soon as Garcia turned off his office light, they all sprang into action.

Making sure no one was loitering in the vicinity, they snuck across the street and assumed their positions. Two minutes later, right on cue, Garcia peered out of the rear door of The Palace a few feet

109

away from his parked car. The small spotlight above the door provided limited visibility, but the coast was clear. He stepped outside, shut the door, and turned to the digital pad on the wall to activate the alarm and internal camera surveillance system.

Before he could punch in the code, Manny emerged from the darkness with a cigarette in hand. "Hey, mister! Got a light?"

Garcia froze when he noticed Manny was wearing plastic gloves. "Oh shit!"

Before Garcia could react, Al came up behind him and slammed a blackjack onto the back of his head, dropping him to the pavement with a fractured skull. Within 15 seconds, Gino and the boys found Garcia's keys, opened the door and dragged the hapless nightclub owner back inside.

While Al and Manny went to work, Gino carefully searched Garcia's office. Taking pains not to disturb anything, he found a file on the desk with various articles and ads promoting Inferno as well as some handwritten notes, detailing his interactions with Gino and Al—including their numerous threats. Smiling smugly, Gino slipped the notes into his pocket, locked the office door and left. Later, he dropped the keys back into Garcia's pocket as Al and Manny finished their little project.

* * * *

By 2:00 a.m., Dante's crew was back at Inferno celebrating their successful mission by doing tequila shots with lime.

Gino raised his glass for a toast. "Long live the disco king!"

"But I thought disco was dead," laughed Al.

"It is now!"

There were high fives all around as they did another shot.

19

Sands Point
Midnight

Tony's private residence was at the far edge of the Conti estate along The Sound. Built of stone and covered in ivy, it was larger than the other servants' cottages and more secluded.

Inside, the cozy one-bedroom home was sparsely decorated with overflowing bookcases filled with classics and pulp fiction, a few old photos, and oil paintings of faraway places. It was Tony's retreat from the world where he had lived alone for almost twenty years—a modest sanctuary where he could read, rest, and reflect.

He maintained a quiet, reclusive home life and rarely entertained. Very few women had ever spent the night. Instead, he reserved those intimate encounters for hotel suites in the City or perhaps the woman's residence.

He cherished his privacy.

Tony's only regular caller was Buddy, the Conti family wolfhound. Buddy joined Tony for short walks through the compound's gardens and woods and along the shoreline, where he loved to chase sandpipers across the beach. Afterwards, Buddy usually curled up at Tony's feet for a short nap before returning to the mansion.

* * * *

Nursing a glass of port, Tony sat in the small kitchen nook in the dark. He was still on edge from his walk through the old neighborhood and couldn't sleep.

Gazing through the window, Tony could see the Conti mansion a hundred yards away. The lights were out in the second-floor master suite where Mario and Carla slept.

Despite his positive comments about Mario's health to Angela and others, Tony was deeply worried about him. Now in his late seventies, Mario was weak and tired all the time. Tony didn't want to accept it, but his dear old friend and mentor had the aura of death about him. He could see it in his eyes, his trembling hands, his labored breathing.

Death was no stranger to Tony. From an early age, his life had been transformed by its cold touch. In contrast to a freak accident, medical malady, or the inevitability of old age, most of Tony's interactions with the Grim Reaper were abrupt, violent, and terrifying:

A suicide in a NYPD prison cell. A murder near Central Park. Countless firefights in the bloody jungles of Southeast Asia. The legendary shootout in Little Italy.

In fact, death was the catalyst that originally brought Tony and Mario together.

20

In the winter of 1959, death crossed the Tucci family threshold for the first time. Tony was only nine years old, living in old East Harlem with his parents, Fabio and Rosalie, and his older sister Sophia.

During an outbreak of virulent Asian flu, Sophia became very ill and then contracted a severe case of pneumonia. It was the only time Tony had ever watched someone close to him slowly die. She passed away on Christmas Day.

Her death had a devastating impact on the entire family, but his mother suffered the most. Rosalie quit her job as a seamstress to stay at home and dote over her young son. Every time Tony left the house, his mother gave him a stern safety lecture—to watch out for cars and avoid strange men who offered candy.

Still, Tony was a handful. When he wasn't running around Jefferson Park, playing stickball in the street, or roaming the neighborhood with his buddies, he accompanied his father to his retail shop over on Eighth Avenue.

Originally, Fabio worked at a large import company as an accountant, where he learned the business and developed contacts in different parts of the world. After he married Rosalie and the kids were born, he wanted to establish his own business to better provide for his young family. He saved enough money to rent a small retail space with a warehouse in the back and purchased his first container of goods containing sculptures, ceramics, and copper artifacts from South America that he sold for a tidy profit. Fabio built his business by paying finder's fees to the doormen at some of the fancy condominiums on the Upper East Side to send their art-crazy residents to his little shop instead of the more expensive downtown stores.

Soon, Fabio was importing a container a month from a mysterious middleman named Diego Zapata, who lived in Bogota, Colombia. For years, their relationship functioned smoothly, with nary a problem. Fabio's steady and growing income allowed him to lavish gifts on his family—a color TV, new family car, and a bicycle, transistor radio and baseball glove for Tony. Life was good.

But in the fall of 1964, everything changed…

* * * *

One Saturday afternoon, Tony, fourteen years old at the time, was helping his father in the shop when Diego Zapata made a surprise appearance. Fabio warmly greeted the fastidious man, dressed in a black suit and pork pie hat.

Tony made coffee for their special guest, and the men chatted for a while until a flashy Lincoln Continental pulled up in front of the store. Two huge black men, thick as granite slabs with shaved heads, emerged to hold open the rear car door for a scary-looking gangster named Willie Duke, the most dangerous drug lord in Harlem. A mulatto with a perfect Afro and brutish brown eyes, Duke ruled the lucrative ghetto drug trade with an iron fist.

As his beefy bodyguards waited outside, their boss entered the shop. Sensing danger, Fabio told Tony to go work in the warehouse while the men talked. Tony left, but he hid in a corner by the door where he could watch and listen to their discussion through a small hole in the wall.

Zapata explained to Fabio that each of the future shipments would now contain a special package exclusively for Duke—a large clay jar. Once the container cleared customs, Fabio would call Duke to arrange for the pick-up of the jar. It was that simple.

A hard fist of nausea hit Fabio below the belt, but he found the courage to ask the most obvious question. "And what will be in those jars?"

"That's none of your business," Zapata said. "All you have to do is turn it over to Mr. Duke, and everything will continue the way it's been for the last several years."

Fabio was being drawn into the jaws of criminal enterprise. He knew those jars would contain illegal contraband, most likely cocaine. There was very little nose candy on the street compared to the enormous volume of heroin being distributed at that time. Thanks to the enterprising Mafia drug dealers over on Pleasant Avenue, and scum like Duke who sold heroin in the ghettos throughout the City, there were already thousands of junkies looking for their next fix. The untapped market for a powerful new drug like cocaine was an entrepreneur's dream.

Somehow Zapata and Duke had teamed up on this dangerous new venture and would split the vast profits—while Fabio was being set up as the fall guy. If the police or the Feds ever caught him with that much cocaine, he would spend the rest of his life in jail.

Fabio was scared to death, but he played dumb.

With his head hung down, Fabio pleaded, "But if it's anything illegal, my family and I could be at risk."

"You'll be in more shit if you don't do everything we say," Duke sneered.

Fabio knew nobody crossed Duke and lived to talk about it. He'd heard a few stories about the foolish wannabe gangsters who tried to horn in on Duke's turf and ended up with flaming Viking funerals out on the East River—while they were still alive.

Realizing this was his last chance to possibly get out before it was too late, Fabio cleared his throat and lied. "My parents back in Sicily are in very poor health. I have promised to move there temporarily to care for them and —"

Before Fabio could react, Duke grabbed him and pulled a stiletto from his jacket pocket. He put the long, cold blade to Fabio's throat, drawing a trickle of blood. "You ain't going nowhere, motherfucker! And if you try anything, I'll carve up your kid like a Christmas ham. Got it?"

Fabio went limp in Duke's grasp as he resigned himself to the inevitable.

Tony almost pissed his pants.

Although he witnessed the entire interchange between the men, Tony never said a word to his father, who was ashamed of his impotence in the face of true terror. For the first time, Tony saw the dark side of life, how the strong and ruthless preyed upon the vulnerable and weak.

Fabio was a simple, God-fearing man who loved his family above all else. He knew Duke's threat was not an idle one. If he did not play along, Tony was dead. Fabio did flirt with the notion of packing up the family and moving away in the dead of night, but their roots were deep within the community, and they had many debts. Leaving was just not possible.

Over the next two years, Fabio followed Zapata's instructions. After every new container arrived at the port and cleared customs, Duke's thugs picked up the contraband from Fabio's shop without saying a word.

The constant fear of getting caught by the authorities took a terrible toll on Fabio. He suffered from insomnia, weight loss, and stomach ulcers.

Meanwhile, Duke sold his new stash and made a fortune. Soon, there were a half-dozen jars in each shipment, then a dozen, each filled with fifty pounds of pure cocaine. Everything remained the same for Fabio's business; however, the new flood of cocaine on the streets caught the attention of the police and the media.

As his drug empire expanded around the City and then across state lines, Duke exploited his personal notoriety. Keeping a low profile did not mesh with his flamboyant persona. With his fair complexion and role as the biggest distributor of the popular white powder, Duke actively promoted his new moniker: "White Willie." Surrounded by a pack of intimidating bodyguards, he dressed in outlandish costumes, like his trademark cape and hat fashioned from the hide of a snow leopard.

Soon, the Italian drug dealers wanted a piece of the cocaine action, but Duke told the wise guys to "fuck off" and stay out of his business. It didn't take long before the two gangster factions were at war. Using their connections with the crooked cops working in the ghetto, the Mafia had many of Duke's low-level dealers busted and thrown in jail, but they were quickly replaced.

Several contracts were put out on Duke's life, using ambitious young black gangsters who thought they could dethrone "The King of Cocaine." Every attempt ended badly.

Besides the gasoline baths and ghastly amputations, Duke employed a sinister mixture of torture and terror on a grand scale. Rumors spread that there was a secret dungeon somewhere in Harlem where the vanquished were castrated, flayed, and gutted. When the headless bodies of two soldiers in the Beneducci family were dumped onto Pleasant Avenue in broad daylight, the Feds finally stepped in.

Shortly thereafter, one of Duke's bodyguards got nailed on a murder charge, and he spilled his guts about Fabio's involvement with the importation of cocaine. One late night, while Fabio waited alone at his shop for Duke's cohorts to pick up the latest delivery, the Feds kicked in the front door.

Fabio was booked on drug trafficking charges that carried a life sentence. The very next day, an emissary from Duke's gang came to visit him in jail. He reminded Fabio of Duke's earlier threat and told him not to say a word—or Tony and Rosalie would pay the ultimate price. Faced with the prospect of either keeping his mouth shut and spending the rest of his life in prison or testifying against Duke and having his family slaughtered, Fabio hung himself in his cell.

Someone in the NYPD leaked all the details of the big bust to the press, including rumors that Duke's threats against Tony's family resulted in Fabio's suicide. The story was splashed across the front pages of every newspaper in the City; but the authorities did not have enough direct evidence to arrest and prosecute "White Willie." After his ex-bodyguard was brutally stabbed to death in jail, everyone was terrified of testifying against the ruthless drug lord. Duke survived and his organization expanded.

Fabio's death sent Rosalie into a deep depression. She stopped eating and spent most days curled up in the fetal position on their living room couch with all the curtains closed. Until the bust, Tony had been a stellar student in high school, where he excelled in math, but he dropped out in his junior year to take care of his mother.

When he wasn't helping Rosalie, Tony hung out at Remo's Gym on 2nd Avenue. Remo, a crusty old trainer, taught Tony the basics of "The Sweet Science." Boxing became the perfect catharsis for Tony. Soon, he was channeling his anger about what happened to his family into his intense daily workouts—running every morning, lifting weights, and working the speed and heavy bags for hours on end.

Mostly, he enjoyed getting into the ring to test his skills against other teens in the greater New York area. With fast hands and a powerful right hook, Tony was quite cunning in the ring, using excellent defensive skills and smarts to outmatch his bigger and stronger opponents. He won several amateur matches and showed some promise as a potential Golden Gloves boxer until a Puerto Rican kid broke his nose while they were sparring. Tony wanted to keep working out and competing, but his mother begged him to stop. As a good son, he did as she asked.

By late fall 1967, Rosalie had literally lost the will to live and finally passed away. With all the family money spent on medical costs, legal fees, and burial expenses, Tony was evicted from the family apartment on a frigid December morning. Besides the clothes on his back and a heavy silver ring he inherited from his father, featuring the motif of a demonic Mayan god— Tony had nothing.

He stayed with some friends on and off for a few weeks until he ended up living on the streets. Knowing the East Harlem neighborhood so well, Tony slept on the floors of abandoned buildings and tenement hallways to avoid the severe winter chill, and worked different day jobs to earn enough money to eat. Although Tony had many opportunities to steal and rob to improve his situation, he never committed a crime against anyone. He also never forgot who destroyed his family and put him on the street.

In Tony's imagination, "White Willie" Duke was a terrifying specter, forever hovering in the shadows with his knife, ready to carve him to pieces. Tony's revenge fantasies got him through many long, cold nights as he shivered in the dark. But in reality, Duke was untouchable, protected by his henchmen, while Tony was just a destitute, seventeen-year-old high school dropout.

21

One of the few places he felt at peace was Our Lady of Mt. Carmel Church. Father Cerruti, the young priest who managed the church, chatted with Tony a few times. The father offered to help get him off the streets, but Tony refused, saying there were others who needed the Church's assistance more than he did.

In February 1968, about six weeks before his eighteenth birthday, Tony sat on a pew in the back of the empty cathedral, staring up at the vaulted ceiling illuminated by hundreds of candles.

A gentleman approached, crossed himself, and sat down beside Tony. He wore a dark pinstripe suit and an expensive-looking camel hair overcoat. Lowering his head, the man said a silent prayer.

Embarrassed by his shabby clothes and bad hygiene, Tony stood up to leave.

"Please sit down, Tony," the man said softly.

Tony was stunned that the stranger knew his name. He carefully studied the man's face. He was a handsome thirty-year-old with hazel eyes and a friendly smile. The man looked vaguely familiar, but Tony couldn't quite place him.

Tentatively, Tony sat back down.

"You're Tony Tucci," the man said matter-of-factly. "Years ago, you and your buddies used to play around this neighborhood, right?"

Tony's mind raced back in time, searching for any recognition of the man. "Yeah. I grew up here."

"I did too," the man replied, casting his eyes upon the classic sculpture of Madonna and child in the glowing gold alcove above the front altar. "In fact, I knew your father."

Tony was suspicious, but he was also curious about anything related to his father.

"Really?"

"I played handball with your father a bunch of times. He was fast, agile. Nice guy, too... Anyway, one day a big Irish kid who lived several blocks away snatched our handball and ran off. Your father tracked him down and, about an hour later, he returned with our ball—and a black eye. We never asked Fabio what happened, but I never saw that Irish prick in our neighborhood again."

The story made sense to Tony. Despite his forced alliance with Zapata and Duke, his father had been a devout Catholic, who adamantly believed in the Ten Commandments. There was no gray area between right and wrong. And if Fabio was ever placed in a position where someone needed help, he jumped in without hesitation.

They sat in silence for a minute. Finally, the man said, "Father Cerruti told me you liked to come here at night."

Tony nodded.

"You're living on the streets."

"What of it?" Tony said defensively.

The man stared straight ahead. "I know the true story about what happened to your family. I know Duke threatened to kill you and your mother if Fabio testified against him. Your father killed himself because he saw no way out ... Such a terrible thing."

Weary of rehashing the sad story of his family's demise, Tony said nothing.

"Well, if I were in your shoes, I'd want to get a little payback. You know, to make things right."

Tony shrugged, knowing his revenge fantasies about Duke were childish and far-fetched.

"I came to see you out of respect for your father, Tony. He was a good man and not a vengeful person; however, there are times when evil must be confronted and destroyed."

Tony was getting antsy. The church closed at midnight, and he had to search for shelter on the snowy night.

"What exactly are you saying, mister?"

The man turned to face Tony. "I know where Duke will be tonight. And he'll be alone."

A cold drop of sweat rolled down Tony's spine.

"Where?"

"He's banging a white woman on the Upper East Side. Apparently, she's a former stripper, a real babe. Her husband is a NYPD watch commander on the graveyard shift. Dumb schmuck doesn't even have a clue," he said with a small chuckle. "Duke usually shows up around one o'clock in the morning for a romp in the hay with the wife and then leaves no later than three a.m. The beauty of it is that he always comes alone. No bodyguards. He probably wants to keep a low profile so the neighbors won't suspect anything."

Everything was happening too fast. Tony needed more time to think, but the man continued, "Look, kid, one way or another, this is Duke's last night on the planet. Tomorrow, some people I know are going to whack him. Duke murdered two of their crew in an unspeakable manner. He's a rabid animal that needs to be put down."

Tony stared into the man's eyes. The warm hazel sparkle was gone, replaced with a gaze cold and black. "Duke is a dead man. He just doesn't know it yet."

Then Tony remembered where he had seen this gentleman before. He couldn't recall his name, but he was some big-shot bookie from Pleasant Avenue. Some of Tony's friends used to run small errands for him, picking up betting slips or delivering pizza and pastries to his colleagues around the neighborhood. Tony always kept his distance, knowing his parents would disapprove if he took money from a known wise guy.

"Do you have a black Caddy convertible with red leather interior?" Tony asked him, to be sure.

"Yeah, it's an older model, but it still runs great. It's parked right outside." The man smiled. "Want to go see where Duke will be in about an hour? It's not far from here."

Tony's pulse quickened as he tried to focus his thoughts. What could he possibly do to a killer like Duke?... Beat him with a tire iron? Broken arms and kneecaps! Yes, that would feel good.... Or maybe shoot him? No way. He had never even fired a gun. And what if Duke carried a gun too?... Maybe he could use a knife? Then he remembered the long stiletto Duke pulled on his father years ago.

Another drop of sweat rolled south.

Father Cerruti began to extinguish the candles near the front altar with a long snuffer. The man stood and buttoned his overcoat. "Do you want to take that ride?"

Feeling small and powerless, Tony stared down at his feet. "Thanks, but no thanks."

The man bent down, placing some money and a matchbook into Tony's hand. "If you change your mind, there's cab fare and the address... Good luck, kid."

Tony looked at all the cash, which totaled more than two hundred dollars. It seemed like all the money in the world to the homeless boy.

As the man turned to walk away, Tony gently reached for his sleeve. "Excuse me, sir, but what's your name?"

A broad smile crossed the man's face and his eyes were bright again. "Mario Conti."

22

Tony shoved the cash into his pocket and opened the matchbook. An address on East 94th Street was handwritten on the top inside flap. His hand began to shake as he stared at the matchbook. In his gut, he knew this moment in time, this strange confluence of events, was somehow a turning point in his life.

On a certain level, he wanted to avenge the death of his father and the destruction of his family, but "White Willie" Duke was such a frightening and intimidating presence. He was the bogeyman incarnate, a monster that would surely feed on Tony's psyche and soul for the rest of his life.

Tony had been through Hell over the last few years, losing his parents and his home. It was all long gone. There were plenty of times when he just wanted to be a kid again, to cry and lash out at the unfairness of it all, but he would not let himself show weakness. He would not let evil men like Zapata and Duke beat him.

Alone and afraid, the emotional toll was too much to bear… Tony did something he had not done in years. He prayed.

Then, without saying a word to the priest, Tony got up and left.

Snowflakes drifted down as he stepped out onto East 115th Street. The temperature was dropping fast as the snow began to stick to the slick sidewalks and streets. Tony pulled up his ragged coat collar and rubbed his hands together, wishing he had a pair of gloves.

He started walking southwest towards 94th Street. As he stumbled along the near-empty roads, Tony wondered what he should do. Perhaps nothing. Just let the Mafia hitmen do the dirty work. After all, Duke would be dead and his hands clean.

What would his father expect him to do? And how would Tony himself feel later if he didn't do something—anything to avenge his family? He felt compelled to go see Duke, but he had no idea how it would play out.

Fate seemed to be pushing him forward toward a destiny he could not control.

23

A frosty wind blew as he approached Central Park. Only the homeless were out on this blustery, snowy night. As Tony came across one destitute street person after another, cowering in doorways and sleeping on metal grates over steam vents, he pulled money from his pocket and generously distributed it. After he had walked the last few blocks down 5th Avenue along Central Park, he had less than a hundred dollars left.

He checked the address on the matchbook again and veered down East 94th Street. Standing in the shadows, Tony watched as a dark sedan pulled up in front of the suspect brownstone. Tony froze as a man got out of the car and walked briskly up to the front door.

The porch light was out, but he could clearly see it was "White Willie" Duke, a cigarette dangling from his lower lip and a bottle of booze tucked under his arm. He looked much bigger and stronger than he had when he'd threatened Tony's father four years earlier.

Duke glanced around the neighborhood to make sure no one was watching, and knocked softly on the door. A moment later, it opened and he slipped inside.

For the next two hours, the snow continued to fall, covering everything in pure, surreal white. Tony lingered in various doorways and alcoves along the block, shuffling his feet to keep warm.

His favorite childhood memories of the family came flooding back... His tenth birthday, when his father traded a valuable Colombian art piece for two tickets for opening day to watch the Yankees beat the Red Sox 15-10… When he and his parents rode rental bikes through Central Park and had the best picnic ever in the Great Meadow… And that hot August night on Coney Island when they rode the Ferris wheel, and he thought he was on top of the world…

After standing around for hours, he was exhausted and his limbs were numb. Nervously, he twisted his father's heavy silver ring on his right hand, round and round, as he lurked in the shadows.

Around 2:45 am, a large sedan slowly rolled down the street. It was dark, but Tony could see four men inside. They were probably the hit men Mario Conti mentioned earlier in the church. The sedan stopped beside Duke's car, pausing for a moment before moving on.

Snow continued to drift down. Tony was cold, weary of waiting, and not sure why he was even there. Fed up, he walked over to Duke's car, ready to smash the windshield with his fist, when he heard Duke's girlfriend's front door open and close. Silently, Tony hid behind a large maple tree right next to the car.

With his back pressed against the tree, Tony heard footsteps coming closer. Despite the freezing temperature, he began to perspire as his heart pounded. A moment later, Duke was standing beside him, just a few feet away. Duke shook out a Salem from a cigarette pack and cupped his hands to light up. As the lighter flared, he suddenly noticed Tony.

"What the fuck?" Duke said with total surprise.

Simultaneously, Tony unleashed a devastating right hook to Duke's left temple. All the pent-up anger that had smoldered inside him for years exploded behind that vicious haymaker. Stunned and confused, Duke dropped to his knees. He grabbed his throbbing head with both hands, trying to get his bearings.

"I'm going to kill you!" he snarled as he tried to rise to his feet.

Tony was in shock, too. He hadn't planned on cold-cocking Duke, and now he was in a life-or-death confrontation.

Tony saw Duke reach into his pocket, fumbling for his stiletto. Just as Duke whipped it out and snapped open the blade, Tony kicked him hard in the groin. The air went out of the older man, and the knife slipped from his hand, falling into the soft snow.

In one fluid motion, Tony lunged forward, picked up the switchblade, and drove it deep into Duke's chest.

Duke clutched the knife with both hands—his eyes wide and watery. He wondered: *How could this little punk get the better of me?*

"Who are you, kid? Who sent ya?" Duke managed to blurt out.

Tony hesitated for a moment and said, "I'm the son of Fabio Tucci. Remember? The kid you promised to cut up."

Blood trickled out of the corner of Duke's mouth, "Yeah... I remember... Too bad about your Daddy."

Tony leaned in closer and said, "Well, who's the Christmas ham now?"

Duke's face contorted with rage. He started to yank the blade out of his chest but stopped when a small stream of blood spurted out.

Another spurt. And then another.

As the life slowly ebbed out of him, Duke's hands fell to his sides, and he tumbled face first into the gutter with a sickening thud. The weight of his body drove the knife deeper into his chest and blood spread out around his corpse like a crimson halo.

Time seemed to stop as Tony loomed above Duke's corpse. He didn't know what to do. He thought about turning him over to grab the knife, but there was too much blood.

Tony slowly backed away…

The next thing he knew, he was running west toward Central Park. He almost knocked over a young couple at the end of the block, dodged a few cars as he darted across 5th Avenue, and disappeared into the park.

24

For the rest of the night and all the following day, Tony walked the streets of New York, contemplating what he should do.

Thinking it would be wise to get rid of his clothes, he used the last of the money Mario Conti had given him to buy a new parka, jeans, boots, and some leather gloves. He went into a YMCA to shower and change clothes, and then scattered his old bloodstained garments and shoes in several garbage cans.

Later that evening, Tony returned to the church in East Harlem, emotionally and physically burned out. When he entered, he saw Father Cerruti sitting next to the confession booth reading the Bible. Given the late hour, the church was empty.

The priest smiled at Tony and beckoned him to come over. "How are you, Tony?"

"Okay, I guess."

Cerruti noticed Tony's new wardrobe and gestured to the bench beside him. "Please sit down."

The priest said, "Looks like you've been out shopping."

Tony shoved his hands into the pockets of his new parka. "Yeah. My old clothes were beginning to stink. I needed a change."

"I saw you talking with Mr. Conti last night. Can I ask what it was about?"

Tony looked away. "Nothing much. He told me he knew my father."

After his mother died, Tony had confessed to the priest he wanted to kill the man responsible for destroying his family. Cerruti was sympathetic to the young man's plight, but warned Tony about the high moral price of sin, particularly murder. The priest told him that instead of seeking revenge, he should put his faith in God. Tony did not respond well to the sermon, and their relationship had been chilly ever since.

The priest looked closely at Tony's face. "You look tired. Have you been awake all night?"

"I couldn't find a decent place to sleep."

"I told you, I can get you into a shelter whenever you want."

"Save it for somebody else. I can take care of myself."

"Really?" Father Cerruti asked. "The police were here this afternoon, looking for you."

Tony tightened up.

"Apparently, a notorious drug dealer was murdered last night over near Central Park," Cerruti said. "They said he was complicit in the death of your father."

Tony shifted on the wooden bench but kept quiet.

Cerruti pulled a NYPD business card from his pocket. "The police asked me to contact them if you came by... Should I call them?"

"Do whatever you want, Father."

Cerruti placed his hand on Tony's shoulder. "You *really* need to trust in the Lord, my son. He'll help you through the darkest of times."

"Right. He's done a super job so far," Tony said sarcastically. "Go ahead. Make the call. I'm not going anywhere."

Tony was done. He had lost the will to keep trudging through the streets of New York. His legs felt like bags of sand, his head and heart were heavy. He just wanted to curl up and sleep.

And forget.

25

A short while later, two detectives arrived. They asked him about the night before, but Tony said nothing. They cuffed him, put him in the back of their unmarked car, and drove him downtown, where he was fingerprinted and placed in a holding cell.

The interrogation started at 9:00 a.m. and lasted for hours. The detectives laid out their evidence against Tony. Based on a review of his father's arrest records, they knew all about Duke's involvement in the destruction of Tony's family, which they claimed provided a "very compelling motive for murder."

The detectives surmised that Tony stalked Duke, sucker-punched him, and then used the switchblade to finish him off. Forensics confirmed that a partial fingerprint found on the blood-soaked handle of the knife matched Tony's right thumb. Also, the nasty indentation on Duke's left temple was "consistent" with the Mayan motif on the large silver ring found on Tony's right hand.

The detectives believed it was basically a crime of passion—a grieving son avenging his father's death. If it had been a routine robbery, the perp would surely have searched Duke and found the bulging billfold in his coat pocket, stuffed with more than $2,000 in cash.

There was also "premeditation" on Tony's part. He was wearing a complete new set of clothes, which in their minds proved he knew what he was doing and wanted to cover-up the whole thing.

And to compound matters, Tony offered no alibi.

Throughout the interrogation, Tony never said a word. Nor did he ask for a lawyer. After the detectives conferred with an Assistant District Attorney, Tony was arrested on a first-degree murder charge. He was arraigned in juvenile court later that day and ferried to Spofford Juvenile Center in Hunts Point to await trial.

Tony's court-appointed defense attorney was an earnest but unproven young litigator. Based on the evidence and alleged motive, he told Tony there was an excellent chance he'd be convicted, so he pushed him to take the plea bargain offered by the DA: If he pleaded guilty to a second-degree murder charge, he would receive a reduced ten-year sentence. If he kept his nose clean, he'd be out in five years.

Tony felt like he was being railroaded by the entire system. Although he was guilty of attacking Duke, Tony had never actually planned to kill him and was forced to act in self-defense. There was no way he was willing to accept any kind of murder plea. He also questioned the validity of some of the so-called "evidence," particularly the alleged ring mark on Duke's temple. And there were no witnesses to the crime. The couple he almost knocked over as he sprinted toward Central Park never came forward.

Tony was mulling over what he should do when he got jumped by a pack of black gang members who used to sell drugs for Duke in the hood. They beat him senseless. He was transported to the hospital, where he was treated for numerous cuts and lacerations requiring dozens of stitches.

His attorney went to Judge Lewis Randolph, a legendary jurist who had been prominent in the City of

New York Children's Court for decades, to ask that his client be moved to a safer facility.

The judge, known as a thoughtful and compassionate man, took an interest in Tony's case. When he learned that Tony was a top student until his father's suicide, how he'd cared for his ailing mother, and had a spotless record despite being destitute over the last several months, the judge decided to get the case resolved fairly and quickly.

On the eve of Tony's 18th birthday, Judge Randolph arranged for a meeting in his office with the prosecutor, the defense attorney, and Tony. After discussing the various legal aspects of the case, he spoke with Tony privately.

He carefully reviewed the consequences of each legal scenario, and then offered Tony a chance to walk down a different path. If Tony agreed to enlist in the military the very next day, Judge Randolph promised to reduce the charges to involuntary manslaughter and waive any additional jail time. And if he left the military with an honorable discharge, the judge would expunge his juvenile record.

Two days later, Tony was on a bus heading to boot camp at the Marine Corps Recruit Depot at Parris Island in South Carolina. After graduating thirteen weeks later, he was shipped to Camp Geiger in North Carolina for advanced infantry training.

Tony served two tours in Vietnam, earning a Silver Star and two Purple Hearts. After three long, brutal years in the military, Sergeant Tony Tucci was honorably discharged.

As promised, Judge Randolph expunged his juvenile criminal record and returned the solid silver ring that Tony inherited from his father.

* * * *

Still sipping his glass of port in his cottage, Tony watched a bank of ominous clouds drift across the night sky behind the Conti mansion.

He was anxious and tense. All his instincts told him his world was about to implode. Tony had experienced the same feelings when he was in Vietnam. He had learned to be keenly aware of his environment at all times and always trust his gut.

As a squad leader, Tony often led night patrols deep into hostile territory in search of the elusive enemy. There were countless instances, as his troops crept along a riverbank or jungle trail, when he sensed danger ahead and ordered his men to retreat back into the bush. That sixth sense saved the lives of many of his men from deadly ambushes, land mines, and booby traps. Later, when he worked with Mario and came into contact with shady and dangerous characters, those well-honed instincts for survival had come in handy again.

Now, Tony's intuition told him Dante was desperate and out of control. He needed to gather more information about that possible arms deal before reporting back to Mario, but he couldn't push the river.

Just as when he laid in wait for the enemy in the jungles of Vietnam, Tony had to be vigilant, alert... and patient.

WEDNESDAY

26

Phoenix, Arizona
10:00 a.m.

Jake Crowley entered Homeland Security Headquarters and went directly to his boss's office. A small engraved plaque outside the door read: "Roger Hamid, Director of Special Investigations." Crowley knocked and entered.

Special Agent Hamid, an intense, middle-aged Arab-American, and ex-Army Ranger in a short-sleeve dress shirt and tie, sat at a table facing five stacks of files. A credenza behind him was covered with family photos and various military memorabilia.

Two younger agents, who looked like Mormon missionaries, shuffled papers and scanned their laptops.

"Pack your bags, Crowley. You're going to New York," Hamid said abruptly.

"What? No big kiss hello?"

The two agents laughed, but their boss was all business.

Hamid pointed at the files. "We got the forensics reports from Sheriff Royal earlier this morning and your field report."

"Paperwork. It's what we do best," Crowley said, winking at the other agents.

"We've also reviewed the case files from the other four border killings, as well as your interview with the burn victim in Tucson last night," Hamid continued. "It's pretty obvious that at least ten Arab militants have been smuggled into the U.S. And based on the extreme measures used to conceal their entry, we have to assume we're dealing with some kind of terrorist plot."

"But where did they all go?" Crowley asked.

One of the young agents offered, "We got a break this morning."

"Yeah, Allah smiled on us," the other agent quipped.

Hamid shot the agent an angry look. Then he picked up a folder and walked to the door. "Come on, Crowley. I'll show you."

They walked quickly through a gray cube farm filled with solemn people busy at work.

Hamid talked as fast as he moved. "Two Iraqis, a brother and sister who came to the U.S. a few years ago, contacted the police this morning with a very disturbing story. The sister is married to another Iraqi, a long-haul truck driver for a local food company. He makes round trips from Phoenix to New York every two weeks."

They went through a door and veered into another hallway. "She claims her husband was approached at their mosque by some 'evil men' about three months ago. They threatened his family if he didn't help smuggle some foreigners across the country in the back of his truck."

After passing through a few more doors, Hamid and Crowley arrived at an interrogation suite. They entered a dark, soundproof space with a glass partition looking into the adjacent room. It hummed with recording equipment as two other agents videotaped the Iraqi brother consoling his distraught sister.

"Apparently, her husband left Phoenix early Monday morning with his fifth set of smuggled men. The trip to New York City usually takes about two days, and he always calls her right after each drop, but he never checked in this morning. Fearing the worst, she called her brother, who insisted they immediately come in to talk with us."

The agents listened as the brother and sister spoke softly in Arabic. Hamid looked at one of the agents who monitored the sound recorder. "Have they said anything else that's relevant?"

The young Arab-looking agent shook his head.

Crowley asked, "Have you already checked them out?"

"Of course. They both came here legally after the surge began in Iraq in 2007. The brother worked as a translator for the military for four years before he was granted U.S. citizenship. Two years ago, his sister came to join him. She married an Iraqi-American, the long-haul truck driver, and they all settled here in Phoenix. They've been model citizens."

"Have you checked her cell phone records to trace her husband's calls?"

"An FBI team in New York is putting the maps together right now," Hamid said.

"Did her husband tell her anything about his passengers?"

"The details are pretty sketchy. He had virtually no contact with the men stashed in the back of his rig. Their handlers put them on and took them off."

"Did he overhear anything?"

"They all spoke Arabic, but he did hear one brief discussion in Pashto."

"So—they could be Afghanis, maybe Taliban," Crowley mused.

"Possibly."

Crowley walked over to the window and peered down at the sobbing woman. "Have you located her husband yet?"

"No. The NYPD is searching for his truck right now... We've booked you on the red eye tonight to JFK. Your contact at 26 Federal Plaza in New York is Special Agent Hank Kline. He's head of the FBI's Counterterrorism Unit and expects to see you tomorrow at 1:00 p.m. sharp. In the meantime, clean up all your case files. You may be gone for a while."

Crowley said, "You know, this could turn into a monumental clusterfuck."

Hamid nodded sternly. "Watch your back, Crowley."

27

The janitorial service arrived at The Palace to spiff the place up before a planned private party that evening. When the team boss went to disarm the alarm and surveillance system on the keypad by the rear door, he noticed it wasn't activated as usual.

Strange, he thought.

Once inside, the team was shocked to find the giant disco ball had fallen from the rafters, crashing onto the center of the dance floor. To their horror, only the feet of a dead man wearing Air Jordans protruded out from under the shattered glass sphere.

The police were immediately summoned to investigate.

After many hours of forensic evidence gathering, it was determined the excessive weight of the huge disco ball had stripped the threads on the support bolts, which eventually caused it to fall to the floor.

It would take about a week to analyze all the evidence from the scene and conduct an autopsy on the disco club owner, Raul Garcia. In the interim, the newspapers speculated it was probably a freak accident—albeit, an ironic one.

28

Tony leaned against the passenger side of the limo at the entrance of Saint Carmen High School on the Upper East Side. He casually held up a handwritten sign that read:

Sheila Burns
Gloria Payne
Pamela Smith

The school's closing bell rang and the students began to pour out of the classic, granite-faced building. Hundreds of teenagers funneled down the staircase and onto the sidewalk, talking and texting as they made their way home.

Amid the torrent of students, Tony spotted three girls standing at the top of the stairs. With their perfect noses pointed high into the air and their designer wardrobes, they projected an air of power and entitlement. As if they were walking the red carpet at the Oscars, they glided down the stairs until one of them spotted Tony's sign. The girls stopped and looked him over, whispering among themselves. They continued down the steps and walked up to him.

The tall brunette said, "Excuse me, I'm Sheila and these are my friends, Gloria, and Pam. What's going on?"

Tony bowed and said, "I'm Carl, your driver. It appears you have a secret admirer."

The girls marveled at the sleek new limo and giggled among themselves.

"Well, tell us! Who set this up?" demanded Gloria, a bottle blonde.

Tony gave them his best Cheshire grin. "Sorry, ladies. It's a surprise. Climb in, and you'll find out soon."

He opened the door, and the eager girls jumped in, squealing in anticipation of unknown delights. Tony pulled the limo out into the busy mid-afternoon traffic and headed south.

"There's a chilled bottle of French champagne in the ice and some glasses. Please help yourselves, ladies," Tony said.

"You know we're underage, right?" said Sheila.

"I won't tell if you don't."

"Let's party!" chortled Pamela, a little redhead.

Sheila pulled out the bottle, popped the cork, and poured three full glasses.

Tony eavesdropped on their conversation.

"Who do you think is paying for this?" Sheila whispered.

"I think David Helmsley set this up," Gloria said. "You know, his father is a heavy at Goldman Sachs, and he's got a huge trust fund. And I *know* he wants to get into my pants."

"Well, I think it's Michael Kerry," Pamela chimed in. "His parents are billionaires. He rents limos all the time and parties at those fancy nightclubs."

Tony rolled his eyes as the girls poured another round of champagne and continued their adolescent chatter. After driving for a while, the limo came to a dilapidated building under renovation. Suddenly, Tony swerved the limo past the scaffolding and down a steep ramp into a secluded underground parking area. He pulled to a stop beneath dim fluorescent ceiling lights.

"Hey, where are we?" Gloria asked.

"I thought we'd be going to some fancy restaurant or hotel," Pamela said.

Sheila chimed in. "What gives, Carl?"

Tony got out and opened the back door of the limo. "No worries, ladies. Like I said, it's a surprise."

Reluctantly, the girls climbed out of the limo into the empty parking lot. They clutched their champagne glasses, and Pamela held the bottle. Huddling together and peering into the darkness, they exchanged furtive glances.

"Listen, Carl. I think you should just take us back to school," Gloria said.

"Yeah! This is some sick joke," said Pamela.

Tony spread his arms and sighed. "Everything is fine." He gestured at a bench a few yards away. "Please have a seat."

The girls froze.

Sheila pushed back. "No! You need to…"

"Sit down!" Tony demanded.

The frightened girls quickly obeyed. Tony pulled a folding chair from out of the shadows and sat down to face them. He glared at the anxious girls for almost a full minute before speaking.

"This is no joke. It's a reality check," he said in a low, steady voice.

The girls looked at each other nervously.

"You know Gina Ricci, of course."

The girls smirked at the mention of her name.

"I understand you've been bullying her. She's very upset about it and —"

Sheila cut him off. "So that fat, dumbass bitch is behind all this? Just wait…"

"Shut up!" Tony bellowed, his words echoing loudly throughout the garage.

He rose to his feet and leaned on the back of the chair. "As good Catholic girls, you know The Golden Rule, right? *'Do unto others as you would have them do unto you'*… Sadly, some people don't think it applies to them. They say and do cruel things to those less fortunate."

As the girls twitched uncomfortably on the hard bench, Tony continued. "And when that happens, another Biblical saying comes to mind: *'An eye for an eye.'*"

He let that vague threat hang there for a moment and then looked out into the darkness. "Sal?"

A cigarette lighter flashed in a dingy corner, illuminating a face. The girls couldn't see him clearly in the shadows, but the man's presence was breathtakingly ominous. His heavy footfalls came closer. Sal walked into the dim light. He wore a wife-beater t-shirt underneath a scuffed leather jacket, filthy jeans, and black Doc Martin boots. His hard face was pockmarked and scarred.

Tony pointed down at the chair. "Good to see you, Sal. Have a seat."

Sal slumped into the chair and blew some smoke rings at the anxious young women.

"I'd like you to meet Sheila, Gloria, and Pam," Tony said. "The girls I told you about."

Standing behind his guest, Tony continued. "Sal is Gina's avenging angel. Of course, Gina never has and never will meet Sal, but if you keep tormenting that poor girl, you'll all spend some quality time with him."

Sal leered at the girls, revealing rotten teeth and emitting foul stale-beer breath.

"Sal is also what you'd call a 'sexual predator,'" Tony said.

"Yeah ... I'm a bad, bad boy," Sal growled in a deep voice, his eyes crawling over the girls' shapely young bodies.

They cringed.

Pam accidentally knocked the champagne bottle off the bench and onto the floor, where it shattered, bouncing ear-piercing shards of sound off the concrete walls.

"Sal has spent about half his life behind bars. He's been convicted of kidnapping, rape, sodomy—you name it," Tony said. He looked down at Sal. "You just beat a rap for an aggravated sexual assault on a woman in Queens, right?"

"Yeah, yeah. After a buddy of mine had a little chat with her, she refused to testify. Imagine that!" Sal laughed. "Praise the Lord!"

The girls did not find it amusing at all.

Sal leaned forward and, with a menacing look, lifted up the hem of Sheila's dress to look at her crotch. She shuddered in a near panic. Urine dripped down her leg and pooled on the floor.

Sal smiled. "You just peed your pants, sweetheart. But it doesn't bother me. I *lick* it—I mean *like* it."

Even Tony was grossed out. "Knock it off, Sal."

"What the fuck, man? I thought you said we were going to party!"

"Maybe later," Tony said, pushing Sal back down into his chair. "Just relax."

Tony faced the distraught girls. "Here's the deal. You stop harassing Gina and start treating her with respect or..." he patted Sal on the shoulder, "I'll give Sal your home addresses and hangouts."

Shaking, the girls eagerly nodded.

"And if you tell anyone about this meeting, you'll meet some other guys who make Sal look like a priest... Now get back in the limo."

As the girls dashed away, Sal lifted one of the abandoned champagne glasses to make a toast. "Let's hook up soon, girls! I got *a lot* to teach you!"

Tony pulled Sal into the shadows, out of sight of the limo.

"So how did I do, Tony?" asked Casey Flynn, the young actor who had played his chauffeur during the shakedown of The Turk.

"It was an Academy Award-winning performance, Casey. Bravo!"

Casey removed his gross cosmetic dentures and flashed a perfect smile. "Aren't these great? Found them at a costume shop last night."

"It was a brilliant touch."

"Do you think they bought it?"

"Hook, line, and sinker."

"I hope I didn't scare them too much."

"Hey, they pushed poor Gina to attempt suicide. She's the victim, not them," Tony said. "They got off easy."

Casey wiped the makeup from his face, removing the fake pockmarks and scars. Then he pulled out a small theater flyer from his pocket and handed it to Tony. The name of the production read: *Titus Andronicus Goes to Washington.*

"Check it out. It's an off-Broadway comedy, and I've got the lead role," Casey said excitedly.

Tony studied the flyer and nodded. "Congrats! I'll be there on opening night. Then I'll take you and your parents out to dinner. Sound good?"

"I'll make sure your ticket is waiting at Will Call."

Tony pocketed the flyer, peeled off several hundred-dollar bills, and handed them to Casey.

"Thanks for the gig, Tony."

"Break a leg, Titus!"

He watched Casey disappear into the blackness and returned to the limo.

* * * *

Tony drove the girls back to Saint Carmen High School. Still unnerved, Sheila, Gloria, and Pamela huddled together in the back seat. Not a word was spoken.

As the limo pulled into the loading zone in front of the school entrance, Tony peered at the girls in the rearview mirror and said, "Remember—there's always a bigger bully."

29

A young Muslim named Ali sat in a small sidewalk café sipping sweet Yemeni tea. As the sun set, the sidewalks and streets began to fill with people on their way home from work.

Across the street, loudspeakers at the local mosque sounded the Adhan for the daily Maghrib prayer, the fourth of five daily devotions. As worshippers streamed up the steps of the mosque and disappeared inside, Ali pretended to check email on his smartphone. Actually, he was keeping watch over a small stretch of street, looking for a wanted international terrorist named Mustafa Al-Anazi.

A master of disguise, Anazi was a legendary figure in the clandestine world of Islamic terrorism. Prominently displayed on the FBI's 'Most Wanted Terrorists List,' his exploits around the world included embassy bombings in Africa and assassinations in Europe. He fought with Al Qaeda in Iraq, Syria, and Afghanistan. On several occasions during the prolonged Iraqi civil war, Anazi had slipped away from U.S. military forces after he detonated IEDs (improvised explosive devices) that killed hundreds of police recruits and innocent civilians.

With darkly handsome features and a lean, powerful build, Anazi did not look particularly dangerous or stand out in a crowd. But on closer examination, one could see a key distinguishing feature: a glass left eye.

Two weeks earlier, Ali had seen Anazi moving through the crowd at about this same time. During a fleeting glance, he made eye contact with the infamous "Ghost of Fallujah" as they passed on the sidewalk. By the time Ali realized it was Anazi, the wanted man had disappeared.

Ali, born and raised in America, was a college student pursuing a degree in law enforcement. Disgusted by the murderous acts of Islamic extremists around the world, Ali went to the FBI to volunteer to work as an informant. He hung out in cafés and attended prayers at the nearby mosque, listening for conversations about possible terrorist activities. Over the past year, Ali had heard a lot of grumbling about U.S. actions in the Middle East, but never a serious threat or plot.

When the young informant first saw the terrorist, Mustafa Al-Anazi wore a baseball cap and a dark windbreaker. Now, sitting at the sidewalk café, Ali scanned the passing crowd, hoping to catch sight again of one of the most sinister men on earth.

Ali finished his tea and walked down the street away from the mosque. As he passed in front of the old Monroe Hotel, the decaying ten-story building on the corner, Anazi suddenly brushed by him and turned down the side street. Ali stopped cold in his tracks as a jolt of primal fear gripped him.

Recovering quickly, he texted his FBI handler, a woman named Elizabeth Ross, with a short message:

just saw the ghost again_ following

Ali paused at the corner and peered down the side street, which was nearly abandoned and much darker than the main thoroughfare. Moving slowly, he crept along the east side of the hotel, passing the rear service dock and several large dumpsters. The remainder of the block was a mix of shuttered businesses, rundown properties, and a large abandoned warehouse.

Anxious and afraid, Ali ducked into a narrow alley. Scanning the street for any sign of Anazi, he started to text again. Before he could finish, a muscular arm wrapped around his neck, and he was dragged back into the shadows.

30

New York City
6:00 p.m.

Tony walked along the busy sidewalk packed with holiday shoppers. The retail stores were bustling with pre-Christmas activity, and tipsy revelers filled the bars and restaurants. As he passed an upscale café on Fifth Avenue, Tony glanced in the window and spotted his ex-wife, Anne.

Stylishly dressed, the statuesque brunette sat alone at a table, drinking a glass of white wine. He paused and watched her for a moment, wondering if he should approach. It had been two long decades since they last spoke, and it had not ended well—at least for him.

His curiosity and sense of civility got the best of him, so he walked inside to greet her. As she finished her wine and stood to pick up the numerous shopping bags at her feet, Tony said, "Hello, Anne."

For a split second, she didn't seem to recognize him and then a smile spread across her lips. "Tony."

They hugged awkwardly.

Gesturing at the bags, Tony said. "Looks like you're getting a jump on your Christmas shopping."

"You know me. Always thinking ahead."

How true, he thought.

"Can I buy you another glass of wine?"

After a momentary hesitation, she replied, "Why not? After all, it's the holidays."

She sat back down. Tony waved at the waiter and ordered two glasses.

"It's been a long time," she said softly.

"Yes," Tony replied, leaning back in his chair. He took a moment to really look at her. She was an elegant woman with a regal manner. "You look good, Anne. The years have treated you well."

"Thank you. You know, the last time we saw each other you were in rehab at the hospital."

"How could I forget? You came to say goodbye."

"It was a difficult time for both of us," she replied, looking away.

"And later that day you had me served with divorce papers."

Anne shrugged. "I was a coward. Still am."

She glanced at his fancy cane. "How's your leg?"

"It gets stiff and painful as the climate gets colder. Want a weather report?"

"I see you still have a sense of humor."

"Like they say: You've got to laugh to keep from crying…"

"… like you've got to breathe to keep from dying," she added.

They both smiled.

The waiter arrived with the wine, and they touched glasses.

"To the future," Tony said.

"I'll drink to that."

"Tell me. How are your parents?"

"Mom passed away a few years ago. I just moved Dad into an assisted living facility. His mind is still razor sharp. Reads everything."

"He's a good man, even though he never approved of me or our relationship."

"Dad always liked you as a person, Tony, but he hated your association with the Conti family."

"Believe me, it cut both ways. Having a father-in-law who was a federal judge put me in a very tough spot with certain people."

They sipped their drinks in silence.

"Twenty years... That's a lot of water under the bridge," Tony said. "Tell me about your life."

"Well, after we split up, I married a Yale grad named Alex Simon. He's now a senior V.P. with IBM."

Tony knew about their relationship. Shortly after he was released from the hospital, about a year after Anne had left him, Tony hired a driver to go to Albany to where her parents lived. Still in love with her, he intended to reveal his decision to leave the mob life once and for all. Tony desperately wanted to start fresh with Anne, rebuilding their relationship away from the dark domain of organized crime.

His timing could not have been worse.

As Tony's car pulled up near the Judge's colonial home, Anne and her fiancé embraced on the front porch. Watching them through the car's tinted window, he could tell their affection for each other was strong and pure. At that moment, he knew he'd lost her forever.

"We have two great kids. Kyle is a freshman at Fordham and Kaitlyn is a sophomore in high school," Anne said, reaching for her purse. "Would you like to see some photos?"

"No thanks."

"I understand," she demurred. "Anyway, we live in Scarsdale. A big house, country club membership, Junior League. It's a comfortable life."

After a long pause, Tony asked, "Are you happy, Anne?"

She hesitated. "Content would be a better word."

They sipped their wine. Anne noticed Tony's shopping bag. "Are you shopping for anyone special?"

"I just bought some scarves for Carla and Angela Conti. And a good bottle of cognac for Mario."

"Still the loyal soldier... Are you seeing anyone?"

"I've had a couple relationships over the years, but they never seemed to work out. I guess I've got too much baggage."

Anne gazed at him with a reserved affection. "You know, Tony, I have a lot of misgivings about how I handled things between us at the end. After the trauma of the shooting, all the surgeries and those long days in intensive care watching you hover at death's door, I was pretty wrung out."

She removed a tissue from her purse. "Miraculously, you survived, which filled me with great joy. I loved you, but that horrible experience forced me to think about our future together. I despised the life you'd chosen and most of the people in it. Plus, I was terrified there would be more trips to the hospital—or worse. It was all too much for me. I needed to get out and find a new life."

He touched her hand. "I don't blame you for leaving me. You deserved better."

They looked deep into each other's eyes. There was still a spark there, an eternal flame.

Tony's phone buzzed, and Anne pulled her hand away. Reluctantly, he took the call.

"Yes?

"Where are you?" Gino asked.

"Downtown."

"Good. Dante wants you to pick up a couple of working girls at Blackie's and bring them over to the Nottingham Palace Hotel, Suite 1650."

"Since when does he want *my* help?"

"Just do it, Tony," Gino demanded. "Their names are Destiny and Godiva."

"When?"

"Now. They're waiting in the bar."

Tony clicked off and slid the phone into his pocket.

"Do you have to go?"

He swirled the wine around in his glass. "It can wait."

They sat in silence, watching the crowds.

"And what about you, Tony? Have you found peace? Happiness?"

"Peace? Perhaps... Happiness? Not really... After the shooting, Mario wanted me to be made, but I didn't care about it anymore. I was a changed man, and I wanted out. As luck would have it, Mario also wanted a new life to protect himself and his family. He sold his criminal interests and pumped all the proceeds into his construction company. I worked closely with him for over ten years building a legitimate business until Dante forced me into early retirement. Now, I'm just the driver for the family—among other things."

Tony took a long sip of wine. "I still have guilt about certain things I did in my younger years, but... well, I've learned that having power is not about taking—it's about giving."

A solitary tear rolled down Anne's cheek.

"It really is good to see you, Tony," she said, reaching for his hand. "Would you like to get together again? Maybe lunch or..."

Slowly, Tony pulled his hand away. "I don't think that's a good idea."

Her lips pursed in disappointment. "You're probably right."

She smiled at him for the last time. It was genuine and heartfelt. "Well, I'd better be going."

She stood and gathered her shopping bags.

"If it's okay with you, I'd like to visit your father sometime," Tony said.

"I know he would like that. He's at Shady Acres up in White Plains."

They brushed cheeks.

"Take care, Anne."

"You too."

And he watched her vanish into the crowd.

31

Destiny and Godiva stood behind Tony as he knocked on the door of Dante's suite at The Nottingham Palace. Al ushered them into the plush anteroom and took the women's coats, revealing sexy evening dresses and high heels.

Gino greeted Tony. "Thanks for picking up the girls."

"Sure," Tony said, peering through a half-open door into the living room. A well-dressed, Slavic-looking man with a nasty crescent-shaped scar on his right cheek and slick black hair was doing Stoli shots with Dante.

Dante picked up a bottle of vodka. "Another round?"

"Always!" replied the man with a heavy Russian accent.

Tony wondered if the man was involved in the arms deal Mario mentioned. Perhaps, but he was an international money launderer or drug dealer. One never knew with Dante, who was always dabbling in dangerous transactions for a quick payday.

Al and Frank led the girls towards the back bedroom.

"Come on, girls. Before you meet our special guest, you can polish *our* knobs," said Al. "It'll be good practice."

Gino patted Tony on the back and guided him to the door. "Thanks, Tony. We'll call again if we need ya."

Wanting to gather more information about exactly what was going on, Tony offered, "I don't mind sticking around. I can drive the girls back later."

"Nah. Once we're finished with them, they can get their own fuckin' cab," Gino said.

Careful not to be too pushy, Tony relented. "Sure. Catch you later."

32

Dante's guest, Victor Volkov, lit a long Cuban cigar.

"Tell me about your client," Dante said.

"Sorry, but I never talk about who I'm working for. It's bad for business."

"Tough shit. Give me a hint," Dante replied, lighting a cigarette with his solid gold lighter.

"Let's just say, they are one of the largest Mexican drug cartels."

"Well, why the hell do they need surface-to-air missiles?"

"I didn't ask, but I'll bet they'll target both the Mexican military and their rival gangs. They're in a full-blown war down there." Laughing, Volkov added, "If I could get them a nuke, they'd buy it."

"Fuck 'em all! But let's get our deal done *first*," Dante said. He smeared black Beluga caviar onto a cracker and gulped it down. "Hey, you gotta try this. It's fabulous!"

Volkov dug in.

"Listen, I doubt my client will pay half a million dollars for each package. For five sets, that's two and half mil. Very expensive! After all, when Muammar al-Qaddafi fell, thousands of those launchers disappeared into the desert. Now, they're a dime a dozen."

"I don't think so," replied Dante. "Those lousy Libyan launchers are stuck over there with the sand monkeys. Instead, I can deliver five U.S. manufactured Stinger launchers and ten missiles in two days—just like we discussed. But you'll have to take delivery here. We're not moving that kind of hardware down to Tijuana."

"We can take delivery here. It's just the price," Volkov said as he scooped up more caviar. "Man, this shit tastes better than pussy!"

Dante did another vodka shot. "Okay. Two million for the whole package. Take it or leave it. And you get your cut from the Burrito Brothers."

"I'll run it by my client tomorrow," Volkov said, pouring a double shot.

"I can have the package ready for delivery on Friday afternoon."

"Good. I think I can convince them to proceed," Volkov said with authority.

They stood and shook hands.

Dante added, "And I want to be paid in washed $100 bills—not tortilla chips!"

"Very funny!"

Glancing around the suite, Volkov asked, "Didn't you mention something about female company?"

"Yeah, now it's time to fire *your* missile," Dante said, slapping him on the back. "Hey, Gino! Get the girls!"

A moment later, Destiny and Godiva waltzed into the room, holding a magnum of champagne and a silver platter piled high with cocaine.

And the party began.

THURSDAY

33

New York City
2:15 a.m.

Tony sat in the limo outside the Nottingham Palace Hotel, reading the *Journal* and keeping a watchful eye on the entrance. His right leg throbbed with a deep, unrelenting pain. He wasn't used to sitting still for so long. Grimacing, he massaged his leg and chewed several aspirin.

He was about to get out and take a short walk when the heavily intoxicated Volkov emerged from the hotel. The concierge summoned a cab and the big Russian crawled in.

With Tony following a short distance behind, the cab drove uptown, eventually arriving at a posh boutique hotel called The Majestic Inn, hidden away in a quiet neighborhood—the kind of place one could keep a low profile.

The doorman, a young Asian, held the door open and Volkov stumbled inside. Tony parked out front and approached the hotel. The doorman greeted him outside.

"Excuse me, I spoke with that gentleman earlier today about using my limo service, but I didn't catch his name."

The doorman looked at him suspiciously until Tony slipped him some cash.

"His name is Victor Volkov."

34

Gino Marino and Frank Salvadore stood in the hallway of a shabby flophouse in the bowels of the Bronx. Graffiti covered the walls and trash littered the floor. Loud music and angry voices could be heard from behind the paper-thin walls.

"What a dump," Frank said.

"It sure ain't the Nottingham Palace," Gino replied, a toothpick dancing in the corner of his mouth.

Impatiently, Gino pounded on the room door again. Waiting for a response, they watched a big rat scurry across the floor at the far end of the hallway.

"Nice touch," Frank sneered.

Finally, the door opened a crack and Tommy Mancini peered out. "Oh, Gino! What's happening?"

"Let us in before we catch the plague."

Tommy unbolted the door, and they entered.

The one-room apartment was disheveled, dirty, and dark. The only illumination came from the exterior hotel sign outside the window and an old TV sitting in front of a tattered couch.

Wearing a sweatshirt, cargo pants, and untied boots, Tommy rubbed his bloodshot eyes. "I just got back from my shift at the Armory. I'm fried, man."

"This is Frank. A friend," Gino said.

Tommy nodded at him as he sipped from a can of Pabst Blue Ribbon. He looked stoned.

167

"Gino says you're in the Guard," said Frank.

"Yeah."

"I was a weapons officer over in the Sandbox. Glad to meet you."

Frank and Tommy bumped fists.

"Ditto, dude."

Gino glanced around the filthy studio apartment. "Why the hell are you staying here? Your father's house has got to be much nicer."

Tommy avoided Gino's glare. "Oh, I just wanted a place for myself. You know, somewhere I can chill."

Gino walked over to the TV and turned down the volume on the mixed martial arts match. Drug paraphernalia, including a burnt spoon, bag of weed, and ceramic bong were spread out on the coffee table, along with a few empty beer cans and an overflowing ashtray.

"We came by to tell ya that the heist has gotta go down tonight. That a problem?" asked Gino.

"Fuck no. I got everything set," said Tommy.

"Tell us."

Tommy plopped down on the couch and took a swig of beer. "The Armory is overflowing, man. You can't believe all the shit that's pouring in from the drawdowns in the Middle East. Weapons, explosives, tons of supplies stacked up everywhere. It's chaos."

Frank chimed in, "Sounds like the military. Totally FUBAR."

"You got that right, brother."

Gino asked, "What about the stuff we talked about?"

"I've got the launchers and missiles already hidden away."

"Stingers?" asked Frank.

"Oh, yeah. You know, I fired one over in Afghanistan. They're pretty easy to operate."

Gino circled the room. "How do you plan to get the stuff out of the Armory?"

"It's all stashed in a secluded spot near a rear exit, ready to load into my van."

"What about the guards inside the Armory?"

"I *am* the fuckin' guard," Tommy laughed. "We're running a skeleton crew over the Thanksgiving weekend. Only the two guys in the video surveillance room could possibly see me, but that ain't gonna happen 'cause they'll be fast asleep."

Gino was suspicious. "How do ya know that?"

"I'm gonna drug them. Over the last two weeks, I slipped some low-dose sleeping pills in their coffee around midnight. I've done it three times, and it works like a charm. It knocks them out for a couple hours. That's how I was able to hide the launchers and missiles the other night."

"And how about the guards at the front gate?" asked Frank.

"One of my buddies will be on duty there. We got it all worked out," Tommy said with smug confidence.

Gino walked over to Tommy. "Does your friend at the front gate know about us?"

"No way! He doesn't even know what I'm stealing. He just wants the ten grand I promised him. He's got a gambling problem."

A big grin crossed Gino's mug. "Really? What's his name?"

"Randy Jones."

Gino made a mental note.

Tommy asked, "So where's the down payment?"

Gino pulled out an envelope and handed it to him. "Here's the first twenty-five grand. You get the other half when we take delivery."

"What about the heroin? You promised me a pure ounce."

Looming over him, Gino looked down at the burnt spoon on the TV table. "I thought you didn't shoot that shit."

"Nah. I ain't addicted," said Tommy nonchalantly.

Gino rolled the toothpick to the other side of his mouth. "That's what every junkie says."

Suddenly, he lunged at Tommy, yanked him off the couch and got in his face. "Listen, there can't be any screw-ups. Got it? You better be straight or—"

Tommy tried to play it cool, but he was shaking so badly he dropped his beer can onto the floor. "I will, Gino! I will!"

Gino slowly released Tommy and handed him a note. "We'll meet you at this address right after your shift ends. You'll get your money and the H. And don't fuck it up!"

"I'll be there! I promise!"

Without looking back, Gino and Frank exited, slamming the door behind them.

* * * *

Still trembling, Tommy fished out a small baggie of smack from his pants pocket and sat down on the couch. In the muted light from the TV, he checked to see how much heroin he had left to get him through the next 24 hours.

Junkies like to say the heroin high is like: *"getting a hug from God."* Tommy readily agreed. He desperately needed that ounce from Gino because his regular dealer had just been busted and was in jail.

Using the utmost care, Tommy stashed away just enough dope to ingest right before his graveyard shift at the Armory the next morning. Then he placed the remaining small pile of brown powder into the burnt spoon on the table. He wanted to cook it all, shoot it into his arm and forget all about the arms heist, but Gino's wicked warnings were still too fresh in his mind.

Mainlining was too risky until the deed was done.

Instead, he sprinkled some of the heroin onto a piece of tin foil and heated it from below with a cheap plastic lighter. As wisps of the potent smoke drifted up and into his nostrils, he got an incredible rush.

For the next hour, he chased the dragon, doing one hit after another—until he passed out.

35

Parked across the street from Volkov's hotel, Tony kept an eye on the entrance while he scanned his iPad, where streaming stock prices and financial news flashed across the screen.

Tony had managed to sleep in the limo for about four hours before his internal alarm clock went off just as the sun was rising. He was a light sleeper, needing only a few hours a night to feel good the following day. He had already bought the morning paper, and grabbed a cup of coffee and a croissant.

While a reporter on CNBC discussed the day's latest market trends on the dashboard TV, Tony perused various charts and financial statements. He was tracking several international stocks he believed had major upside potential in the coming new year. With the press of a button, he purchased a series of options to further diversify his portfolio.

He smiled to himself, knowing he had just made money.

Around 11:00 a.m., a Lincoln Town Car arrived in front of the hotel. Sensing it could be there to pick up Volkov, Tony put away his computer and papers. A moment later, Volkov exited the hotel and climbed into the back of the car on the driver's side. As the Lincoln pulled away, Tony followed at a safe distance.

Since it was Thanksgiving Day, traffic was very light throughout the City, except for the main shopping districts and the inevitable Macy's Parade snarl around the west side of Central Park and down Broadway.

The Lincoln drove east and turned south onto FDR Drive. Although its windows were tinted, Tony could see there was another man sitting in the back seat with Volkov.

After passing the Williamsburg and Manhattan Bridges, the Lincoln swung onto the Brooklyn Bridge. Tony wondered if Volkov and his mysterious passenger were having a limo meeting or if they were on their way to a specific destination. Tony became more curious when the Lincoln veered off onto the Gowanus Expressway toward Bay Ridge, home to a growing Muslim community.

Lurking a half block behind the Lincoln amid the midday traffic, Tony followed the car into a robust neighborhood filled with halal butcher shops, restaurants, bakeries, religious bookstores, and specialty shops selling incense and perfumes.

At a busy four-way traffic light, the Lincoln pulled to a stop and the other man in the back seat slipped out onto the street. He had dark Middle Eastern features and wore a parka, baseball cap, and sunglasses. After carefully glancing around, he pulled up his coat collar and ran across a lane of traffic onto the bustling sidewalk.

As the Lincoln started to drive away through the intersection, Tony had to make a quick decision about who he was going to follow. Since he knew where Volkov was staying, he chose the mysterious man on foot. The man's gray parka blended in among the other winter overcoats on the sidewalk, but Tony was still able to follow him for several blocks.

As he approached a large mosque in the middle of a block, the man moved back across the street as if to avoid being seen amid the crowds gathering for the midday prayer. After passing by the Monroe Hotel, he suddenly turned down the adjacent side street.

Tony pulled into the loading zone in front of the Monroe and got out of the limo. He walked to the corner of the hotel and looked down the long, nearly deserted side street. The man was gone, but Tony lingered there for a few minutes, hoping to catch another glimpse of him.

Tony was about to give up when he saw a homeless man slowly emerge from a small alley halfway down the block. The man wore a thick, tattered overcoat and his head was wrapped in a frayed scarf that revealed only his eyes. Carrying a shopping bag in each hand, he shuffled along the sidewalk in an aimless way.

After passing some empty storefronts, the man trudged across the street towards a large, two-story warehouse that anchored the end of the block. The old brick building looked like it had been condemned. The windows on the bottom level were either blacked out or boarded up while rock-throwing vandals had shattered most of the upper story panes.

As the homeless man stepped up onto the curb, the gray sleeve of the missing man's parka slipped out from the back of one of the bags.

Tony did a double take.

Afraid the artful dodger would spot him, Tony moved farther back to hide. The man glanced around to make sure no one was watching or following him. Then, he squeezed through a narrow gap in the chain-link fence topped with razor wire surrounding the warehouse and knocked on the side door. Someone inside opened it a crack and let him in.

Perplexed, Tony returned to his car.

"What the hell is going on?" he asked himself. One moment the man is cruising around in a fancy towncar and the next he's disguising himself in rags? And what exactly was Volkov's relationship to him?

Tony needed time to think.

Looking around, he noticed that the upper floors of the ten-story Monroe Hotel had a decent view of the warehouse.

Tony found a secure, attended parking lot a block away. After removing a pair of opera glasses from the glove compartment, he walked to the hotel entrance

36

Brooklyn
Noon

Even in its heyday, the Monroe Hotel had been a dump. Several months after it opened its doors in early 1929, The Great Depression hit, and the facility was forced to convert most of its plush new suites into low-rent apartments to repay the staggering construction costs. It never recovered and now was in permanent disrepair.

Tony entered the foyer and walked across the seedy lobby to the front desk. Looking into the drab room behind the counter, he saw the clerk watching a porno movie. He rang the bell and looked around. A few residents milled about, including an older woman having an animated conversation with an invisible friend.

The clerk sauntered up to the desk, tucking in his shirt and pulling up the suspenders on his pants. "Yeah?"

"I'd like a room facing the street on the east side of the hotel."

Noticing he carried no luggage, the clerk asked, "How long do you need it for?"

Tony had to get back to Sands Point in time for Thanksgiving dinner. "Just for the afternoon."

The clerk checked the room keys hanging on the wall behind him. "Got a nice room on the sixth floor. Just had it fumigated."

"Okay. How much?"

The clerk eyed Tony's expensive suit and classic cane. "Hundred bucks."

Tony didn't like being ripped off. "Fifty. Take it or leave it."

The clerk stared at him. "You got a date coming, mister? If we have to change the sheets, it'll cost you another twenty."

Tony peeled off the cash and dropped it onto the counter. "It's just me."

The clerk handed him the key and returned to the back room.

After riding up the noisy elevator to the sixth floor, Tony found the dreary room at the end of a hallway. With double beds and a small table and chairs in the corner, it provided a decent view of the quiet side street.

He used the opera glasses to scan the warehouse at the end of the block. There were no signs of life.

Tony dragged a chair over to the window and settled in for the afternoon.

37

**New York City
1:15 p.m.**

Jake Crowley got out of a cab in front of 26 Federal Plaza—the forty-one story, steel and glass monolith near the bottom of Broadway.

Since it was his first trip to FBI headquarters, he wore a new tie. He hated ties, especially the one he had just bought at some upscale men's clothing store for a hundred bucks—but he had to look somewhat professional. Maybe it would help to offset the rest of his outfit: Levis, cowboy boots, and sports coat with leather elbow patches. He was never going to grace the cover of GQ, but at least he was wearing clean socks and boxers.

Inside the spacious lobby, the security checkpoints were extensive. That was hardly a surprise. The Jacob K. Javits Building was one of the juiciest targets for a possible terrorist attack, housing the offices of the FBI, Homeland Security, Immigration Services, and, as rumor had it, clandestine bases for the NSA and CIA.

On regular weekdays, the lines were long and, at times, very acrimonious. Foreign nationals who came to deal with citizenship and immigration matters had a separate entrance with even more stringent security.

Since the regular offices were closed for the Thanksgiving holiday, the foyer was practically deserted. At the employee check-in area, Crowley showed his credentials and presented his 9mm Sig Sauer pistol and backup clip.

He was scanned and patted down by two guards who took their jobs very seriously. Luckily, he had left his computer and overnight bag back at the hotel because it would have been subjected to another time-consuming search, and he was already late for his meeting.

Only after another security guard called up to the 23rd floor to confirm Crowley had an appointment with Hank Kline, Special Agent in charge of the New York Counterterrorism Unit, was he allowed to get on the elevator.

With an armed guard standing behind her, the FBI receptionist checked Crowley's credentials once again and called Agent Kline to inform him his guest had arrived.

Waiting, Crowley walked over to the windows overlooking the lower Manhattan skyline. The new One World Trade Center gleamed majestically a short distance away. His heart ached as he remembered the chilling events of 9/11. He wanted to visit Ground Zero to pay his respects, but didn't know if his schedule would allow it.

Crowley had no idea what his future held over the next days, weeks, or months. He only knew he was committed to tracking down the smuggled terrorists and kicking some ass.

"You must be Jake Crowley," said a voice with a heavy Southern accent.

Jake turned to see a big man, maybe 6'4" and 250 pounds, with a friendly smile, standing in the doorway. "I'm Hank Kline. Welcome to New York."

They shook hands and entered. Kline led Crowley through a maze of offices.

"How's your boss, good ol' Roger Hamid? Is he still as tight as a frog's ass?"

"You know him?"

"Hell, yes. We go way back," Kline said, holding a door open for Crowley to pass through. "We worked together down in Tennessee for a few years. I used to call him 'the only Muslim in Memphis' just to piss him off."

"That would do it alright."

"Well, Roger gave as good as he got. He called me 'Ku Klux Kline.'"

They entered a large conference room. A young female FBI agent with a shapely athletic build and blonde ponytail stood in front of a large flat-screen TV featuring a digital map of Brooklyn.

Kline said, "Jake Crowley, meet my assistant, Agent Elizabeth Ross."

She smiled. "Nice to meet you."

Crowley nodded, subtly checking her out. "My pleasure."

Wasting no time, Kline said, "We've traced all the truck driver's cell phone calls for the past several months. Fill him in, Ross."

"So far, we've confirmed he called his wife from these four locations right after he dropped off his smuggled aliens," she said, pointing at four blue markers grouped together on the screen. "Of course, there should be five markers, but he never got to make the last call home."

"Has the NYPD located him yet?" asked Crowley.

"Unfortunately, yes," Ross said and pointed at a red marker a few miles away from the others. "His body was found in this industrial area early this morning."

She typed on a laptop linked to the TV monitor. A series of grisly crime scene photos popped up. "He and his truck were set on fire, just like those vans down on the border."

Crowley swallowed hard. Gruesome images of the other torched victims began to cycle through his mind like a grotesque slide show.

"Fire," Kline said. "The nastiest but most efficient way to cover up a crime scene."

"Whoever did that should burn in Hell," Ross said.

Trying to push the carnage out of his mind, Crowley changed the subject. "I saw the truck driver's wife and brother-in-law back in Phoenix yesterday. If they hadn't come forward, our investigation would be dead in the water."

"Agent Hamid is placing them into protective custody until this thing gets resolved," Kline said.

Ross gestured at the five file folders on the table. "The field reports and forensics you supplied from the border van burnings are very informative, Agent Crowley," she said.

Kline agreed. "We spent all morning reviewing everything with our crisis management team. Clearly, some kind of terrorist event is imminent, but we don't have a clue what it could possibly be. Every agent and asset we have is humping it. Washington has been alerted. NSA is closely monitoring online and cell phone activity. So far, we've got nothing to go on except the truck driver's cell records. But at least now, we can narrow the search."

Again, Ross circled the area around the blue markers. "We believe your stowaways are in this general vicinity. It has a high concentration of Muslims, and one of the biggest mosques in Brooklyn."

"Has that mosque been involved in any subversive activities?"

"No," Kline replied. "In fact, the head cleric is one of the few Islamic leaders brave enough to condemn the 9/11 attacks. He's been a good partner for local law enforcement, but he can't control who comes and goes at his mosque."

"Two weeks ago, we got a break. We received a tip that a major international terrorist could be in that area. His name is Mustafa Al-Anazi," Ross said.

"Yeah, I read about him on your 'Most Wanted' list."

"He's a very dangerous man."

Crowley studied the map. "Well, it sure looks like they have the personnel and leadership for some kind of attack."

"All of our informants within the Muslim community and other assets are on high alert, looking for anything out of the ordinary—a surge in chatter or whatever. We also have a surveillance post set up across the street from that mosque," Kline said. "We'll go there shortly."

Crowley walked over to the opposite wall, which was covered with the photos and the names of the major organized crime families in the New York area. He casually scanned the mug shots on each family tree.

Kline said, "This is actually the conference room for OCU—our Organized Crime Unit. We're sharing it while our facility is being renovated."

"What about weapons?" Crowley asked. "Those terrorists will want some ample firepower. Any intel about unusual arms transactions?"

"Nothing significant, but we've stepped up our surveillance on all known arms traffickers along the Eastern Seaboard," Ross said.

"Trust me, those terrorists will use anything they can get their hands on. A can of gas and a match is all they need to kill a lot of people," Crowley said coldly.

He continued to walk along the wall until he stopped in front of the Conti Family section. A placard on the top of the family tree read:

CONTI—NEW YORK
Construction
(Drug Trafficking, Extortion, Robbery)

Beneath it were 8x10 glossy photos and the names of each member: Mario Conti, Dante Conti, Giovanni (Johnnie) Conti, Tony Tucci, Gino Marino, Al Franchetti, Enzo Colombo, Leonardo Scarpia, and numerous other low-level associates.

"What about explosives to make bombs? For instance, this family is in the construction business. They may do demolition work and have access to dynamite or C-4. A couple well-placed IEDs around the City could be devastating."

Kline stepped up. "I seriously doubt any organized crime family would knowingly sell explosives to terrorists. Even the Mafia has its standards."

"Well, money talks," Crowley said. "Besides, the terrorists could be using a middleman."

Ross jumped in. "We're already checking with the ATF to get an itemization of all recent sales of explosives. Since 9/11, those transactions are much more closely monitored."

Crowley shrugged. "Well, it looks like you guys have covered every base."

With a note of genuine sadness, Ross said, "By the way, your eyewitness in the burn unit in Tucson passed away this morning."

Crowley winced. "All he wanted was a better life in America. What a waste."

"But when he told you the hijackers used 'Allah Akbar' as a code word, we had confirmation that the smuggled men were probably Islamic extremists," Kline said. "That was crucial intel."

"He deserves an honorable burial and maybe a nice check should be sent to his family in Mexico," Crowley suggested.

Kline nodded at Ross, who made a note.

"I assume you want to see the crime scene where we found the Iraqi truck driver from Arizona," Kline said to Crowley.

"Absolutely."

"And afterwards, we'll go to the stakeout over in Brooklyn. We don't want to blow our cover there, so we'll both need some street clothes to blend in. Come on."

Kline led them to a windowless, wardrobe room next to the FBI gym. There were racks of coats, clothes, hats, and accessories to outfit the most discerning undercover agent.

While Kline donned a bulky overcoat and wool cap, Crowley slipped on a dark hoody and pair of aviator sunglasses.

Sizing him up, Ross said, "The Unabomber. Very stylish."

Crowley flashed a big grin.

38

Behind the blacked-out windows of the abandoned warehouse, Mustafa Al-Anazi and his smuggled comrades were scattered throughout the first-floor. To maintain a hidden presence, they used only small oil lamps and candles to provide light. Propane heaters glowed in corners to warm the sparse rooms. There was no furniture, only prayer rugs and sleeping bags on the cold concrete floors.

Armed with rifles and handguns, the insurgents took turns guarding the various entrances, reading the Quran, sleeping, and cleaning their weapons.

In the makeshift kitchen, a pot of vegetable and mutton stew simmered on a gas camping stove. Bags of fruit and bread were spread out on a metallic counter. Cockroaches crawled around the trash bags stacked in a corner beside an old, broken refrigerator.

Blindfolded, gagged, and hog-tied, the captured FBI informant Ali moaned on the frigid floor as two men watched over him.

In an empty room in a far corner, Anazi sat on the floor in front of a laptop computer and printer running off a portable battery pack. On the small screen, he examined numerous photos of passenger airliners landing and taking off at nearby metropolitan airports.

Anazi's key operative, Kamel Al-Masud, had secretly photographed the various locations, searching for the ideal places where heat-seeking missiles could be launched into the jet engines of commercial airliners. Anazi carefully scrutinized the detail in each photo before printing out a copy and placing it in one of five manila envelopes.

The avowed terrorist had known Masud since they were children growing up in Saudi Arabia. With their handsome features and muscular physiques, they looked like twins and were inseparable until their early teenage years. That changed when Masud's father, a petroleum engineer with a multi-national oil company, brought his family to the United States to start a new life.

For the next ten years, Masud and Anazi kept in close touch; however, after the first World Trade Center bombing in 1993, Anazi went underground into the murky world of international terrorism, and they lost contact. But Anazi kept a photo of his childhood companion in his Quran, knowing they would reconnect one day in the future.

Masud became a successful businessman who owned a string of auto repair shops throughout Brooklyn. Last spring, Anazi came quietly calling. Masud wept at the sight of his long-lost friend.

Anazi, a master manipulator, caught Masud at a very vulnerable point in his life: he was going through a difficult divorce as well as battling a rare form of leukemia. With a cold calculus, the cunning Anazi appealed to Masud's deep-seated ties to Islam and the promise of Paradise to convince him to help in his plot against America.

Since Masud knew the New York area so well, Anazi put him in charge of the operation's logistics. Using funds provided by extremist benefactors in the

Middle East, Masud purchased everything to support his friend's grand scheme.

Their immediate priority had been to procure a safe staging area away from prying eyes, where Anazi and his smuggled cohorts could live until the day of reckoning.

Masud leased the Brooklyn warehouse and went to great lengths to fortify the building, boarding up the first-floor windows and erecting an eight-foot-tall construction fence around the entire perimeter. Shortly thereafter, Anazi took up residence at the warehouse, using the old first-floor offices as his base of operations. Surreptitiously, Masud delivered supplies to the warehouse to feed and clothe the growing ranks of holy fighters being smuggled into the U.S.

Every two weeks, when the long-haul truck driver from Arizona arrived with a new two-man team, Masud met them at a designated drop-off location and transported the smuggled men back to the warehouse. These were always very tense and dangerous journeys, because if the police were to pull them over, things could escalate into a deadly confrontation and their entire operation would be blown.

Anazi left the warehouse only on rare occasions and always in disguise. The only time he accompanied Masud outside was when the final two-man team arrived in New York. As Masud served as the lookout, Anazi quickly garroted the long-haul driver from Arizona, drove the truck to a secluded industrial area, and set it on fire.

Masud had also secured a fleet of five panel vans to transport the two-man teams and weapons to their targets. His chain of auto repair shops offered the ideal cover to purchase and retrofit the vehicles. Each van was bought with cash, registered with the DMV, and fully insured. Unaware of the terrorist plot, Masud's mechanics made sure the vehicles were roadworthy and devoid of any mechanical issues that could draw attention.

To project the image of a legitimate working business, Masud created a sham company called "Tri-State Plaster & Paint." Tongue-in-cheek, he hired a graphic artist to create a logo, featuring a jolly pharaoh dressed in overalls, holding a plaster trowel in one hand and a paintbrush in the other, with the pyramids of Giza in the background. The ad slogan beneath read: *"No job too big or too small."* The logo was applied to the exterior of the vans, along with a toll-free telephone number and business license number.

To complete the ruse, Masud filled the back of the vans with buckets of plaster and paint, brushes and rollers, and numerous drop cloths, which would be used to cover up a deadly cache of weapons. He even hired a master counterfeiter to create fake IDs and green cards for all the insurgents. If a van were to be stopped by the police, it would surely pass scrutiny.

Now, the vans were safely parked in a corner of the warehouse, gassed up and ready to roll.

Lastly, Masud needed to locate, vet, and train five drivers for the vans. In order to find the most loyal and dependable young men, Masud met with radical clerics in the greater New York Area who preached anti-Western extremism. Each brainwashed recruit was required to speak perfect English, have a valid driver's license, no criminal record—and a thirst for the Afterlife.

Over the previous month, Masud had worked with each driver: teaching them how to drive their specific routes, ways to avoid any contact with authorities, where to park to give each two-man crew the ideal place to launch their missiles, and how to navigate to their secondary targets where they would murder their victims face-to-face.

The drivers had just joined the group at the warehouse two days before. Initially, given the language barriers and their American ways, the young drivers clustered together during the first night, but were soon embedded with their designated two-man teams of foreign fighters, bonding and rejoicing together in anticipation of the coming battles.

* * * *

Anazi opened his online browser and entered an obscure Islamic website. He moved the cursor across the elaborately illustrated home page to a small icon in the bottom left corner. Holding down a combination of keys, he clicked the return button. That launched a series of encrypted pop-up pages that filled the screen. He selected a certain page and entered a username and long password, which linked him to a site in the Middle East. A text box appeared, and he entered in Arabic:

confirm_saturday_9am

He hit the return button again, and the message disappeared into cyberspace.

After turning off the laptop, he put all the photos and computer components into a backpack and placed it beside his bedroll in the corner.

A great sense of satisfaction overwhelmed him. Smiling, he lifted his hands to Heaven and quietly whispered, "Praise be to Allah."

Once he and his fellow martyrs secured the launchers and missiles the next day, the final countdown to America's next terrorist nightmare would begin.

But first, Anazi had to deal with the traitorous spy.

39

Brooklyn
5:00 p.m.

As the late afternoon shadows crept across the room at the Monroe Hotel, Tony sat by the window, keeping vigil over the warehouse down the block. He scanned the building with the opera glasses for the umpteenth time, looking for any movement.

He had been in the room for almost five hours, hoping to catch another glimpse of the mysterious man who had gone to such great lengths to hide his identity. So far, it had been a bust. The only thing moving at the end of the block was trash swirling in the cold winter wind.

Tony mulled over what he knew about Victor Volkov and the man in rags…

At this point, it was all conjecture. He assumed the Russian had to be a key player, perhaps the middleman, in the arms deal Mario was so worried about. After Tony was ushered out of the Nottingham Palace suite, Volkov and Dante probably came to terms and then partied hard until the early hours of the morning. Tony surmised that by the time Volkov returned to his hotel, he was too wasted, and it was too late for him to rendezvous with his client; hence, he arranged for the limo meeting the next day. The drive from mid-town Manhattan to south Brooklyn gave them plenty of time to confirm all the final details of their arms deal.

The mysterious man, who jumped out of the limo in the middle of the intersection, was a more troubling paradox. As he snaked through the neighborhood, the man had casually looked back over his shoulder and scanned the street in a practiced, nonchalant manner that attracted no attention—but he still seemed paranoid. The one thing Tony knew for sure was that by disguising himself as a homeless bum before entering the warehouse, the man was hiding something inside.

But what?

Maybe the missiles were stashed there. Perhaps the man was providing the arms to Volkov so he could sell them to Dante, who in turn would resell them to the Mexican cartel. Or maybe the mysterious man was the ultimate buyer. Regardless, Tony needed more hard information.

His smartphone rang.

"Yo, T! It's me, Jeremy."

"I was just thinking of calling you."

"Sounds like we're on the same wavelength. What's happening?"

"You go first."

"Okay. I got the initial workup done on Nicky Bruno," Jeremy said. "It was easy and only took a couple hours. First, I identified his personal IP address at that Fifth Avenue condo you gave me. Then I woke up his computer around three a.m. this morning and had a look around."

"What do you mean you 'woke up his computer'?" Tony asked incredulously.

"Simple. Most people leave their computers on, and they eventually slip into 'sleep' mode. That's when they are *very* susceptible to hacking. People like

Bruno, who live in highly secure buildings know they're safe from the average criminal on the street, but they have no idea what kind of damage a cyber crook can do—so they let their guard down. And this guy has his pants around his ankles."

"What did you do?"

"I copied all his files into the Cloud, dropped in my own spyware, and created a secret P2P file-sharing protocol, which gives me full access to everything on his computer. Now, I can track all his emails, online searches, credit card purchases, and bank accounts."

"Perfect. What did you find out?"

"The guy has money stashed all over the place, but he's done a sloppy job of hiding it. I already found two offshore bank accounts under different names worth over three million bucks. Also, someone is depositing $50,000 a month into one of those accounts using third-party wire transfers, but that's more of a hassle to trace. If I have more time, I can probably track it down."

"Interesting. We can follow up on that later."

"I also got the account codes," Jeremy crowed.

"How did you do that?"

"The greedy fuck likes to check on those accounts every morning. As soon as he logged-in, I could see and record all his usernames and passwords. Now we own it all!"

"Any other good news?"

"His fancy condo, which he owns free and clear, is worth about $4 million. The deed is registered with one of those offshore banks. He also pays the annual property taxes and monthly condo maintenance fees via wire transfers. If you want, we can set up a few major credit lines with other offshore banks using the equity in his condo and then borrow against it. I should be able to free up several million on that transaction alone."

"It's something to consider," Tony replied. "But you know the rules, no one gets hurt—except our targets."

"There's more. As a typical old-school Mafioso, Bruno files bogus IRS tax returns. He only declares the income from a partnership in a retail dry cleaner and a couple domestic savings accounts, which is nothing compared to his other hidden assets. He has a checking account and one credit card for basic purchases. I figure that he's got an unreported income stream of at least $1 million annually. He spends a lot of time gambling in the Bahamas and Vegas. And he always uses private jets. Everything is paid in cash."

"Of course."

"You know, we could just toss this guy to the IRS. Those bloodsuckers would drain him dry and throw his sorry ass in the can for years."

"That's an enticing thought, for sure."

"Like I told you the other night, I don't know what Bruno's got under his bed, but he'll need it when we lower the boom."

"*If* we lower the boom."

"What?" Jeremy was genuinely stunned. "Of all the jerks we've shadowed together, I thought this was one guy you'd really want to fuck over. I know I would."

"I plan to meet him soon. Let's wait and see what happens."

"One more thing... Bruno is a real pervert."

"How so?"

"He spends a lot of time trolling the Dark Web—the underbelly of the Internet that's inaccessible by normal search engines. Using special software, one can find drugs, hard pornography, snuff videos, even killers for hire. Bruno's appetites are of the twisted sexual variety. Want the details?"

Tony said nothing.

"What? Too much information?"

"You can never have too much information, especially when you're dealing with a low life like Bruno. But it's going to have to wait."

"Okay, I'll keep digging in my free time."

"I appreciate it. By the way, something else has just come up. I need some info on a guy named Victor Volkov. I think he's a Russian arms dealer."

"If he is, I'm sure the NSA, CIA, and FBI have fat files on him. However, I would have to enter my official ID info to access it, which could raise some red flags."

"Forget it. I don't want you to do anything to jeopardize your job."

"But I do know a well-connected spook who owes me a favor. Let me make a call."

"Any intel would be helpful. Just be careful."

"No sweat, T. I'll get back at you soon."

"Thanks, Jeremy. I owe you."

"More meatballs from Mancini's!"

"I'll be in touch."

Tony ended the call and stood to stretch. He checked his watch and realized he needed to get back to the Conti estate to prepare for Thanksgiving dinner. There was still no activity around the warehouse, so he put on his overcoat, slipped the opera glasses back into his pocket, and left the room.

At the end of the hallway, Tony moved to the back of the rickety elevator to make room for a woman in a black hijab with three young children.

When the elevator doors opened down in the lobby, two men were waiting to board: Hank Kline and Jake Crowley, wearing their undercover attire. They moved aside to allow the passengers to exit.

As Tony walked past them, something caught Crowley's attention. He carefully watched Tony as he dropped his room key into the lock box on the front desk and left the hotel.

"Something wrong, Crowley?" Kline asked, holding open the elevator doors for his tardy colleague.

"That guy... he looked familiar..." Crowley said, shaking his head. "But I just can't place him."

"Maybe it will come to you later."

"Perhaps."

40

Crowley and Kline took the elevator to the top floor and made their way to the undercover FBI stakeout in the front corner suite. Kline tapped twice on the door, paused, and then rapped twice again.

Agent Steve Watkins, weary and unshaven, peered through the peephole and unlocked the door to let them in.

"Hey, boss," said Watkins, a techie in a short sleeve dress shirt and Clark Kent glasses.

"What's the good word?" Kline asked as he led Crowley into the living room filled with hi-tech surveillance equipment.

Another agent, Nuri Al-Bashir, said, "Nothing new since we spoke earlier." Bashir was a young man with Arabic features, a longish black beard, and Apple t-shirt.

Both agents had Glock .40 caliber handguns strapped to their hips.

"Gentlemen, meet Jake Crowley from Homeland Security. These are two of my best agents, Steve Watkins, and Nuri Al-Bashir."

They all shook hands.

Kline carried a grocery bag filled with snacks and sodas. Handing it to the agents, he said, "Since it's Thanksgiving, I thought you would appreciate some turkey sandwiches to celebrate."

Like two hungry dogs, they ripped into the bag.

Crowley took a look around the large suite. There was a digital camera with a huge telephoto lens and a video camera mounted on tripods, pointing out the window down at the mosque on the other side of the street. In the center of the room was a long table stacked with laptops, printers, police radios, and more high-tech toys. Fast-food wrappers, empty energy drink cans, and coffee cups littered every counter top. In the dark adjacent bedroom, there were twin beds heaped with rumpled sheets, blankets, and dirty clothes spewing out of suitcases. The place had the typical musky, messy ambiance of a long stakeout.

Eating as they continued working, Watkins snapped some photos of a group of men on the street with the digital camera while Bashir aimed a parabolic microphone down at two men having a heated discussion in front of the mosque. All the agents listened to the loud Arabic conversation on the speakers in the room.

With a slight Middle Eastern accent, Bashir commented, "Looks and sounds suspicious, doesn't it? But those guys are just arguing about that controversial call from Sunday's New York Giants game with the Niners."

"Watkins is our tech guru, and Bashir is one of our undercover agents," Kline said. "Bashir speaks three different Arab dialects and makes a mean falafel."

A comic at heart, Bashir flashed the peace sign.

Kline pointed at the laptops on the table. "This is a state-of-the-art digital recognition system. Every photo and voice track we capture on this equipment is recorded on those computers and immediately sent to our new biometric database in Washington, which scans for various identification markers and then matches them to criminal and terrorist profiles in a matter of seconds. It's an incredible tool."

"In the last several weeks," Watkins said, "we've scanned thousands of faces through the system. We've had a handful of matches, but they're mostly small-time felons. We're looking for much bigger fish like Mustafa Al-Anazi."

Kline nodded at Crowley and said, "He's got to be close by."

Crowley walked over to the windows and looked directly down at the mosque. "Is this your only stakeout?"

"Yes, but we've got numerous informants in the neighborhood," Kline said, who suddenly looked ill. "Sad to say, —"

All the FBI agents hung their heads.

"What?" Crowley asked.

"Yesterday, we received a text message from Ali, the informant who saw Anazi two weeks ago. He claimed he had just seen 'The Ghost' again and was following him... Ali has disappeared."

Bashir added, "Since then, I've attended prayers at the mosque several times, listening for any word about him. And I've checked with every source in the neighborhood. No one has heard a thing."

"This looks like the end of the trail, Crowley. At least, for now," Kline said, heading for the door. "I've got to get back to the office for a meeting with my counterpart at the NYPD to review our contingency plans in case of an attack. Want to come?"

"If it's okay with these guys, I'd like to hang out here for a while," Crowley said.

"Be my guest, but they'll probably put you to work."

Watkins and Bashir eagerly nodded their consent.

"Great. Let's git-r-done!" Crowley replied, picking up a pair of high-power binoculars to scan the street scene below.

41

It was time…

Anazi picked up his Quran and a long knife with Islamic writing scrolled along its glistening blade. Slowly, he moved through the warehouse offices and into the kitchen where his captive lay on the floor.

The other men slowly gathered around, including Masud, who held a small video camera with a blinking green light.

Anazi ripped off Ali's blindfold.

His face was a bloody mess, and several of his fingers were missing from the interrogation the day before. The torture session had been particularly long and brutal—just the way Anazi liked it. He had no mercy for those who betrayed his warped version of Islam. Of course, young Ali had quickly confessed to working for the FBI and begged for a swift execution, but Anazi still wanted his pound of flesh.

Anazi leaned in close to his prisoner and showed him the knife. "It is time to pay for your treachery."

Ali's eyes filled with sheer terror. He tried to scream, but the gag was too tight.

Calmly, Anazi held up his Quran and quoted its scripture in Arabic: "As to those who reject faith, I will punish them with terrible agony in this world and in the Hereafter, nor will they have anyone to help."

As the circle of terrorists tightened around the condemned man, his muffled screams turned into a low guttural wail as the knife sawed through soft tissue, arteries, muscle, and bone of his neck.

Eventually, it was over.

42

After spending the previous night in the limo and half the day at the Monroe, Tony needed a long hot shower and a fresh, pressed suit. As he adjusted his tie in the bathroom mirror at his cottage, his phone rang.

"Hello?"

"Tony! It's Dominic."

Dominic Romano, a jovial, heavy-set man, sat at the end of a busy bar in Philadelphia. The Flyers played hockey on the TV above his head.

"Thanks for calling back, Dom. You're a tough man to reach."

"Sorry, but I change cell phones all the time. Don't want to take a chance Big Brother is listening in. Is your line secure?"

"No one in law enforcement gives a shit about me. I'm too far down the food chain. We can speak freely," replied Tony. "What are you up to?"

"I'm just sitting here handicapping this weekend's games. Are you still betting on sports?"

"No, I'm focused on stocks now, but sometimes that seems even riskier. Anyway, how's life in Philly?"

"You know. Same shit, different day. And you?"

"Getting by," Tony said. "Listen, the reason I called was to find out if you know a guy named Frank Salvadore."

"A young, tough-looking guy, right?" Dominic asked as he arranged a stack of bookie slips in his bulging billfold.

"He's hanging out with Dante's crew. Just arrived."

"Yeah, I met him at a Phillie's game last year. I was up in the De Luca's suite watching the Yankees get their ass kicked," Dominic laughed. "It was beautiful."

"Hey! Go easy on my team!" Tony chided. "Tell me, what's Frank's story?"

"The De Lucas brought him in after he got canned from the Army. He was some big-shot weapons expert. That is until he got caught stealing."

"Stealing what?

"Fancy machine guns, explosives, you name it. While Frank was still in the military, the De Luca family always had fire sales going on for that shit."

"Interesting."

"You guys going into the arms biz?"

"I wouldn't know."

Dominic tipped back a cold beer. "To tell ya the truth, Tony, I thought you were calling me about… well, Dante's gambling markers."

Tony sighed. "What's the damage?"

"It's serious dough. He borrowed a mil from Joey Martini here in Philly back in early September to finance some new nightclub in Manhattan. Then during the World Series, he bet two hundred-fifty large with a friend of ours in Boston and lost his ass. Plus, he stopped paying the juice on both loans weeks ago. People are royally pissed."

"Jesus Christ!" Tony cursed, wondering how much more Dante had borrowed to finance the nightclub and his gambling addiction.

Dominic whispered, "Hey, you didn't hear this from me, but if it's not repaid soon, Dante's old man is gonna get squeezed for it. Nobody wants that, but you know the rules: Everyone pays."

Tony exhaled wearily. "I'm too old for this shit."

"Yeah, we're just a couple of old timers waiting for the next issue of AARP Magazine, right?"

"I wish."

Tony checked his watch. It was almost time for dinner. "Well, Happy Thanksgiving, Dom. The next time you're in New York, let's break bread."

"Now that's an offer I can't refuse."

They both chuckled and hung up.

43

Tony slipped on his suit jacket and overcoat, removed a chilled bottle of expensive champagne from the fridge and headed over to the Conti mansion.

As he walked through the gardens above the shoreline, small waves broke along the beach in a soft, melodic rhythm. It was a crisp, clear night, and an invigorating briny scent filled the air.

Tony watched as a small, beat-up sedan pulled up in front of the mansion. Wearing a tailored Brooks Brothers suit and holding a large bouquet, Dr. Hali Dia climbed out. He looked a little on edge.

"You must be Angela's friend," Tony said, extending his hand.

"Yes, I'm Hali Dia," he said with a distinct British accent.

"And I'm Tony Tucci. It's a pleasure to meet you."

A large smile brightened Hali's face. "So you're the famous Uncle Tony? Angela speaks very fondly of you."

"She's sweet. We're not related, but I love her like a daughter."

Tony gestured to the imposing front door. "So, are you ready to meet the rest of the family?"

Hali hesitated. "Frankly, I'm a little nervous."

"About what?"

"Come on. I didn't just get off the boat from Senegal. I've been studying here for many years. I know that no matter how good a physician I am, they're going to take one look at me and..."

Interrupting him, Tony said, "Let me ask you one question. Do you love Angela?"

"Yes."

"Then you just have to trust that everything will work out."

44

Dr. Hali Dia looked around the massive foyer as Tony closed the front door behind them. The air was heavy with the rich scents of fresh roasted turkey, stuffing, and rosemary.

In the dining room, two maids in traditional black dresses with white trim laid out silverware on the table while a chef placed freshly baked pumpkin and apple pies on a silver desert cart.

Tony cleared his throat. "Our guest has arrived."

The servants looked over to see Hali, exchanging concerned looks. Carla emerged from the living room and froze in the doorway, her mouth agape in shock. Hali approached her with the bouquet of red roses just as Angela appeared behind her mother.

"Oh, Hal! You brought me roses!" Angela said as she ran to him with her arms outstretched.

They hugged briefly.

"Actually, these flowers are for your mother."

Carla graciously stepped forward and accepted them.

"Thank you. They're beautiful."

He took her hand and bowed. "I'm Hali—or Hal—as your beautiful daughter likes to call me. It's so nice to meet you."

Warming to the reality of the situation, Carla forced a smile.

"I brought your favorite champagne, Carla. It's perfectly chilled," Tony said. "Shall we open it?"

"Yes," Carla said. "I'm sure we could all use a drink."

Carla waved at the servants, who quickly delivered a tray of champagne glasses. She handed the roses to one maid with instructions to place them in the center vase on the dining room table.

"Where's Mario?" Tony asked as he popped the cork.

"I'm afraid he's still under the weather," Carla said, studying the tall African physician standing before her.

Hal turned serious. "May I be of some assistance, Mrs. Conti?"

"Thank you, but his doctor was here earlier. Mario is resting now."

As the champagne was poured, Angela said, "You'll just have to meet Papa next time."

"I'll look forward to it."

Tony raised his glass. "Cheers to Mario. To his good health and long life."

They clinked glasses and drank.

Looking through the front windows out onto the circular driveway, they watched Dante pull up in his Ferrari.

Clutching Hal's sleeve, Angela whispered. "That's Dante, my brother."

"This is the first year his wife Maria and my grandchildren won't be here for Thanksgiving," Carla sighed. "Divorce can be so tragic. And Dante is not handling it very well."

Angela gulped down her champagne in anticipation of dealing with her brother. "I'm sure he'll find solace in the arms of one of his many girlfriends."

They all waited for Dante's entrance. The front door opened, and footsteps followed, echoing through the entryway. A moment later, Dante, who looked flushed and drunk, waltzed into the living room. He stopped abruptly when he saw Hal. "What the hell is going on?"

Sensing trouble, Carla said, "Everything's fine, Dante. Please join us."

Dante lurched toward the group. Tony tried to intercept him gently, but Dante shoved by him to get closer to Hal. "Who's this fuckin' moolie?"

Hal recoiled.

"Dante!" Carla exclaimed.

Dante turned to Angela. "Don't tell me this is the guy you've been screwing. I thought he was a surgeon!"

"He *is*, you jerk!" she said, pushing her brother away.

Carla started to tear up. "Please!"

"What's happening to this family? First that whore wife of mine kicks me out and now my little sister is shacked up with Kunta Kinte? Well, happy fuckin' Thanksgiving."

Tony stepped in. "Knock it off, Dante!"

Dante shoved by him and looked around the room. "Where's Dad?"

Trying to compose herself, Carla said, "He's upstairs resting."

"Does he know what's going on down here?" Dante asked as he staggered out of the room towards the staircase.

"Don't you dare disturb him, Dante!" Carla said angrily. "In fact, I think you should leave."

Wiping some spittle away from the side of his mouth, Dante turned back to face the group. He glared at Hal. "Fine! I lost my appetite anyway."

He stomped out of the house and slammed the front door behind him.

Tony said, "Excuse me. I'll be right back."

He caught up with Dante in the driveway.

"Can you believe that shit?" Dante asked, lighting a cigarette.

"You need to calm down," Tony said sternly.

Dante paced around. "Calm down? I should go back in there and kick his ass. You can't trust those motherfuckers!"

"Let it go, Dante. Besides, you've got bigger problems."

That surprised Dante. "What are you talking about?"

"Just what do you know about the man you met with last night?"

"He's a businessman. That's all."

"His name is Victor Volkov, right?"

Dante took a drag. "That's my deal, Tony. I don't need or want your input."

"Your father is very worried about it."

"Well, it's none of your fuckin' business!"

"It's affecting his health."

"The old man will be fine. Everything is under control."

"Really? This morning I followed Volkov and..."

Dante exploded. "I'm warning you. Stay out of it!"

To emphasize the point, Dante flicked his lit cigarette right past Tony's ear—a brazen act of disrespect.

Then he leaped into his Ferrari and sped off into the night.

45

After a few more glasses of champagne and wine, Carla, Angela, Hal, and Tony recovered from the earlier pyrotechnics and enjoyed an excellent dinner.

The conversation was dominated by the story of Hal's life story: how he was rescued from an orphanage in Senegal at a young age by Christian missionaries, and later adopted by an English couple who raised him, and sponsored his studies at Oxford until he came to America to study medicine at Johns Hopkins. By the time dessert and coffee were served, Carla and Tony were quite fond of Angela's charming boyfriend.

As the servants began to clear the dishes, Tony leaned close to Carla. "If it's okay with you, I'd like a word with Mario."

Carla nodded. "Okay. But if he's asleep, please don't wake him."

* * * *

Tony climbed the stairs and entered the spacious anteroom fronting the master bedroom suite. A maid came out of the bedroom carrying a tray of untouched food and turned down the hallway. He found Mario propped up in his bed, looking out the window at the moon with an open Bible beside him.

"Mario?"

"Oh, Tony… Please come in."

Mario looked very weak and pale.

"How are you feeling?"

"Like shit."

Tony poured a glass of water from the nightstand and handed it to him.

"I'm sorry I couldn't come down to dinner. Tell me about Angela's boyfriend."

"Seems like a fine young man."

"We could use a doctor in the family," Mario said, smothering a deep, rumbling cough. "Any news about Dante's latest scheme?"

Tony had planned to tell him about what he'd learned about Dante's meeting with Victor Volkov, the mysterious Arab man, and his son's huge gambling markers—until he saw Mario's hand shake uncontrollably as he tried to sip from his water glass.

He had never seen Mario look so fragile, so vulnerable.

"Nothing yet," Tony said.

As he took the glass from the Don's hand and set it on the table, he flashed back to that fateful night when they met in the old neighborhood church almost fifty years ago…

* * * *

Confident and charismatic, Mario wore expensive clothes, drove a fancy car, and was building a vast gambling empire. He was young, strong and handsome. A man in full. On the flip side, Tony was a grungy, troubled seventeen-year-old kid—homeless, scared, and lost.

Tony did not fully realize it at the time, but Mario gave him his manhood by telling him where to find "White Willie" Duke. And six years later, after Tony returned from Vietnam and his travels around the country, Mario gave him his first real job within the organization.

The rest was history.

But now, the tables were turned. Tony was the strong one, and he had to look out for the Don's best interests.

Mario closed his eyes and drifted off. Tony grasped his hand. "Goodnight, Mario."

FRIDAY

46

Brooklyn
1:30 a.m.

All was quiet inside the warehouse. Guards were posted at each of the three doors to secure the facility. While the rest of the men slept, Mustafa Al-Anazi knelt on his prayer rug on the chilly office floor. He was wide-awake, anxious and excited about the next thirty-six hours. After years of careful planning and execution, Anazi was on the verge of realizing his goal of orchestrating an attack on America that could transcend the events of 9/11.

As he performed the Tahajjud prayer ritual in the flickering light of a single candle, he reflected on his path to a historic jihad...

* * * *

In 2012, Anazi hatched his diabolical plan in a crude field hospital outside a war-torn town in Northern Syria. While fighting with a small band of al-Qaeda insurgents against the military of Syrian President Bashar Assad, he was hit in the leg with shrapnel from a government artillery shell. The wound became infected and Anazi plunged into a semi-delirious state. During a feverish dream, he imagined a spectacular two-stage strike on America. The plan was simple in concept, but pulling it off would be a complicated proposition, requiring operatives and resources from around the globe.

Anazi's first order of business was to put together his own army: five two-man teams composed of seasoned fighters who were experienced with MANPADS (Man-Portable Air-Defense Systems)—shoulder-launched surface-to-air missiles designed to destroy low-flying planes and helicopters.

Like most modern-day jihadis, Anazi knew the value of propaganda and media manipulation. He believed Osama bin Laden made a public relations blunder by using so many Saudis for the 9/11 attacks. To underscore the widespread solidarity for jihad, Anazi wanted each of his teams to be from a different country in the Middle East. He found many of his men on the killing fields of Syria:

Amal and Hasan were cousins from Iraq who served in a tank division of Saddam Hussein's Republican Guard before they joined the deadly Sunni resistance during the post-war period of ethnic cleansing after the second U.S. invasion.

From Yemen, Abu Bakr and Kafil shot down a U.S. cargo plane near Al Asad Airbase in Iraq using a shoulder-launched missile, then crossed the border to terrorize and murder Christians in Syria.

Hailing from Saudi Arabia, Mahdi and Sakhr fought alongside bin Laden in the Battle of Tora Bora and later trained Somali terrorists on how to use RPG (rocket-propelled grenade) launchers against armored personnel carriers.

Two brothers from war-torn Libya, Ahmed, and Sayid, were experts in urban warfare and torture, and especially proud of their murderous roles in the attack against the U.S. consulate in Benghazi.

All were eager to kill as many Americans as possible.

One night, Anazi brought these eight men together around a fire in the desert, away from the other insurgents. Without getting into specifics, Anazi told them he had a master plan to strike America at its core and asked them to stick closely together until he contacted them. They all agreed.

A few months later, Anazi traveled to Afghanistan to learn the latest techniques for building IEDs and suicide vests from a master bomb-maker. He had the good fortune to meet his final two-man team—Taliban fighters who were ambushing U.S. troops on a daily basis.

Abbas, a lean and steely man in his mid-sixties known far and wide as "The Scorpion," would become the oldest and most experienced fighter of the five teams. In 1987, when the Mujahedeen were at war with the Russians, Abbas was trained by special U.S. operatives to use Stinger missiles. His reputation grew after he shot down two Russian assault helicopters and a fighter jet within a three-month period. After the Russians were driven out, Abbas returned to grow opium poppies in his village in Helmand Province. As the Taliban grew more powerful in the days leading up to 9/11, Abbas refused to join their ranks, preferring a quiet life. That all changed when an errant U.S. drone missile strike killed his wife and his brother's family. Abbas returned to being a full-time soldier, his heart hardened by the endless struggle against the foreign occupiers. Along with his grandson, Turan, a formidable young warrior and skilled assistant, he shot down a helicopter transporting an Afghani general. Once again, "The Scorpion" had fatally stung his enemies on the battlefield, and his reputation was revived.

Recruiting a great warrior like Abbas for his mission was a public relations masterstroke for Anazi. Not only would Abbas serve as a symbol of strength and inspiration to the younger warriors—his eventual martyrdom could be exploited to lure more jihadis to the cause.

In late 2013, Anazi was back in Iraq when ISIS (Islamic State in Iraq and Syria) took control of Ramadi and Fallujah, his old stomping grounds. In the face of their swift and bloody advance, the cowards in the new Iraqi Army shed their uniforms, dropped their weapons, and tried to disappear into the general population. During the ensuing chaos, Anazi discovered a Stinger launcher, battery packs, and a small cache of missiles at an unguarded government ammo dump. He quickly loaded the munitions into an SUV and sped off to a secret al-Qaeda desert camp in remote southeast Iraq.

Anazi summoned all five teams to join him to train with the pirated state-of-the-art weaponry. Once they were all assembled, they traveled to the nearby Tallil Airbase for a little target practice. The airbase had been much busier during the U.S. occupation, but there were still plenty of Iraqi air sorties to pick off. Using the Stinger launcher, Anazi's warriors took turns downing planes and helicopters before vanishing back into the desert.

To complete his plan, Anazi needed to transport his insurgent army to the U.S. and secure the necessary weapons. Luckily, he knew a sympathetic, high-ranking Iranian intelligence officer named Hashemi. Hashemi was a rabid Shiite, who generally despised Sunnis like Anazi, but they had met and bonded in Iraq while fighting U.S. forces in 2008. While Iranian-backed Shiite militias were fighting the Americans in Sadr City, Anazi attacked the Green Zone (the main U.S. military base) with a lethal barrage of mortar fire. It shifted the battle and saved the lives of many Shiite fighters as well as several Iranian secret operatives. Hashemi praised Anazi's actions and vowed to repay the debt at a future time.

When Anazi told Hashemi about his plan to attack America, the ruthless Iranian agreed to help smuggle his terrorist teams to Mexico and put him in touch with Victor Volkov—an international arms dealer who had brokered numerous deals for the Iranian Army, Third World warlords, and terrorist organizations.

Eventually, Anazi and his men boarded an Iranian cargo ship out of the port of Abadan. The long trip included covert ship changes in Tanzania and Venezuela before they finally arrived in the coastal city of Tampico in eastern Mexico. Later, Anazi's well-paid operatives moved the smuggled terrorists north to the porous U.S. border where they were stashed in safe houses until it was time for the Mexican cartel coyotes to ferry them into the belly of the beast.

Anazi crossed over first, months before the others, to rendezvous with two sleeper al-Qaeda agents living in the Southwest. The agents were radicalized American Muslims who had travelled to Syria and Iraq to fight with al-Qaeda before returning home. They were the killers who ambushed the cartel coyotes along the Texas and Arizona borders before placing the smuggled insurgents in the semi-truck for their cross-country journey to New York.

In early September, Anazi spoke with Volkov, who claimed to have a reliable source for Stinger launchers and missiles in the New York area. Within days, the first terrorist two-man team crossed the border.

Thanks to the financial help from his extremist benefactors abroad, the ever-growing international web of hardcore terrorists, the logistical support of his close friend Kamel Al-Masud, and Volkov's black-market connections to secure the sophisticated weapons required to create mass murder and destruction, Anazi was brimming with confidence about the pending attack.

47

Mustafa Al-Anazi was hardly a selfless, highly principled Muslim. Like many other vicious extremists who preached Islamism to rationalize their own narcissistic agendas, he was far more interested in promoting himself and his own jihadi exploits.

He aspired to be as famous and feared as Abu Musab al-Zarqawi, the murderous thug who ran al-Qaeda in Iraq and was the godfather of ISIS. So far, Anazi had proven himself to be far more slippery than the hapless al-Zarqawi, who was killed by a pair of laser-guided 500-pound bombs in 2006, courtesy of the U.S. military.

While Anazi routinely spouted the standard platitudes about jihadi camaraderie and the good fight against all infidels, he regarded himself as far superior to his loyal band of brothers. Anazi knew his terrorist teams were on a suicide mission, but he planned to escape to fight another day. However, the one thing they all had in common was a fascination with the anticipated rewards and carnal delights of Martyrdom.

After he finished his prayers, he blew out the candle, laid down on his bedroll, and finally fell asleep—dreaming of Paradise after his own celebrated death...

Surrounded by rivers of milk and honey, Anazi strolled through lush gardens that stretched to the horizon and beyond. Along the way, he sampled succulent fruits, the most delicious he had ever tasted. Eventually, he came to a great palace of gleaming pearls filled with a multitude of ruby-encrusted courtyards and green emerald mansions. Inside each dwelling, there were seventy-two beds of every color where voluptuous, black-eyed virgins waited for deserving martyrs.

Anticipating an eternity of endless pleasure, Anazi became sexually aroused as he entered one of the luxurious abodes. Confidently, he approached one of the willing women. Bathed in a golden light, a young brunette in a silk robe sat with her back to him.

She whispered, "Come hither, friend of Allah."

His heart raced wildly with erotic expectations, but as she turned to face him, Anazi recoiled in horror. Instead of the lovely, full-breasted virgin of his dreams, she was a hideous leper—rotten and foul. As she reached out to embrace him, the floor became a raging river of blood, and the undertow swept him off his feet, dragging him deeper and deeper into the horrifying Netherworld.

Anazi awoke with a terrible shudder. Despite the freezing environs of the warehouse, he was drenched in sweat, and nauseous. He rolled onto his side and dry-heaved violently. For the first time in his long career as a serial terrorist, Anazi's faith was shaken to the core.

For the next several hours, he lay in the darkness, wondering if his nightmare was an omen and he was somehow unworthy of the promise of Paradise. But like the true sociopath he was, by the early light of day he had convinced himself his mission of mayhem and murder was holy and justified. He overcame his brief crisis of confidence by focusing his anger and hatred onto the American infidels.

Yet, despite his rationalizations, Anazi knew dreams were now his enemy, too.

48

Dressed in fatigues and toting an M16, Tommy Mancini patrolled the sprawling National Guard Armory. It was an enormous edifice filled with all sorts of military equipment and thousands of weapons, boxes of ammunition, grenades, land mines, and other battle supplies.

Tommy turned up the sound on his headphones to hear the latest Snoop Dog release as he walked down corridor after corridor overflowing with deadly military munitions.

It was time to get to work.

Tommy circled back to the security command center at the front of the Armory. Inside, there was a wall of video cameras and recorders monitoring the entire facility. As planned, the two soldiers responsible for overseeing the surveillance systems were sound asleep at their posts. Silently, Tommy pushed the pause buttons on the cameras aimed at the storage area near the loading dock and the parking lot.

Minutes later, Tommy pulled a tarp off five crates labeled as FIM-92C Stinger Missile Launchers and ten tubes containing the actual missiles. He loaded the weapons into his van, parked right outside the back door. Noticing that there was still plenty of room, Tommy impulsively helped himself to two RPG launchers and a box of grenades. Lastly, he carefully covered his lethal stash with the tarp, placed an envelope filled $10,000 on the floor and locked his van.

Tommy returned to the Command Post, where his fellow soldiers were still fast asleep and restarted the cameras.

Mission accomplished, he continued his patrol around the Armory, stopping in a hidden spot away from the video monitors to smoke some weed.

8:15 a.m.

Tommy's van rolled to a stop at the main security gate of the Armory. Two fellow National Guardsmen, Corporal Randy Jones and Sergeant Otis Hayes, exited the guardhouse and approached the van.

"Well, if it ain't Seal Team Six," Tommy said with a big grin.

Jones was a nervous, gangly kid in baggy camo fatigues with an M16 slung over his shoulder. "Hey, Tommy, how's it hangin'?"

"Long and low. Your sister ought to know."

Jones laughed, but Sgt. Hayes's face never changed from deadpan stillness.

A few days earlier, when the work shifts were posted for the holiday week, Jones told Tommy that Hayes was a hard ass who went strictly by the book. Tommy also learned Hayes was a gym rat with an enormous appetite.

"This is Tommy Mancini," Jones said, looking over at Hayes. "We served together outside of Kandahar."

Hayes stared at Tommy as Jones walked around the front of the van to the open passenger's window.

Jones continued. "His family owns that famous restaurant in East Harlem I told you about. It's called Mancini's."

"Nice to meet ya, Sarge," Tommy said, delivering a half-assed salute.

Hayes nodded and glanced around the front seat area.

Jones asked, "Is the back open, Tommy? Got to check it."

Making steady eye contact with the serious Sergeant, Tommy replied. "Sure. Knock yourself out."

Jones walked around to the rear of the van.

"You like Italian food, Sarge?" Tommy asked.

"Love it."

"You married?"

"No, but I got a girlfriend."

Jones opened the van's rear doors. The envelope filled with cash lay on the floor. He shined his flashlight over the tarp that covered the stolen arms.

Tommy kept Hayes engaged. "Why don't you take your girlfriend there for dinner this weekend? My dad loves to entertain the troops. He'll comp the whole thing. The food is fantastic, and the wine will flow!"

Jones stashed the envelope into his coat pocket. "All clear back here, Sarge. Want to take a look?"

Tommy tried to play it cool, but he was anxious and paranoid. The marijuana he smoked earlier to steady his nerves had worn off and he was getting withdrawal symptoms from the lack of heroin in his system. His palms were clammy, and his stomach churned. Still, as Hayes continued to look him squarely in the eyes, Tommy smiled and did not blink.

After what seemed like an eternity, Hayes finally said, "Nah, just close it up."

Jones slammed the doors and walked back to the driver's door, where he stood behind Hayes. He winked at Tommy.

Tommy smiled. "Great. I'll let my father know you and your girlfriend are coming. I promise. He'll treat you like a king!"

Hayes and Tommy bumped fists.

Jones slapped Hayes on the back and said, "Sounds like you're finally going to get laid, Sarge!"

Hayes gave the wisecracking corporal an annoyed look as Tommy's van rolled through the gate.

49

Sands Point
6:20 a.m.

The door to Mario Conti's bedroom suite burst open.

Disheveled and terrified, Carla ran to the top of the staircase and yelled, "Mario is having a heart attack! Call an ambulance!"

50

Tommy arrived at the address Gino had given him. It was an industrial area near Bowery Bay, one of several vast staging areas for Conti Construction throughout the greater New York area.

Beyond the tall chain-link fence, Tommy saw row after row of tractors, dump trucks, and concrete mixers. No one seemed to be around.

He pulled up to the entrance and flashed his lights twice beneath a security camera. A moment later, the gate slid open and he entered.

Tommy drove past mountains of metal scaffolding, concrete forms, and porta-potties until he came to a large mobile office trailer in the center of the yard. Only a black Escalade was parked nearby.

He got out of the van and lit a cigarette. Gino, Al, and Frank emerged from the trailer, rubbing their hands together in the early morning cold.

"How'd it go?" Gino asked as he sipped steaming black coffee from a Styrofoam cup.

"Piece of cake. Just like I said," answered Tommy.

Al and Frank moved to the back of the van and opened the doors. Frank tore off the tarp and handed Al one of the RPG launchers.

"What the hell is this?" Al asked, holding it up so Gino could see.

"It's a rocket-propelled grenade launcher," Frank said.

"What the fuck?!" yelled Gino. He dropped his coffee and turned to Tommy in a sudden rage. "You were supposed to steal Stingers, not RPGs!"

Tommy spread his arms. "Relax, Gino, relax! All five Stingers are there. I just grabbed those two RPG launchers and a box of grenades, hoping you'd slip me an extra ten grand. After all, I had to take care of my friend at the front gate of the Armory out of my end."

Gino lightened up. "Smart thinking, kid. I'll ask Dante about it, but I'm sure he'll pony up some extra cash."

He looked back over to the van just as Frank opened a Stinger crate and removed a launcher. Frank carefully checked it out and said, "This is Grade-A shit. Perfect condition. The battery packs are fully charged too."

"Only the best for my bros!" Tommy said, taking a long, well-deserved drag on his cigarette.

"Looks like we have a winner!" Gino said as he playfully wrapped his arm around Tommy's neck. "Come on! Let's go inside and get you paid. I'm freezing out here."

Gino and Tommy entered the warm trailer, filled with construction charts and maps on the walls, tables covered with blueprints, desktop computers, and filing cabinets. Gino sat down behind a desk facing the front door, a toothpick bobbing in his mouth. Tommy sat down across from him.

"You did good, Tommy," Gino said. He removed a brown paper bag from a drawer and dropped it on the desk. "There's the balance. Twenty-five grand. Want to count it?"

"I trust you, Gino. And you will talk to Dante about the extra ten thousand for the RPGs, right?"

"You bet. I'm sure we can sell that shit to someone and make a tidy profit." With a menacing chuckle, Gino added, "Or maybe we'll just save them for a rainy day."

Tommy asked, "What about the ounce of H?"

Gino placed a plastic baggie of heroin on the desk. "Are you sure you really want it?"

"I really don't need it. It's just that... uh, it helps me sleep," Tommy stammered. "I got really bad nightmares from the war."

Al and Frank silently slipped into the trailer directly behind Tommy.

Gino reached back into the drawer and placed a loaded syringe of heroin on the desk. "I took the liberty of preparing this for you. You know, to celebrate."

As Tommy stared down at the syringe, the toothpick slipped in and out of Gino's mouth like the tongue of a serpent.

"I appreciate it, Gino, but... I really should be going."

Tommy stood up and reached for the cash and dope, but Gino pinned his hands down on the desktop. Simultaneously, Al and Frank rushed forward and slammed him back down in his chair.

Al yanked up Tommy's sleeve to reveal a patchwork of needle tracks.

Gino shook his head in disgust and gave Tommy a long, cold stare. Slowly, he held up the syringe and tapped it a few times with his finger, preparing for an injection. "Sorry, Tommy, but you're a junkie, and that's a big liability for us. I'm sure you understand our concern."

Tommy flailed around, but Al and Frank held him tightly in place.

"You can trust me, Gino! I'll never say a word about the heist. I swear it!" Tommy pleaded, tears streaming down his contorted face.

"You're right. You'll *never* say a word again."

Gino plunged the syringe into Tommy's arm and drained it. "See ya on the other side, kid."

The shot sent a massive jolt through Tommy's body. He gagged violently, foaming at the mouth as his eyes rolled back into his head. Soon, he went limp, and his breathing stopped.

Gino wiped off the empty syringe with a tissue and placed it in Tommy's hand to collect his fingerprints. Then he dropped the syringe into a baggie and handed it to Al.

"You know where to dump him and the van," Gino said to his cohorts. "Make sure it looks like he overdosed."

As Frank and Al dragged Tommy's lifeless body towards the door, Gino gave a short salute. "Hey, Tommy. Thanks for your service to our country."

Once again, they all cracked up.

51

In the wake of Mario's heart attack at the Conti estate, the paramedics stabilized and transported him to the Manhattan Medical Center. Following the ambulance, Tony drove Carla and Angela into the City.

The trauma had taken its toll on everyone. Sitting in the waiting room outside the surgery unit, the two most important women in Mario's world were distraught, their faces drawn and swollen from crying and exhaustion. As Carla and Angela consoled each other and waited for the doctors to give them an update, Tony brought coffee and offered reassuring words.

Tony also took a few calls, including one from Jeremy. One of his contacts within the intelligence community had confirmed that Victor Volkov was an international arms dealer who worked with many different dictatorships and terrorist groups around the world.

Eventually, Dante burst in, still wearing the same clothes from the night before and nursing a wicked hangover. "How's he doing?"

"We're still waiting for the doctor," Carla said.

For the next few minutes, Dante paced around the waiting area with an unlit cigarette dangling from his mouth. Finally, he walked over to the empty nurse's station and slapped his hand down hard on the counter, which jolted everyone in the room.

In a loud, obnoxious voice, he yelled, "Excuse me! Anyone home?"

As if on cue, the double doors to the surgery suite opened and Dr. Shelton Fritz, a distinguished white-haired surgeon in blue scrubs, entered the waiting area.

"Mrs. Conti?"

The family quickly gathered around. "I'm Dr. Fritz."

"How's Mario doing?" Carla asked as Angela anxiously clutched her arm.

"He's better. His heart attack was a result of severe symptomatic aortic stenosis, which is a narrowing of the aortic valve opening. We inserted a Transcatheter Aortic Valve Replacement."

"That sounds serious," Tony said.

"It is. It's also a new, non-invasive technique that allows us to implant a device into a heart valve without open-heart surgery. It only works with certain patients, but we got lucky with Mr. Conti."

Everyone sighed with relief.

"So—he's going to be okay?" asked Angela.

"He's stable for now, but still very weak. We'll know more in a day or two after some additional tests.".

The doors opened again, and Hal came out.

"I understand you know Dr. Dia," said Dr. Fritz. "He assisted me today in surgery. He's one of our finest cardiac residents, and he'll be Mr. Conti's attending physician. I'm sure he can answer any of your questions."

"Super," Dante said, barely controlling his contempt for Hal.

Fritz offered a curt smile and exited.

Carla collapsed into a chair, and Tony sat down beside her. Angela gave Hal a hug.

Dante walked over to Hal. "That doctor just said my father is going to survive. Is that really true or just the sugar-coated version?"

Hal squared his shoulders and faced Dante. "I have studied medicine for the last eight years. I know there is more to a man than just tissue, bone and blood. I can tell you that your father is a real fighter."

"Tell us something we don't know."

"For now, the new valve is functioning well. The next twenty-four to forty-eight hours are crucial. He's not out of the woods yet."

Angela inquired. "And after that?"

"He is going to need all his strength to make a full recovery."

With a condescending leer, Dante said, "Well, I think we should get a *second* opinion."

Tired of her brother's endless attacks on Hal, Angela exclaimed, "Oh, shut up, Dante!"

Carla brushed off the outburst and turned to Hal. "Can I see Mario?"

"Yes, but just for a few minutes and then we'll move him to Intensive Care."

Dante checked his watch. "I've got an important meeting. I'll be back later." He turned and walked down the hallway.

Tony excused himself and followed. He caught up with Dante just as he was passing a small hospital chapel.

"We need to talk, Dante."

"What is it now?"

They walked into the empty chapel.

"I'm very sorry about your father."

"He'll make it just to spite me," Dante replied as he shot his cuffs and adjusted his shirt collar.

"He loves you, Dante. That's why he doesn't want you involved in that arms deal. It's very dangerous."

"You don't know shit."

"I know that Victor Volkov is an international arms dealer."

Dante wiped some lint off his shoulder. "You're *not* involved! Capiche?"

"I don't want to be, but tell me one thing: Who do you think those weapons are going to?"

Dante gave him a dismissive look.

Tony said, "I think they could be going to Islamic extremists."

"Bullshit! Volkov assured me his client is some Mexican cartel."

"And you believe him?"

Annoyed by Tony's persistence, Dante asked, "Are we done?"

"No. I tailed Volkov yesterday morning, and he met with a very suspicious guy, who's hiding out in a Muslim neighborhood in Brooklyn."

"Volkov has lots of clients. Anyway, it's too late. As of this morning, that deal is half done. It'll all be wrapped up later today."

Dante started to leave, but Tony grabbed his arm. "Please, Dante! I think you're making a huge mistake."

"Frankly, I don't give a rat's ass what *you* think." He pulled away and pointed his finger menacingly at Tony. "I'm warning you for the last time. Back off!"

"Yeah, that's your problem, Dante. You never want to take responsibility for your actions."

"Fuck you," he replied, turning towards the door.

"And now you're running away again, just like after the hit and run."

Dante spun around. "That was fifteen years ago, but you'll never let me forget it."

"The kid you ran over can never forget either. He's paralyzed for the rest of his life. Remember?"

"I was going to take care of it until you butted in."

"How? His family needed money for his long-term care. Big money."

"Somehow I would have gotten it."

"When? After you finished that month-long coke binge down in Rio? As usual, you were acting like a selfish little prick."

Seething with anger, Dante said, "You didn't have to tell my father about it. You violated our trust."

"Trust is earned—not inherited."

Trying to calm down, Dante measured his words. "Out of respect for your long-term loyalty to our family, I'm going to let this slide. Just stay out of my business!"

Tony was not going to back down. "Your dangerous business activities threaten the family."

"Yeah, *my* family! Not yours!"

Tony taunted him. "And what about all your loans and gambling debts?"

Scoffing at Tony's allegations, Dante said, "After this deal is done, I'll be rolling in cash. Everything will all be paid off in the next few days."

"And what if you're wrong, Dante? What if there are complications?"

"Hey, just stick to what you do best—running shitty little errands and driving my mom and kid sister around."

As Dante walked out the door, he added, "Face it, Tony. Your time has passed."

Viscerally upset by the encounter, Tony sat down on one of the pews in the small chapel. As usual, Dante was thinking only of himself. Although Tony was extremely worried about the arms deal, there was nothing he could do.

Right now, his thoughts were with Mario.

52

As he sat alone in the hospital chapel, Tony recalled when he was in the hospital after the assassination attempt. Seventy-two hours after the shooting, Tony lay in the intensive care unit—barely clinging to life.

Hooked up to a cluster of IVs and pulsating machines, he stared up at the ceiling. Slowly, the acoustical ceiling panels began to blend together, morphing into a swirling white abyss that looked like the eye of a hurricane. It was mesmerizing, and Tony felt drawn to it. Soon, he was floating above his bed, looking down at his broken body, swathed in bandages and plaster, and connected to a complicated traction system. His pain was gone, and he felt at peace. In this brief moment of lucidity, Tony repented his many past sins and silently vowed to become a better person.

Then, he turned toward the bright light in the eye of the storm and surrendered to its warm embrace. As he drifted away, he heard the faint emergency beeping of a machine as his heart flat-lined. Looking back down with a calm indifference, he saw a frantic team of hospital personnel burst into the room with a defibrillator and gather around his body. There was a flash of metallic paddles and, suddenly, Tony felt the worst pain in his life…

Later that day, while recovering from his latest dance with death, Tony had an epiphany—he wanted out of the mob life and a chance for a fresh start. By saving the Don's life, Tony figured Mario would grant him any wish, but he was mistaken. Mario had always respected Tony's sharp mind, but now there was an extra special bond between the two men. Mario did not want to lose Tony's loyalty and friendship under any circumstance.

The Don tried to visit Tony twice in the hospital immediately after the shooting. The first time, Tony was still in a coma. On a subsequent visit, Tony was undergoing emergency surgery for arterial leakage in his ravaged right leg.

Finally, one late night, Mario and two other powerful men came to see Tony in his private room. Before the door was closed, Tony saw the silhouettes of several bodyguards standing in the hallway. He immediately knew this was a visit of some importance.

The flashing red and green lights on the monitors surrounding his bed cast an eerie glow across the room. In the faint light, Tony could see his distinguished visitors. He recognized Carmine Bertoli and Vincent Leone, the dons of other prominent New York families.

Mario sat down in the chair beside the bed while Bertoli and Leone stood on the other side, looking like two morticians glaring down at their next customer.

Gesturing to the two men, Mario asked, "You know my friends, don't you?"

"Of course," Tony nodded wearily. Of all the families on the East Coast, Mario trusted these men the most. They had all known each other since the early years, and they now shared similar business interests. Like the Conti clan, the Bertoli and Leone families were mainly involved in gambling, money laundering, and major financial scams. They shunned the more despicable Mob enterprises like drugs, prostitution, and the protection rackets.

Mario clutched Tony's right hand and whispered, "I'm sorry I haven't seen you before now, Tony. I tried, but you were always indisposed."

"Yes. I heard you came by. Thank you."

Mario let out a small laugh and spoke to his colleagues. "Can you believe this guy? He saves my life, and now he's thanking me for coming to visit him in the hospital. Benedica il suo cuore!"

The other men smiled tersely but did not speak.

Mario asked, "Are you doing okay, Tony? Need anything? Anything at all?"

Floating serenely in a pool of morphine, Tony shook his head.

Mario surveyed the massive traction system that held Tony's right leg rigidly in place. The cast stretched the entire length of his limb, which was tenuously held together by titanium rods, countless screws, and bolts. Plastic tubing poked out of the cast in two places and funneled down into hanging drainage bags. Only part of his right foot was visible, showing ominous discoloration and emitting a foul smell.

Mario swallowed hard. "Listen. When you get out of here, Tony, we'll talk at length about what happened. In the meantime, we've been trying to find out who was responsible for the hit. So far, it's a dead end."

Tony did not respond. In his more lucid moments, he wondered who would attempt such a bold assassination in broad daylight, but the chronic pain, drugs, and other hospital horrors overwhelmed his ability to concentrate for any period of time. Instead of revenge fantasies, Tony had to focus on just surviving the next few weeks, the additional surgeries, and then the long road of rehabilitation. Besides, he wanted to change his life and did not want the emotional weight of retribution.

And then came the moment of truth.

Mario reached into his pocket and removed a card with the image of St. Francis. Tony immediately knew what Mario intended to do: formally induct him into the Mafia and make him a "made man."

"You've been a trusted member of my family for years. And you certainly made your bones the other day. After what you did to save my life, I feel it's appropriate, and frankly long overdue, to open the books and bring you in."

If such an overture had been offered before the shooting, Tony would have welcomed the honor, but now everything was different. The whole ritual of being "made," the commitment to *omerta* and the rest of it, now seemed like an empty charade to him. He also knew once you were made, you never got out of the business—alive.

As Mario calmly waited for him to reply, Tony looked up at the other dons who peered down at him.

Ghouls in a wax museum.

He did not want to embarrass Mario in front of his friends by refusing his offer to join the brotherhood.

Slowly, he turned back to face Mario.

"I killed those men because they wanted to kill you. I acted out of a deep and abiding friendship. And I'd do the same thing again to protect you, but —"

At that moment, as if throttled by the hand of God, a spasm jolted through Tony's body, and he bucked backwards in his bed. The startled men watched as Tony suffered an intense, violent seizure.

The machines all started to beep and buzz.

Mario leapt to his feet and yelled, "Get a doctor!"

* * * *

As the tremors subsided, Tony remained unconscious until long after his visitors had left. When he awoke, alone in his hospital room, he saw the St. Francis card lying on the bedside table and remembered everything that had transpired.

In retrospect, that last seizure could not have happened at a better time. Tony had avoided what would have been a clumsy and humiliating rejection of Mario's offer.

* * * *

… Now, sitting alone in the chapel at the Manhattan Medical Center twenty years later, Tony bowed his head and whispered a silent prayer for Mario and the entire Conti family.

He should have said one for himself because this day would be the longest and most challenging of his life.

53

Upon returning to the hospital waiting area, Tony found Angela sitting alone.

"Is Carla still with your father?"

"Yes... Do you think Papa will be okay?"

Tony sat down and wrapped his arm around her. "He's getting the best medical care, plus Hal is here to watch over him. He'll be fine."

Carla returned and sat down.

"How's he doing, Mom?"

"He looks much better. He was so ghostly pale after the heart attack, but now his color has come back."

"That's great news, Carla," Tony said.

"Yes," she said with a heavy sigh. "Mario wants to see you."

"Are you sure he's not too tired?"

"The anesthesia is still wearing off, so he's a little groggy. You should go see him now before they take him to Intensive Care."

Tony nodded.

"Angela and I have decided to spend the day here. We'll call you when we want to go home."

Tony hugged both of them and left.

* * * *

Entering the surgical recovery area brought back unpleasant memories for Tony. Over the last two decades, he had endured a few minor outpatient surgical procedures, but he would forever loathe the cold, antiseptic atmosphere of hospitals.

Tony was pleased to see Hal filling out paperwork next to the nurse's station.

"Hey, Hal."

"Hello, Tony. I can only give you a few minutes to speak with Mr. Conti." He nodded at the curtain across the hall.

"Thanks for everything—and welcome to the family."

Hal smiled and raised his hands in mock surrender.

"Trust me, things will improve with time. And I can tell Carla really likes you."

"That's good to know," said Hal. "See you later. I've got to make my rounds."

Tony slipped inside the curtain to find Mario resting with his eyes closed. A heart monitor, IV drips, and other high-tech medical machinery were clustered around his bed. His breathing was slow and steady.

"Mario," Tony said in a hushed voice.

His eyes fluttered open. "I'm still here, my friend."

"Thank God. You had us going there for a while."

Mario raised his hand, and Tony took it. It was warm and heavy in his grasp.

"How are you feeling now?"

"Better, but... I'm just so damn tired."

"You should sleep. I'll come back later."

"No... I need to ask you a favor."

"Anything," Tony said, softly squeezing his hand.

"Promise that if something happens to me, you'll look after my family."

"That's not going to be necessary."

"Please... promise me."

Tony shrugged. "Of course, but..."

"And I want you to come back to Conti Construction. I want you to run it, not Dante."

"We can discuss that later when you get home."

"No. I've made up my mind," Mario whispered. "It was a mistake to acquiesce to Dante's demands and threats."

Seeing that Mario was parched, Tony held up a glass of water, and Mario drank feebly through a straw.

Tony expected him to ask for an update about Dante's dangerous arms deal, but instead Mario inquired, "Tell me, Tony, have you paid Nicky Bruno a visit yet?"

"Not yet."

"I've given that matter more thought too," Mario said clearing his throat. "He needs to be confronted about his treachery against us."

"It can wait."

"No. It's unfinished business," Mario said wearily. "I want you to go see him today. I have a strange feeling about it."

"Why?"

"I want him to know that I'm still alive, and I haven't forgotten. He needs to be reminded of what he did, especially to you."

"But you said you were too old for revenge."

Mario became very solemn. "Last night, I had a horrible nightmare. The hit on me had a much different outcome. You were killed in the opening volley. Then the gunmen hovered over me and emptied their guns. I was blown apart—piece by piece."

"It was just a dream."

"It gave me a fuckin' heart attack!" an agitated Mario shouted.

His heart monitor began to beep loudly.

Tony placed his hand on Mario's shoulder. "Easy now. Just relax."

Suddenly, the curtain was pulled back and a nurse burst in. "What's going on?"

"He's okay," Tony said, watching Mario's pulse rate slowly return to normal.

The nurse moved in to check his vitals.

A moment later, two orderlies appeared. "We're here to transport Mr. Conti to Intensive Care. Is he ready?"

"Yes," the nurse replied and turned to Tony. "I'm sorry, but you have to leave."

"I'll see you later, Mario."

"Go see that asshole now… Let's resolve it."

54

After dealing with Mario's harrowing heart attack and the anxious hours at the hospital, Tony needed to freshen up. He went to the City's premiere private athletic club to shave, shower and change his clothes.

For two decades, he had been a member in good standing. Originally, he joined the club to wine and dine the clients of Conti Construction, but now it was his favorite Midtown hangout. Tony enjoyed swimming in the fitness center, taking long saunas, reading and trading securities in a quiet corner of the library.

He kept a few pressed suits, shirts, and other fashion accessories in his locker for emergencies. Tony wanted to look sharp for his surprise rendezvous with the man who tried to kill Don Mario.

* * * *

On the east side of Central Park off 5th Avenue and East 74th Street, the Conservatory Water was originally constructed as a reflecting pool; however, when the plan for the grand conservatory was abandoned, it became a popular model sailboat pond. Inspired by similar pools in Parisian parks, the Conservatory Water was a beautiful spot where kids and adults had played with their toy sloops for more than 135 years.

Mario said Nicky Bruno would probably be there and Tony was ready to confront him.

Tony approached the Park on the north side of the Conservatory Water. He passed a small group of avid bird watchers, clutching binoculars and staring up at a high-rise condo at the nest of "Pale Male"—the most famous red tail hawk in the world.

Circling west around the serene pool, Tony scanned the spectacular landscape for a sign of the aging mobster. Locals walked their dogs. Tourists marveled at the tall, regal condos poking up behind the barren trees along Fifth Avenue. And wealthy young mothers pushed their kids in designer strollers in the low winter sun.

Tony noted the temperature was quite pleasant for late November. The coldest winter months were right around the corner and soon the pond's water level would be lowered to create a free public ice skating rink.

Tony paused near the famous Hans Christian Andersen statue, removed the smartphone from the pocket of his overcoat, and dialed. As two sailboats skimmed gracefully across the glassy pond, "The Kid" updated Tony on the status of his research into Bruno's finances. Jeremy's spyware was working like a charm, and he confirmed everything was in place to destroy Bruno's credit and steal the bulk of his fortune.

Jeremy added, "If you pull the trigger, we just have to decide who gets all that loot."

"Stand by, bro," Tony said, ending the call.

As he strolled south along the edge of the pool, Tony spotted a squat, older man passing by the Boat

House, followed by a young Neanderthal carrying a four-foot-long model motorboat. Tony figured it had to be Nicky "The Runt" Bruno.

As the old man walked up to the pond and sat on a park bench, his monstrous manservant bent down to place the boat in the water.

"Be fuckin' careful, Jimmy!" Nicky warned as he removed a remote control unit from his overcoat pocket.

"I know, I know," groaned Jimmy, who struck Tony as a bumbling bodyguard who spent all his time being a go-fer for his demanding, geriatric boss. His short, sloped forehead, uni-brow, and 350-pound girth made Jimmy look intimidating but incredibly dim-witted.

"I'm gonna smoke a cigar," Jimmy said. "Okay, boss?"

"Fine! Just keep that stinking stogie away from me," Nicky snapped as he steered his boat out into the pond.

Jimmy walked over to another bench about twenty yards away.

Tony approached Nicky. "Mind if I sit here?"

Nicky, a pugnacious, troll-like man scrutinized the elegantly dressed stranger and shrugged. "It's a free country."

Tony sat and watched Nicky steer his boat around the pond. His model yacht was much larger and more powerful than the small sailboats bobbing in the water. With a few quick flips of Nicky's remote throttle, the sailboats were partially flooded in the motorboat's huge wake.

"That's a powerful boat," Tony said.

"Yeah, it's an exact replica of a Riva 122 Mythos—one of the most beautiful yachts ever built. My brother, rest his soul, had it custom made for me a few years ago."

On the other side of the pond, the owners of the half-submerged sailboats pointed angrily over at Nicky and yelled a few choice obscenities.

Nicky just shrugged them off.

"I didn't think powerboats were allowed here," Tony said.

"They're not. From April to October, this place is packed with all those pussies and kids with their stupid sailboats. But now it's winter and the big dogs get to eat."

Nicky spun the menacing motorboat around in a huge arc on the water, making sure to thrash the swamped sailboats once again. One forlorn sailboat skipper, trying to rescue his battered boat, gave Nicky the finger. And Nicky reciprocated.

For a few silent moments, Nicky and Tony just sat there, watching the sleek model yacht rip around the pond with astonishing speed and agility.

A homeless woman pushed an overflowing shopping cart up beside a nearby garbage can. Pawing through the trash, she found a pizza box buried halfway down. As she mumbled incoherently to herself, she removed a partial piece of pizza and took a hungry bite.

Nicky sneered, "Look at that! Eating from a garbage can. Disgusting!"

"Maybe she's just down on her luck, or mentally ill."

"If you ask me, they should all be rounded up and executed," Nicky said, turning back to his boat. Tony cringed at the man's insensitivity.

The beautifully-carved, antique ivory head of Tony's cane caught Nicky's eye.

"That's an amazing walking stick. Looks like it should be in a museum or something."

"It's about 150 years old," Tony said, spinning it around so Nicky could study it more closely. "It used to belong to a Prussian diplomat."

"May I see it?"

Tony handed his cane to him. "Of course."

Nicky gave the boat's remote control to Tony. "Take it for a spin. Just keep it out in the middle and away from the sides of the pond."

Tony started to maneuver the miniature yacht around as Nicky carefully examined the cane's craftsmanship. "It's exquisite."

"And deadly," replied Tony as he tried to master the nuances of the remote control.

Nicky was taken aback. "Really? How so?"

Tony pointed to a small, semi-hidden button under the handle. "Press that."

Nicky pressed it and pulled up the handle to reveal a two-foot long sword. With an evil smirk, he said, "Nice. This could come in handy!"

Tony smiled.

Jimmy saw the long blade and leapt to his feet, but Nicky waved him off. "It's okay."

Still concerned, Jimmy sat back down but kept his eyes glued on Tony.

Nicky slipped the sword back into the cane. "Tell me. Where did you get it?"

"It was a gift from a dear old friend," Tony said, steering the yacht around the far side of the pond. "I think you know him."

Nicky eyed him suspiciously. "Really?"

Tony faced him. "Mario Conti."

Nicky turned white.

"And I'm Tony Tucci."

Nicky continued to stare at him, trying to hide his utter surprise. Finally, he said, "What do you want?"

"I want the last twenty years back, Nicky. I want to be whole again."

"Sorry. I don't know what you're talking about."

Tony gave Nicky a stony look. "Drop the pretense or this thing is going to escalate fast."

Nicky took a deep breath, trying to control his anger. "That move against Conti all those years ago was my brother Benny's idea, not mine."

"So now you're throwing your dead brother under the bus? Even after he gave you that nice little motorboat?"

"What happened to you was an unintended mistake."

"But it was *your* mistake, Nicky. And I've been living with it ever since."

"Who are you to lecture me?" said Nicky, his lip curling up like a window shade. "I oughta call Jimmy over here to break your legs."

"Go ahead, but thanks to you, I only have one good one left."

"What is this shit? Are you here to kill me with your fancy hidden little sword?"

Tony didn't reply. Instead, he looked back over to the homeless woman who was rummaging deeper into the garbage can.

"To tell you the truth, when I came here this morning I wasn't sure how this was going to end, but now I do."

Tony let that statement hang there as he spun the boat back across the pond.

"Are you familiar with St. Anthony's over on 78th Street?"

Annoyed, Nicky said, "Yeah, what about it?"

Tony watched the bag lady extract a half-full Gatorade bottle from the trash. She unscrewed the top to smell it.

"To help the growing homeless population in the City, the diocese is building a new kitchen, expanded sleeping quarters, and a job training center. It's very impressive."

"Who gives a shit."

Tony flashed a big smile. "You do. Because you're going to make a million-dollar donation to the project."

Nicky looked at the pathetic woman drinking the leftover Gatorade and laughed out loud. "The hell I am!"

Tony turned the boat back towards them. "You're filthy rich. You live in a multimillion dollar condo, which you own free and clear. And you've got millions stashed away. You can easily afford it."

"How the hell do you know that?" Nicky fumed.

Tony did not reply, but he did push the speed control to the max. The toy yacht shot across the pond straight at them.

"Hey! What the hell?!" Nicky yelled. "Quick! Give me the goddamn remote!"

Slowly, Tony handed the remote control back to Nicky, who tried in vain to turn the speeding boat, but it was too late. It had too much momentum and crashed violently into the pond's cement side with a loud crack.

"Oops," Tony said.

Badly damaged with a ruptured front hull, the boat listed to its side, taking on water. Nicky jumped to his feet, looking down at his broken boat. "Motherfucker!"

The two men with the sailboats on the other side of the pond burst out laughing.

Jimmy came running over, huffing and puffing. "Holy shit! What happened?"

Casually, Tony picked up his cane and stood. Addressing Nicky, he said, "You have until Monday at 5:00 p.m. sharp to make that donation to St. Anthony's. An old friend of mine, Father Cerruti, is heading up the donation drive. I'll be checking with him."

"And if I don't do as you say?"

Their eyes met.

"What's your life worth, Nicky?"

Flexing his ham-sized fists at his side, Jimmy asked, "Is this guy bothering you, boss?"

Nicky didn't hear him.

Tony added. "Just get the cash or a check to Father Cerruti and all will be forgiven. You have my word."

They watched Tony limp away, never looking back.

High above them, "Pale Male" soared across the sky with a dead pigeon in its claws.

55

Jake Crowley snapped awake from a deep sleep. The room was dark and foreign to him. For a moment, he didn't know where he was. Laying on one of the beds amid a mess of pillows and sheets, he realized he was still at the FBI stakeout at the Monroe Hotel.

He walked to the bedroom door and opened it. A blaze of mid-morning light enveloped him as he stepped into the main room where Agents Watkins and Bashir operated the surveillance equipment.

"How long have I been asleep?"

"About five hours," Bashir said.

Watkins said, "Hey, thanks for pulling the all-nighter, Crowley. We appreciate your help."

Crowley rubbed his eyes. "I just remembered something. When I was in the FBI conference room, I saw all those photos of the organized crime families on the wall. I think I may have seen one of those guys here yesterday. Do you have those photos in your computer system?"

"Sure, I can access them. What's the family name?" asked Watkins.

"I think it was Conti."

Crowley and Bashir stood behind Watkins as he opened a series of files on a laptop. He found the Conti crime family tree and scrolled down through the various headshots until Tony's photo appeared.

"That's him! I saw him getting off the elevator downstairs."

They read the condensed biography:

Antonio Maximo Tucci

Born: February 28, 1950, East Harlem, NY

Parents: Fabio and Rosalie Tucci

Siblings: Sofia (died in 1959 at age 10)

1966: Father indicted on conspiracy charges to import cocaine. Hung self in jail while awaiting trial.

1967: Dropped out of high school (junior year) to care for dying mother.

1968: Arrested for the murder of "White Willie" Duke, a reputed heroin and cocaine dealer from Harlem.

1968-1971: U.S. Marines. Staff Sergeant. Served 2 tours in Vietnam. Decorations: Silver Star, Bronze Star, Purple Hearts (2) and Vietnam Service Medal. Honorable Discharge.

1972-1974: Whereabouts unknown.

1975: Joined the Mario Conti crime family. Involved in gambling and money laundering.

1982-1984: Sentenced to 36 months in Sing Sing Correctional Facility for illegal gambling. Released after 24 months for good behavior.

1988: Married Anne Greeley. Divorced in 1995.

1995: Thwarted assassination attempt on Mario Conti, killing the three assassins. One bystander killed. No charges filed.

1996-1997: Extended hospitalization to treat injuries, multiple surgeries, and rehabilitation.

1998-2008: Worked for Conti Construction as CFO. Replaced by Dante Conti.

2009-Present: Family chauffeur. Active stock trading. IRS-audited in 2012 and 2013. No issues found.

"The family chauffeur?" Bashir said. "Maybe his presence here yesterday was just a coincidence."

Crowley frowned. "I don't believe in coincidence."

"The Conti family could still be involved with gambling," Watkins said. "Maybe he was in the neighborhood collecting on a bad debt."

"Most Muslims don't gamble, and he's too old to be strong-arming some deadbeat gambler," Crowley said.

Watkins suggested, "Maybe he was just trying to get laid."

"I doubt it. Old Italians don't slum for sex in Islamic neighborhoods. Something else is going on," Crowley said. "Agent Ross is checking with the ATF to see if Conti Construction does demolition work.

They could have extra explosives for illegal sales. For all we know, this Tucci character met with that terrorist Anazi yesterday—right here under our noses."

"Building bombs in Brooklyn?" Bashir mused. "Now, that's scary."

Crowley said, "I'm going to catch a cab back to headquarters. I want to talk with your experts in the organized crime unit about drilling down on the Conti family immediately."

As he slipped on his hoodie and sunglasses, Crowley asked Watkins to print out the headshots of Tony and Anazi so he could show them to the hotel clerk downstairs.

Crowley said, "I've got a feeling things are about to heat up."

* * * *

After flashing his Homeland Security credentials, Crowley showed the photos to the clerk at the front desk of the Monroe Hotel.

The clerk claimed he'd never seen Anazi, but he verified that Tucci had rented a room the day before. He also remembered that Tucci had specifically asked for a room on the east side of the hotel.

Crowley got the room key to check it out.

Moments later, Crowley stood in the stuffy little room. It seemed like the perfect place for a secret meeting. Had Tucci met with Anazi there to finalize some deal involving explosives?

Perhaps...

Staring out the window, Crowley also wondered why Tucci would specifically request a room that overlooked a street filled with empty storefronts and an abandoned warehouse.

It was a mystery that would be solved soon.

56

Tony sat at his favorite corner table at Mancini's, sipping coffee and reading the *Times*.

Connie Ricci, the waitress, saw Tony and rushed over to his table. Tears of gratitude filled her eyes. "Oh, Mr. Tucci! How can I ever thank you?"

"Hello, Connie. How is Gina doing?"

"She's so much better! Those mean girls not only stopped their harassment, they're actually being nice to her." She pulled a tissue from her pocket to wipe away her tears. "Whatever you did made all the difference."

"Well, I'm glad that it all worked out."

Connie bowed her head. "I'm so curious... How did you convince those girls to change their ways?"

"Let's just say that sometimes people have to be reminded to do the right thing."

"God bless you, Mr. Tucci."

Connie kissed his hand and went back to work.

Paolo swept in behind the bar with a tray of clean glasses. "Hungry, Tony? How about a nice meatball sandwich on some fresh focaccia?"

"No thanks. I'm still full from Thanksgiving dinner last night."

Tony removed a Montblanc pen from his jacket breast pocket to tackle the NYT's crossword puzzle. As he was filling in the first answer, an NYPD patrol car pulled up in front of the restaurant. Two officers emerged from the vehicle and entered the restaurant.

Paolo grabbed some menus and went to greet them.

"Good morning, officers! Here for an early lunch?"

Nervously, the officers both removed their hats. The senior police officer, a burly black man in his mid-forties, said, "No... actually, we're looking for the parents of Thomas Mancini."

Sensing something was amiss, Paolo responded, "I'm Paolo Mancini, Tommy's father. How can I help you?"

Both officers bowed their heads. The younger officer, a Hispanic woman, did not look up. Biting his upper lip, the crusty veteran patrolman looked squarely at Paolo. "Mr. Mancini, there's no good way to say this, but... your son was found dead this morning in his van up in the Bronx."

"Oh, my God!" Paolo gasped and almost fell over.

Tony rush over to help him sit down.

In a state of shock, Paolo started to tear up. "That can't be possible. I just spoke with him a few days ago."

Delivering a death notice was one of the most difficult duties in law enforcement. Both officers were trained to know denial was usually the first response from the family of the deceased.

After a minute of awkward silence, the senior officer whispered, "We're very sorry for your loss, sir."

Tony inquired, "Can you give us any details, Officer?"

"I'm sorry, but that's all I know. Detective Banks is waiting at The Jacobi Medical Center. We need someone to identify the body."

Tony put his arm around Paolo who was shaking and crying. "Paolo, I can handle it. Why don't you just stay here?"

They waited patiently until Paolo could compose himself. After a long, painful pause, he said, "No. I want to see him."

Tony helped Paolo to his feet. "Come on, I'll drive you."

57

Throughout the twenty-minute trip to the Bronx morgue, Paolo never said a word. Adrift in his thoughts, he just stared blankly out the front window of the limo at the back of the patrol car as it wove through traffic.

Upon arriving, the police officers led Tony and Paolo through the lobby to a bank of elevators. Three stories down at the end of a long, cold corridor, they found the entrance to the morgue. Paolo, unsteady and still in shock, was on his last legs as they entered the waiting area. He slumped into a chair while Tony checked in with the receptionist.

Minutes later, Detective Banks, a middle-aged veteran cop with a wrinkled suit and apathetic demeanor, took them inside.

They passed through a chilly room of stainless steel sinks, counters, and examination tables with built-in drains. A coroner and his assistant prepared for an autopsy beside a body covered with a white sheet and toe tag.

The clash of bright, white fluorescent lights, and the pungent stench of antiseptics gave Tony an instant headache.

Banks directed them into an adjacent room with an entire wall of stainless steel square doors—a filing cabinet for the dead.

He nodded at a morgue assistant, who opened one of the doors and slid out a corpse on a metallic shelf. Tony helped Paolo walk over as the assistant respectfully pulled back the white sheet to reveal the upper body of a young man.

"Is this Tommy Mancini?" asked the detached detective.

Paolo looked down at his son with an indescribable sadness in his eyes. "Yes, that's my son."

"I'm sorry for your loss," said Banks.

"Yeah, I know!" snapped Paolo as he shifted into the anger phase of his grieving. He shook his head. "I'm sorry, Detective... I didn't mean..."

Tony gently patted Paolo on the back to calm him down.

The distraught father turned away while Tony stepped in closer to the corpse. Tommy was naked from the waist up. He noticed some purple and yellow bruising on Tommy's neck and wrists, but no other obvious trauma.

Since Paolo was incapable of dealing with the situation, Tony asked the questions. "What can you tell us?"

Banks flipped open his notepad and summarized: "Tommy's van was found by a patrol car in Riverside Park at 10:00 am. The engine was on, and the windows were rolled up. The officers knocked on the driver's window, and when there was no response, they opened the door. Tommy was dead, and there was a syringe in his arm. The officers discovered drug paraphernalia and a quarter ounce of heroin inside the van... Shortly thereafter, I arrived at the scene along with a medical examiner. There was no sign of foul play or robbery. The medical examiner made a preliminary finding that Tommy died from an overdose. I found a business card for Mancini's restaurant in Tommy's wallet and I sent those police officers to bring you here."

Paolo shook his head. "Tommy was no heroin addict."

Banks sighed and pulled on a pair of plastic gloves. Stepping to Tommy's side, he gently rotated his left arm into a palms-up position. Needle tracks along the anterior elbow were clearly visible.

Paolo turned away.

Trying to keep Paolo focused, the detective asked, "Tommy was in the National Guard, correct?"

"Yes."

"Where was he stationed?"

"At the Bronx Armory."

"And what did he do there?"

"He worked as a guard on the graveyard shift."

That revelation almost knocked Tony off his feet. "You never told me that, Paolo."

Wearily, Paolo rested his head in his palm. "What difference does it make now?"

Turning away, anger began to roil deep within Tony. He suddenly remembered a few omens over the past week—indications that something sinister was brewing between Dante's crew and Tommy...

The first clue came on Tuesday evening at the Conti mansion, when Gino and Al looked away nervously when Tony mentioned he was going to Mancini's for dinner... Then later that night, Paolo mentioned that Gino and Al had taken Tommy out to dinner after he returned from his tour in Afghanistan. At the time, it seemed rather harmless since they had watched Tommy grow up and supported the war... But now, Tony saw the real motivation behind the mobsters' dinner invitation. Clearly, Dante and his crew had discovered the young soldier's drug addiction and exploited it to get their greedy hands on those high tech military weapons… And finally, Dante's comment in the chapel that "as of this morning" the arms deal was "half done." Obviously, they had already taken possession of the arms and, in predictable Mafia fashion, got rid of Tommy by making it look like a drug overdose.

Tony was angry with himself for not connecting those dots earlier, but he was infuriated that those heartless SOBs would use Tommy in such a callous way.

As usual, unbridled greed trumped all.

Closing his notebook with an air of finality, Banks said, "We'll be doing an autopsy and a comprehensive toxicology work-up over the weekend, but it'll take a few weeks to get the full reports."

Paolo, looking like he was circling the drain, started for the exit.

Tony said, "What? That's it? Don't tell me that's the end of your investigation?"

Banks gave him the classic blank cop stare.

Tony pointed to the bruises on Tommy's neck and wrists. "And what about those?"

Banks bent down and examined the bruises. "The medical examiner will check them out during the autopsy."

Tony kept pushing. In a whisper, he said, "I think you should also check for fingerprints inside Tommy's van."

Banks looked surprised. "What? You think this was murder?"

"Those bruises look very suspicious and, as someone who knew Tommy most of his life, I just don't believe he would overdose. He wasn't that careless."

"Duly noted," said Banks, his voice dripping with sarcasm. "And, by the way, who are you again?"

"Tony Tucci. A friend of the family."

Banks glanced over at Paolo, who was already walking out the door. "Mr. Mancini needs to make the funeral arrangements. We can release the body soon."

Tony nodded and helped his friend to the car.

* * * *

Tony drove Paolo home. This time, Paolo sat in the back with a double Scotch in his hand.

Again, silence reigned.

Stunned by the crushing reality of Tommy's death, Paolo was practically comatose. A broken, hollowed-out widower, he now had to bury his only child.

Tony could not imagine what it must feel like for a father to see his son laying in a morgue. He wanted to comfort his old friend, but there were no words.

58

Tony dropped Paolo off at his house in East Harlem. He offered to stay with him, but Paolo said he wanted to be alone.

Emotionally, it had already been a brutally long day for Tony too. And it was just starting...

He drove around the City aimlessly, ending up in lower Manhattan. Spotting an old neighborhood bar on Mulberry Street, he pulled the limo in front.

Tony sat by himself at the end of the long, empty bar nursing a cup of coffee spiked with a single shot of Jack Daniels. At the other end, a bartender prepared drink garnishes and chatted with some local patrons. An oldies radio station played in the background as a popcorn machine in the corner next to a pool table burped up a pungent batch of exploded kernels.

"Hey, mister. Need a refill?" the rosy-faced bartender asked.

"No thanks," replied Tony.

He stared down into the cup, slowly swirling around the lukewarm concoction. Tony had always been a very rational, methodical man. He had learned never to speak or act impulsively without due process of thought, carefully weighing all the options before he made a move. Now, he was faced with the biggest moral dilemma of his life.

Dante had taken possession of whatever Tommy stole from the armory, and he fully intended to sell it later that day via Victor Volkov. Tony was convinced the suspicious Arab he followed the day before was the ultimate client, and those weapons could be part of some terror plot, culminating in the deaths of many innocent Americans.

And time was running out.

Tony could either turn a blind eye and let the arms deal proceed, which would solve all of Dante's pressing financial problems—or God forbid, go to the authorities and tell all.

Of course, if Tony chose the latter, he would be walking on the razor's edge. As a convicted felon and close associate of the Conti family, Tony's credibility with law enforcement would be highly suspect from the beginning. His fantastic story involving an international arms dealer and possible Islamic terrorist was all conjecture, and had too many loose ends. After all, he had no real proof of anything, just Dante's statement that the deal would be done by the end of the day. Nor did he have any details about when or where the arms transaction would go down.

Tony also worried about how his decisions would affect the Conti family. Dante and his crew would surely end up in prison for a very long time or even on death row, especially if they could be directly linked to Tommy Mancini's murder. Mario was already clinging to life and losing Dante would probably break his heart permanently. Carla was more fragile than ever. Having both of her sons behind bars would be a terrible burden. Angela knew her older brother deserved to be punished for his crimes and sins, but she would still have to deal with all the fall-out.

Inevitably, she would have to take care of her angst-ridden parents, which could derail her plans for graduate school and any chance for a decent life with Hal.

Tony's personal situation was the least of his concerns, but it was hard not to contemplate the consequences of his choices. If word got out that Tony had gone to the Feds, he could join the likes of Joseph Valachi, Henry Hill, Jr., and Sammy "The Bull" Gravano as one of the biggest Mafia rats in history.

Dante, Gino, and Al all were made men, and betraying them would be unforgiveable. They had many contacts in the underworld, and for the right price, those henchmen would be eager to take revenge. Tony would go from being a respected legend in Mafia circles to a marked man, never knowing when some stranger would walk up behind him with a .22 caliber pistol and pump half a dozen hollow-points into the back of his head.

Tony sipped his spiked coffee, which tasted bitter.

Peering into the mirror through the multi-colored bottles lining the back of the bar, his reflection was unreal and distorted. He felt queasy and lightheaded, afraid he was losing his balance.

After years of relative quiet and stress-free living, the gods were fucking with him. If Mario hadn't asked him to keep an eye on Dante, he wouldn't be in such a difficult position.

Once again, the old Don's fate was in his hands.

59

Reeling back the years, Tony recalled the second time he'd met Mario Conti. It was the spring of 1975. Tony had just arrived back in New York after being gone for more than six years. He was sitting at a small table outside a coffee shop on First Avenue, perusing the classified section of the newspaper for an apartment to rent.

"Hello, Tony."

Tony looked up to see a well-dressed gentleman looming over him. At first, he didn't recognize him, but when Mario smiled, Tony remembered him from the night at the church when he was seventeen.

"Mr. Conti?" he asked, laying down the newspaper.

"It's good to see you again. It's been a long time."

"Yes, it has."

Mario gestured at the empty chair beside the table. "Mind if I sit down?"

"Not at all."

A waiter stopped by, and Mario ordered two cappuccinos.

"I heard you joined the Marines back in '68 and went to Vietnam," Mario said.

"I really didn't have much choice at the time."

"I'll never forget the night we spoke in the church."

"That night changed my life," Tony said sheepishly.

"I don't know what happened between you and 'White Willie' Duke, but somehow you killed him. No one could believe some teenager could get the best of that bad ass."

"It just happened."

"You know, a lot of people I knew over on Pleasant Avenue were quite happy about his demise. It was a blessing for their business." Mario shrugged. "But it doesn't matter now. The Feds and a special police squad busted all those guys."

"I thought you were part of that scene."

"Not drugs. My thing is gambling."

Tony swore he would never get involved with drug dealers. After all, it was the drug trade that got his father killed, destroyed the Tucci family and undermined his future. Gambling was different, and he genuinely liked the action.

"I gambled a lot in the Marines. When we weren't out humping the Cong, there was always lots of dice and card games."

"Really? You win a lot?"

"Let's just say that I was very good at card counting—and it didn't hurt that most of the guys were usually drunk or stoned by the time we cut the deck."

"Sounds familiar," Mario laughed.

The waiter brought their coffees.

Mario kept asking questions about Tony's experiences in Vietnam and what he had been doing the last few years.

Tony told him that during his time in the military, he saved a small fortune. While his buddies pissed away their salaries on booze and prostitutes, he supplemented his income by mastering the subtleties of games like Craps, Five Card Stud, Red Dog, and

Blackjack. He scooped up one large pot of cash after another and stashed the money in a savings account.

After two tours in Nam, he spent his final days stationed at Camp Pendleton in Southern California, where he trained Marine recruits in close-combat warfare. When he was discharged in 1971, Tony had saved more than $30,000. He bought a used Harley Davidson Super Glide and hit the road.

Curious about the whole hippie scene, his first stop was Haight-Ashbury, but the blissful days of free love were long gone and, as a Vietnam vet, he felt very out of place. He headed north along the coast into the Pacific Northwest, where he worked on a fishing boat for a while.

Drifting from state to state, Tony stayed in small towns and big cities, explored local sites, and met all kinds of interesting people. He landed a job on a horse ranch in Montana, crossed the border into Canada to work as a logger, and drove down through the Midwest Plains until he arrived in Texas, where he labored on an oil field. Then, he toured the South and spent the last winter on the sunny, sandy shores of Key West.

"I had some great experiences and learned a lot," Tony said, "but after the last few years on the road, I thought it was time to come home."

"What are your plans now?"

"Since I qualify for the G.I. Bill, I was planning to take some college classes. Maybe math and accounting."

"Hmm… You got a job?"

"Not yet."

Mario gave him a long, contemplative look. "Why don't you come to work for me?"

Taken aback, Tony didn't reply.

Mario leaned in closer and whispered, "I'm running numbers, card and dice games all over the East Side—plus, weekly gambling junkets to Las Vegas. Frankly, I could use a smart, responsible guy to help me with the books. I hate that crap."

Tony figured Mario was associated with one of the large Italian families of New York. He was circumspect about getting involved, but he also needed money. After his three-year, post-Vietnam odyssey around America, his savings were almost gone, and he had no other decent prospects.

Still, he hesitated.

Mario continued. "We've only met twice, but I like you, Tony. I respect that you're a vet and how you dealt with Duke. You probably don't know this, but I tried to visit when they had you locked up in juvie. But since you were a minor, and I wasn't a relative, they denied me access… and then they shipped you off to Nam."

If that was true, it meant Mario was the only person who had been concerned about him when he was going through the darkest hour of his youth. When he was in jail, no one ever came to see him except the police, prosecutors, and his court-appointed attorney.

Mario kept pushing. "Look, I own a small apartment building about two blocks from here. You can stay there for free. For the next two weeks, you hang out with me. I'll show you the ropes, and we'll see just how good you are with numbers. If we both feel comfortable with the arrangement, we'll cut a longer-term deal. Sound okay?"

With the dull roar of FDR Drive in the background, Tony and Mario shook hands, launching their forty-year friendship.

* * * *

Once again, Tony contemplated his reflection in the mirror behind the bar on Mulberry Street.

No matter what decision he made about how to deal with Dante's imminent arms transfer, people were going to get hurt and probably killed. One way or another, he knew Mario would end up suffering the most.

Finally, Tony decided on a course of action.

He left a tip on the counter, picked up his cane and walked out of the bar.

60

Inside the cold, empty offices of the warehouse, candles illuminated a room with blacked-out windows. Mustafa Al-Anazi sat in a circle of sixteen men. It was a very solemn occasion because every man knew that in less than 24 hours, he would certainly die fighting the godless infidels.

Anazi scanned the faces of the men surrounding him. He knew all their personal stories and backgrounds. They were young and old, some untested in the ways of combat; others were war-hardened veterans after decades of jihad. It was his great honor to lead these martyrs into battle.

Seated to Anazi's immediate right was his close friend, Kamel Al-Masud. In remission from leukemia, Masud looked gaunt and tired, but could still pass for Anazi's twin brother. Earlier in the day, Masud had confided to Anazi that he wanted to become a martyr too, and was prepared to do anything to make their mission a success. Anazi assured Masud that Allah would grant his wish.

The five two-man teams, so carefully selected, trained, and smuggled into the United States, were eager for their last fight to begin. If they were back in their homelands, the lean and weathered men would be wearing the long tunics and loose trousers so common in the Arab world. Their faces, featuring shaved

278

mustaches and full beards as prescribed by Mohammed, would be hidden behind headscarves, revealing only their menacing eyes. Instead, the ten men were dressed in casual Western attire: jeans, sweatshirts, and running shoes. Also, prior to their journeys to America, they had shaved their faces to initially pass as Mexicans and later as nondescript Americans.

As prescribed by the Quran, every man had prepared for martyrdom by shaving their bodies and dousing themselves with flower water in preparation for their weddings with the beautiful virgins of Paradise.

They also had the opportunity to record a personal martyrdom video. Sitting in front of a black al-Qaeda flag on a wall, each man gave a last testament, proclaiming "hatred" of the West, "love of death," and "sacrifice for Allah."

A collection of deadly weapons was spread out in the center of the circle. Masud had carefully gathered the guns from underground arms dealers and out-of-state gun shows over the previous six months. It was a lethal cache, including AR-15s, TEC-DC9s, MAC-10s, and even a few cherished AK-47s with clip extensions, plus numerous semi-automatic handguns, plenty of ammo and a box of smoke grenades.

The Stinger launchers and missiles would be their primary weapons, but they needed the smaller arms to protect themselves if confronted by the police, and to use mercilessly on their secondary targets after the initial strikes at the airports.

Anazi spoke to the group in Arabic. "Rejoice my brothers! Fourteen hundred years ago, the Prophet Mohammed established the first Islamic state.

Tomorrow morning, we will take another step in expanding his great empire. And America will feel the wrath of Allah."

Rocking back and forth in a prayer-like rhythm, the would-be martyrs chanted, "Allahu Akbar! Allahu Akbar!"

There was a manila envelope in front of each team, filled with photos from the airports and their secondary "soft targets." Earlier in the day, Anazi had reviewed the information with every team to make sure they understood their objectives to ensure the greatest possible destruction of life and property.

The time had come for Anazi to reveal the full scope and historical significance of his evil plan. With a showman's flourish, Anazi unfurled a large map of the eastern United States and laid it out before the men. He pointed at the key airports: JFK and LaGuardia in New York, Logan International in Boston, Philadelphia International, and Reagan National in Washington, D.C.

"These are the most symbolic, target-rich airports on America's east coast," Anazi said. "We will simultaneously strike each of these facilities tomorrow morning at nine o'clock. You will take the battle to the enemy using your expertise with shoulder-fired missiles. Each team will have two missiles. Use them wisely. Aim straight and true. We will destroy ten airliners in a matter of minutes and rip America's heart out once again."

Until that moment, each of the young drivers had known the details of their personal mission only, but had no idea of the grandiose scope of the planned attack. Their excitement was palpable. The older warriors just smiled with a stoic detachment.

Anazi continued, "If you can evade the police around the airports, you will travel to your secondary targets where you will have an opportunity to slaughter great numbers of infidels with these weapons."

He swept his hand over the firearms spread before them. "We have carefully selected the targets. Some of you will have the honor of attacking synagogues, which should be packed with Jews celebrating their holy day, while others will assault the crowded malls where the American pigs love to shop after stuffing their faces with turkey... Show no mercy!"

The men softly chanted their approval.

"In the next few hours, we will take possession of the launchers and missiles. Then, early tomorrow morning, you will travel to your designated targets to unleash holy hell on America. Afterward, your statements of martyrdom will be dispersed to the press. Soon, the whole world will hear your voices and see your handiwork."

Although he was still haunted by his nightmare from the night before, Anazi gave an impassioned speech declaring that the Worldwide Caliphate was real and predestined, and how he craved the "honors and delights" awaiting all martyrs in Paradise.

In closing, Anazi spread his arms out as if to embrace the entire group. "Remember, 'America is the great Satan, the wounded snake.' And tomorrow, my friends, we will kill it."

61

Jake Crowley stood in the FBI conference room at 26 Federal Plaza, staring intently at the photos of the Conti crime family. Hank Kline and another senior agent walked briskly into the room.

"This is Nicolas Greco, the head of our Organized Crime Unit," Kline said.

Dressed in a dark three-piece suit, Greco was tall and lean with sunken, dark eyes. He offered his hand. "Nice to meet you, Agent Crowley."

Crowley nodded and pointed at Tony's photo. "This is definitely the guy I saw in the elevator at the Madison Hotel yesterday." Turning to Kline, he asked, "Do you remember him?"

"Can't say I do."

Greco cracked a smile. "I've never met him, but I know him well. Tony Tucci has been with the Conti family for over forty years. After saving Mario Conti's life in a mob-related shootout, he helped him build one of the largest construction companies in New York state, which is now run by the Don's son, a dangerous punk named Dante. Supposedly, Tucci is now just the family driver, but he remains a close confidant of the Don—probably his consigliore. He keeps a very low profile and is not involved with Dante's criminal enterprises. Frankly, I still think Tucci is dirty."

"What do you know about their business?" asked Crowley.

"It's basically legit, but they do collect millions of dollars in kickbacks from their subcontractors every year. When Tucci ran the company, the contractors were kicking back a small percentage of their gross profit. Everyone seemed happy, and there was never any rough stuff. But when Dante and his crew took over the collections, they started to squeeze the subcontractors for more and more. Now, after many years, those people are pissed off. So far no one will talk to us on the record. You know, 'the fear factor.'"

Greco added, "We know that Dante isn't kicking up any of that extra cash to his old man, which is a mortal sin in those circles. He and his crew are pocketing it all. And from what we hear on the streets, Dante needs every cent to subsidize all his other scams, gambling debts, and projects like his new nightclub in the city, which opens tomorrow night."

"He sounds like a real shitheel," said Crowley. Turning to Kline, he asked, "Did you ever find out if Conti Construction is in the demolition business?"

"Yes. Agent Ross confirmed that Conti owns a company called Phoenix Demolition & Hauling, Inc. It has a Federal Explosives License issued by the ATF. Records indicate they're in full compliance."

"But they could be selling explosives on the side, right? For instance, let's say their company has a demolition project and purchases a big batch of explosives, but they only use part of it and stash away the rest. After a while, they've accumulated a hefty stockpile of explosives that's worth a fortune on the black market," Crowley hypothesized. "Trust me, it happens. We busted a white supremacist group down in Louisiana that tried to buy five hundred pounds of dynamite from a demolitions contractor to blow up a gay nightclub. It's a lot more common than you think."

Everyone in the room chewed on that for a while.

Crowley continued. "Perhaps Tucci is brokering a deal with Anazi. With enough explosives, they could make some nasty IEDs or dirty bombs."

"That's a distinct possibility," Greco said, "but there's been another interesting development."

He handed Crowley a photo of Frank Salvadore.

"That's Frank Salvadore—a hired gun out of Philly. Our sources tell us he joined Dante's crew about a week ago. He's also a former Army weapons specialist who was busted for stealing arms and ammo. It got him five years in Leavenworth and a dishonorable discharge."

Crowley studied the photo. "Maybe they brought him in as a consultant for some kind of arms deal or to build bombs."

Greco closed his file. "Regardless, we have enough circumstantial evidence to get some wiretaps and start surveillance on Dante and his entire crew."

"Let's get the paperwork done and over to the FISA court ASAP," Kline said.

Agent Ross stuck her head through the door. "You'll never believe who just walked into the office."

62

Sitting alone in a brightly lit interrogation room, Tony calmly stared at the two-way mirror. Kline, Greco, Ross, and Crowley entered the adjacent observation suite, where sophisticated recording equipment glowed and hummed in the dark.

"Whoa! That's him, alright," Crowley said, walking over to the glass for a closer look. "Tony Tucci in the flesh."

Kline asked, "Has he said anything yet?"

"He told another agent that he has some valuable and time-sensitive information," Ross replied. "He wants to talk to someone in charge."

"Well, aren't we the lucky ones," Greco said cynically.

Ross clutched a file folder and computer tablet against her chest. "I haven't had much time, but I did scan most of his file. He seems like an interesting character."

"He's also a convicted felon and killer," said Greco.

"You can add this to the list," Ross said, holding up Tony's cane. "This belongs to Tucci. It's an antique cane with a hidden 24-inch blade."

Crowley examined the walking stick, found the hidden latch under the handle and unsheathed the shiny sword. "Cool."

"It's against the law to carry a cane sword in New York City. Plus, it's a felony to try to smuggle any kind of weapon into a Federal law enforcement facility," Greco gloated. "Now, if we want, we can charge his ass and throw him in the can."

"Actually, the guards at the security checkpoint in the lobby stated that Tucci voluntarily surrendered his cane right when he entered the downstairs lobby and told them about the hidden sword," Ross said. "Just to be safe, they ran him through the scanner system twice. Apparently, his right leg is half titanium."

"Yeah, he's a bionic Mafia ninja," Greco scoffed.

Kline spoke to Greco. "So how do you want to play this?"

Greco looked at Crowley and Ross. "Let's send them in first to soften him up." He asked Crowley, "Have you done many interrogations?"

"I was a homicide detective for many years before I joined Homeland Security."

Kline nodded. "Go get him."

63

Ross and Crowley entered the sparse interrogation room. Besides the hidden cameras and microphones, there was only a small table and three chairs.

Elisabeth Ross spoke first. "Hello, Mr. Tucci. I'm Agent Ross, and this is Agent Crowley. How can we help you?"

Crossing his legs, Tony sized them up. "I assume you've already done a background check on me."

"Of course," Ross said, tapping her finger on the file. "No one gets this far inside an FBI office without one."

Tony slowly exhaled. "You know, it was very hard for me to come here today. I'm not a snitch."

"Then you're a dying breed," Ross said. She opened the file and glanced down. "I see you did a stint at Sing Sing back in the '80s for gambling. You could have done less time if you agreed to testify against your associates."

Tony shrugged. "*Omerta* can be a noble quality, but there are times when such blind loyalty is morally corrupt."

"So now you're a philosopher?" asked Crowley.

"No, just a concerned citizen."

"And that's why you came in today?"

Tony sat up in his chair and faced them across the table. "Look, I've stumbled across something far bigger than me or my family loyalties." He gestured at the file. "Do you have a copy of my military record in there?"

"You're a decorated Vietnam veteran. It's impressive," said Ross.

"A long time ago, I took an oath to protect my country, even if it meant losing my life. That's why I'm here. I think a lot of innocent civilians could be in jeopardy."

Crowley and Ross leaned back in their chairs, ready to listen.

"Two nights ago, Dante Conti and a man named Victor Volkov met at the Nottingham Palace Hotel."

"Who's Victor Volkov?"

"He's a Russian arms dealer."

"And how do you know that?"

"I did a little research. But you should confirm it."

Inside the viewing room, Kline immediately sat down behind a computer monitor and typed Volkov's name into the FBI's criminal databank.

"Were you present at that meeting between Dante and Volkov?" asked Ross.

"I was only there for a few minutes. I'm not part of Dante's inner circle. I just dropped off two hookers for the after party, and then they kicked me out."

"Do you have any idea what they discussed?" she asked.

"Like I said, I didn't hear any specific conversation but based upon other things I've learned, I think they were there to discuss a big arms deal."

"What kind of arms deal?" Crowley asked.

"I heard something about 'missiles.'"

"What kind of 'missiles'?" Ross asked.

"I have no idea, but Dante said it was a multi-million-dollar package."

"And when did Dante say that?"

"I overheard it on Tuesday evening when he was talking with his father."

"Mario Conti sanctioned the meeting with Volkov?" inquired Ross.

"Not at all. Mario is adamantly opposed to what Dante's doing." Turning to the two-way mirror, Tony added, "Make sure that gets in the record."

Inside the viewing room, Greco smirked. "He's jerking us around."

"Maybe, but he's right about Victor Volkov," Kline said as he scanned the search results on the computer screen. "We've got a large file on him. He's definitely a player in the international arms biz with lots of terrorist connections."

Crowley asked, "So is Dante buying or selling those weapons?"

"Selling. He thinks Volkov is the middle man for some Mexican cartel."

"And where is Dante getting those weapons?"

"I believe he got them from the National Guard Armory in the Bronx."

"And how did he pull that off?" Ross asked.

"This morning, NYPD found the body of Tommy Mancini. He's a National Guard soldier who picked up a heroin habit in Afghanistan. His family owns a restaurant in East Harlem called Mancini's Trattoria. The entire Conti clan has been going there for many years. I think Dante and his crew used Tommy's addiction to coerce him to rip off those weapons."

Kline and Greco exchanged concerned looks.

"The cops told his father that Tommy overdosed, but I don't believe it. I saw his body in the morgue at the Jacobi Medical Center, and he had some nasty bruises on his neck and arms. I'm guessing Dante's crew gave him a hot shot to keep him quiet."

Greco picked up the wall phone and dialed an internal hotline. "This is Greco. We have reason to believe some kind of missiles may have been stolen from the National Guard Armory in the Bronx. We need a *rush* inventory of their stockpiles. Get a team over there right now!"

He hung up and turned his attention back to the interrogation.

Crowley leaned forward to face Tony. "Were you at the Monroe Hotel yesterday?"

Tony was surprised at the question. "Yes. How did you know?"

"We passed in the elevator. What brought you there?"

"After Volkov left the meeting with Dante, I followed him to the Majestic Inn near Lincoln Square where he's staying. Yesterday morning he had a limo meeting with a Middle Eastern man. I followed them out of the City and over into that big Muslim neighborhood in south Brooklyn. That man got out of the limo and walked a few blocks over to the area near the Monroe."

"Do you know who he is?"

"No, but he was acting very strange."

Using the computer tablet, Ross scrolled through various electronic files until she found a photo of Mustafa Al-Anazi. She pushed the electronic tablet across the desk to Tony. "Is this the man?"

Tony studied it. "That's him."

Ross glanced nervously at the two-way mirror. Inside the viewing room, Kline smiled. "Bingo!"

He grabbed the wall phone and quickly dialed. "This is Kline. We've got a hot, tactical situation. I want everyone in the hub in five minutes—ready to go on full alert."

Turning to Greco, he said, "Let's go meet our guest."

64

The door to the interrogation room snapped open as Kline and Greco barged in.

Kline walked over to Tony and extended his hand. "Thank you for coming in today, Mr. Tucci. I'm Special Agent Hank Kline, head of the Counterterrorism Unit."

Tony stood, and they shook hands.

"And I run the Organized Crime Unit," Greco said, reaching out too. "My name is—"

"Nicolas Greco," Tony said, ignoring his hand.

The air went out of the room as Greco gave him an icy stare.

"I read a lot," Tony said nonchalantly as he sat down. "You made quite a splash with the press last year regarding the murder of that federal prosecutor up in Buffalo. The only problem is the guy you convicted is innocent."

"Bullshit!" Greco said contemptuously.

Tony continued. "If you had dug a little deeper you would have discovered that the reason the guy confessed was to protect his wife and kids. He was a patsy. "Fast Freddie" Salerno set the guy up and then threatened to slaughter his entire family if he ever said a word."

"And how do you know that?" Greco asked.

"I may be sidelined, but I keep in touch with some people who know things. Look, if you believe anything I say today, believe this: You've got an innocent man rotting away in the Allenwood Penitentiary. Do something about it."

Looking into Tony's unblinking eyes, Greco pursed his lips. "I'll look into it. I promise."

"Okay, let's circle back to the matter at hand," Kline said. He pointed at the photo on the tablet. "Are you sure you saw this man?"

"I'm sure. Who is he anyway?"

Kline nodded at Agent Ross, who said, "Mustafa Al-Anazi, an international terrorist. His nickname is 'The Ghost of Fallujah,' because he's so elusive."

Tony smiled. "He's not *that* elusive."

"Did you see where he went?" Ross asked anxiously.

"Yeah. He's holed up in an abandoned warehouse right down the block from the Monroe," Tony said. "I got real suspicious when he put on a disguise before he entered that building."

"What kind of disguise?"

"He slipped into a side alley and a few minutes later he came out looking like a homeless guy, dressed in rags and carrying shopping bags. Then he crossed the street, snuck through the security fence and knocked on the side door of that warehouse. Someone let him in."

"Could you see the other person?" asked Kline.

"No, I was too far away. I rented a room at the Monroe to watch the place. I sat there all afternoon, but no one went in or out."

Tony turned to Crowley. "I left at sunset. I guess that's when we passed each other in the elevator."

Crowley asked, "Does Dante really think those weapons are going to a Mexican cartel?"

"Apparently, that's what Volkov told him. This morning I tried to warn Dante about Volkov's meeting with that mysterious Arab, but he didn't want to hear anything about it."

"Why not?"

"Dante is in denial because he's in desperate need of cash. Besides getting an expensive divorce, he's deeply in debt to some very scary people. He won't listen to reason and told me to stay out of his business."

"Do you have any idea where and when Dante plans to transfer those weapons?" asked Kline.

Tony shook his head. "That's why I came to you. Dante said the arms transfer is going down later today. I can't stop him by myself."

"Okay, the clock is ticking," Kline said. "We need to identify the kinds of weapons, plus the time and location of that meeting. Can you reach out to any members of Dante's crew?"

"Like I said, they keep me in the dark. If I called any of them, they would smell a rat."

Greco jumped in, "We've got to put tails on Dante and his crew immediately. Can you supply us with any of their cell numbers?"

"Sure," Tony said, removing his smartphone, a small notepad, and pen from the breast pocket of this suit coat.

Kline said, "It took a lot of courage for you to come in today, Mr. Tucci. When this thing is over, I want to buy you a drink."

"If word gets out that I came here of my own volition, I'm a dead man. Dante and his crew will make sure of it," Tony said as he wrote down the names and numbers. "In which case, we may have to order a whole bottle."

Nodding at his colleagues in the room, Kline said. "You have our word we will keep your involvement totally confidential."

Tony made eye contact with Greco, who gave him a sly smile.

Kline added, "Agent Crowley, I'll have someone drive you and Mr. Tucci over to the stakeout at the Monroe to confirm Anazi's exact location. We'll be there soon with the cavalry."

Tony said, "If you don't mind, I need my cane."

Kline nodded. "Done."

Turning to Agent Ross, Kline said, "And let's get eyes on Volkov. Dispatch a team over to his hotel and report back to me."

Ross dashed from the room.

Kline checked his watch and moved towards the door. "The entire staff is meeting in the hub for a briefing right now. We've got to mobilize every asset we've got."

"I'll alert our counterparts at the NYPD. If that arms deal is going down soon, we'll need multiple SWAT teams on standby," said Greco. "Plus, we need to seal the area around that warehouse. We can't let Anazi get away."

65

Tony and Crowley sat in the back of an unmarked Ford sedan as a young, intense FBI agent drove rapidly over the Brooklyn Bridge. The mid-afternoon traffic was light, so they made good time.

Tony asked, "You're not an FBI agent, are you?"

"How did you know?"

"You're the only guy in that office without a white shirt and tie."

"I hate ties, but I do have a few bolos back home."

Tony looked down at Crowley's fancy, lizard-skin cowboy boots. "And J. Edgar would never have approved of those boots."

"Well, I don't particularly care for his taste in dresses," Crowley chuckled. "Actually, I'm with Homeland Security out of Arizona."

He paused and then added, "Since you've been so forthright with us, and this whole thing is about to blow up any minute, it's okay to tell you that I've been trailing some possible terrorists who crossed the border. There's a strong probability they could be from Afghanistan."

Tony asked, "Don't they call that hellhole 'the place where empires go to die'?"

"Arizona or Afghanistan?" Crowley replied with a straight face.

This time, they both laughed.

As they raced towards Brooklyn, Crowley turned serious. "Like Agent Kline said, you did the right thing by coming in."

"Sometimes 'doing the right thing' can get you killed."

"Kline seems like a straight shooter to me," Crowley said. "He'll protect you, but I can tell you don't trust Greco."

"He's just another suit in search of a headline. People who rush to judgment without turning over every rock are dangerous, especially in life-and-death situations. And it doesn't matter what side of the law they're on."

Tony looked out the side window. "If Greco needs to land a bigger Mob fish down the road, he won't hesitate to sell me out or blackmail me by threatening to leak that I voluntarily turned on Dante. He's got a rep for that kind of duplicitous shit."

"If we're able to stop this arms deal, you could end up being a hero. You'd be untouchable," offered Crowley.

"Fat chance."

The car veered south onto the Expressway toward Bay Ridge.

Crowley said, "To be perfectly honest, initially I thought you were one of the bad guys. After I saw you at the Monroe Hotel yesterday and later learned you were involved with the Conti family that owns a demolition company, I convinced myself you were a middleman, handling some kind of explosives transaction with Anazi."

Tony nodded. "I can understand the logic, but…"

"Just ironic, I guess."

"Here's what's really ironic," Tony said. "Tommy Mancini goes to Afghanistan to protect our country against terrorism, but he ends up getting hooked on smack, their biggest export. Then, when he returns home, Dante and his goons take advantage of Tommy's addiction and get him to steal lethal missiles from his country so they can be sold to the same anti-American terrorists."

Crowley shook his head in disgust. "Yeah, it's a real 'circle-of-life' fuck you."

66

Standing in the hallway on the top floor of the Monroe Hotel, Crowley softly rapped on the door using the same signal Kline used the day before. Watkins checked the peephole to see Crowley's face leering back at him.

Crowley and Tony entered.

Watkins and Bashir, who both had their hands resting on their service handguns, looked at Tony with utter disbelief.

Bashir asked Crowley, "Hey, isn't this the guy you saw —"

Crowley cut him off. "Yeah, this is Tony Tucci, a new friend of the Bureau. And per Kline, that's confidential."

Tony nodded at the two dumbfounded agents. "Gentlemen."

"These are Agents Watkins and Bashir."

The Agents relaxed as they shook Tony's hand.

Tony surveyed all the high-tech equipment around the room.

"Mr. Tucci has positively identified Mustafa Al-Anazi," Crowley said. "Apparently, he's right here under our noses."

Watkins and Bashir looked perplexed.

Tony walked over to the windows at the front side of the hotel and peered down at the mosque below. "You guys are looking in the wrong direction."

He crossed the room to the last set of windows overlooking the deserted side street and pointed down at the warehouse at the end of the block. "I saw Anazi go into the side door of that warehouse yesterday afternoon," he said.

Bashir was shocked. "No way!"

A confused Watkins said, "That's an abandoned building. I've scanned it a hundred times and have never seen a thing."

"Ever spot a homeless guy dressed in rags down on that street, schlepping a couple of shopping bags?" Tony asked.

"Maybe once or twice. But that's nothing unique. There are homeless people everywhere," Watkins said. "Why?"

"That's Anazi in disguise."

"Damn!" Watkins exclaimed as he glassed the warehouse with a pair of binoculars.

Crowley and Bashir began to rearrange the surveillance equipment, so it was focused down on the warehouse.

Tony's cell phone rang and he checked the screen. "It's Dante."

"Go ahead. Take it," said Crowley.

Tony answered the call. "Yeah?"

Everyone in the hotel room could hear Dante's deep voice. "Where are you?"

"Brooklyn."

"Good, so am I. I need you to drive me somewhere."

"Since when do you need my help?"

"The boys are busy. Is it a problem?"

Since the limo was back in Manhattan, Tony lied. "Sorry. I'm having some work done on the limo right now."

"Don't worry, I've got a car. Meet me at Pete's Bar. Know the place?"

"Sure, it's on 18th Avenue, but I'll need to catch a cab."

"Just get here fast."

"What's going on, Dante? I need to know."

"Just leave now," Dante demanded. And the line went dead.

Tony looked at the agents. "Sounds like the arms swap is happening right now."

"Great timing," Crowley replied, punching in Kline's number on his smartphone.

Back at the frenzied FBI offices, Kline took the call, "Talk to me."

"It's Crowley at the Monroe. Tucci has confirmed Anazi's location. Plus, he just got a call from Dante, who needs a ride somewhere. He's waiting for Tony at a place called Pete's Bar in Brooklyn. Tucci thinks the arms buy is going down."

Crowley switched his phone to the speaker so everyone could hear Kline.

"First, tell the guys to get a wire and GPS device on Tucci. We don't want to lose him. I'll dispatch a chase team to Pete's right now that can follow Tucci from a distance. We also have four SWAT teams en route, three by ground and one in a chopper, and we're deploying more undercover agents around the neighborhood. The City offices are closed for the holiday, but we're trying to get someone from the building department to get us the blueprints of the warehouse. We'll be at the Monroe shortly."

Tony removed his coat and dress shirt. Watkins and Bashir fit him with a GPS tracking device and wireless microphone that would transmit the audio feed back to the hotel.

Tony warned, "Just make sure those devices are well hidden—or I'm a dead man."

67

About twenty minutes after they spoke, Tony arrived at Pete's Bar. Standing outside the front door under an awning, Dante smoked and waited anxiously. As he climbed out of the cab, Tony noticed a small black helicopter flying high above—but Dante seemed completely unaware of the aerial surveillance.

Tony paid the cabbie and approached Dante, who wore a devilish smile.

"You wanted to know about my deal. Well, like it or not, now you're in," Dante sneered, stubbing out his cigarette with his shoe. "If you want to stay part of the family, it's all hands on deck."

He gestured over at a late-model sedan parked across the street and dropped the keys into Tony's hand. "That's our ride. It's hot so don't get pulled over. Let's go."

With Dante sitting in the backseat, Tony pulled the car out into traffic. At the same time, the FBI chase car, which had been parked down the block, began their covert pursuit.

"Where are we going?" Tony asked.

"Just drive."

For a few minutes, they drifted along with the traffic.

Dante lit another cigarette. "That bag on the seat is for you."

Tony peered down into the partially opened gym bag to see two semi-automatic handguns.

Blowing out smoke, Dante said, "I need "Two Triggers" Tucci watching my back today."

"Don't you mean 'The Gimp'?" Tony said sarcastically.

Dante smirked. "Whatever."

Tony turned his eyes back to the road as they drove deeper into south Brooklyn.

"By the way, they're loaded, and the safeties are off."

"Why do I need them? What's going on?"

Dante said nothing.

Trying to pry more information out of Dante for the benefit of the FBI agents listening to his audio feed, Tony asked, "Where are Gino and the boys?"

"Close by," Dante replied, checking his watch. "Tell me, Tony. When was the last time you fired a gun?"

"Not since that day with your father."

"Don't worry. It's just like riding a bike."

Tony glowered at Dante in the rearview mirror. "You killed Tommy Mancini, didn't you?"

Nonchalantly, Dante looked out the window. "I don't know what you're talking about."

"He was a good kid."

"He was a junkie!" Dante snapped. Trying to compose himself, he took a long drag on his smoke.

Tony and Dante locked eyes in the rearview mirror. Dante gave him a steely glare. "Just keep your eyes on the fuckin' road."

68

Back in the suite at the Monroe Hotel, Crowley and Bashir kept watch on the warehouse as Watkins followed Tony's GPS tracker on a laptop screen.

Agents Kline, Greco, and Ross arrived in their regular work clothes. Given the rapidly unfolding events, all pretenses to maintain an undercover presence were over.

"What's the latest?" Kline asked as he tore off his suit coat and walked briskly over to the windows to look down on the warehouse, which still showed no signs of life.

Pointing at the laptop, Watkins said, "Looks like Tony and Dante are driving back directly toward us, but our chase car says they're alone."

"Where the hell is Dante's crew?" asked Kline.

With a cell phone to her ear, Ross chimed in. "Probably with the five Stinger launchers and ten missiles they jacked from the Armory. The National Guard commander just confirmed it."

"Jesus! Just one of those missiles can easily take down a commercial airliner," Greco growled.

Crowley said, "It all makes sense now. We know at least two of the smuggled men are from Afghanistan, right? Well, back in the '80s, the U.S. trained and armed the Afghani Mujahedeen with Stingers to defeat the Russians. Many of those old warriors are now with the Taliban, and they hate our guts."

"There are plenty of other trained terrorists from the Middle East who know how to use shoulder-launched missiles too," Kline added.

"No doubt about it. Anazi has put together his own jihadi army and they plan to attack us with our own weapons."

They all slipped on wireless headsets to listen to the audio feed from Tony's microphone—and to communicate with their field agents, NYPD, and the SWAT teams converging on the neighborhood.

Bashir asked, "So what's the plan, boss?"

"Our primary objective must be to secure the Stingers. We can't let those missiles fall into Anazi's hands. But we don't want to spook Dante and his boys until they get to the drop spot. By the way, Volkov checked out of his hotel hours ago. We've got to assume he's waiting at the drop too."

Watching his screen, Watkins jumped in. "Tucci's car just turned right onto Columbus Avenue. Looks like they're still heading towards the warehouse."

Kline asked Greco. "Where are those SWAT teams?"

"Three teams are stationed a block back on the east, west, and south corners of the warehouse." Greco pointed across the landscape at the different locations. "They'll move in on our command. We've also got a team aboard a helicopter, ready to drop down on the roof for an aerial assault."

"And where are the snipers?"

"Four sharpshooters are being deployed now around the perimeter of the warehouse," Ross said.

Greco said, "The NYPD is on full alert. They're ready to seal off a three-block radius around the warehouse. No one gets in or out."

69

As Tony drove through an intersection, Dante pulled out his cell phone and made a call.

"Get ready, Volkov. We'll be there in a few minutes." And clicked off.

Then he speed-dialed another number. "Gino, we're here."

Dante hung up just as Tony passed an alley where an unmarked van idled in the shadows. As Al and Frank locked and loaded their guns in the rear, Gino put the van in gear. It lurched out onto the street, narrowly missing a pedestrian.

"Hey! What's the big hurry, mister?!" the startled man yelled.

Gino gave him the finger.

Tony glanced in the side mirror to see the van pull up behind them.

"Looks like your crew just joined the party," Tony said, realizing they were probably heading back to the warehouse for the arms transfer.

Dante said, "Right on schedule."

The FBI chase car edged closer to Dante's sedan and the van. Everyone in the hotel suite heard an agent in the vehicle call the command post. "A white van just pulled in behind the subject's car."

"Stand by to make contact," Kline said.

Tension gripped the room.

Kline adjusted his headset and turned to Watkins. "I can hear Tucci fine, but Dante's voice is muddled. What gives?"

Watkins tried to boost the signal to no avail. "The microphone only has limited reception. Dante must be sitting in the back seat of the car—out of clear earshot."

Crowley spotted Dante's sedan and the white van rolling into view about two blocks from the warehouse. He pointed. "There they are!"

Unaware of the FBI surveillance, Dante called back Volkov. "Open the door now."

As the caravan approached the old warehouse, the main door on the southern side of the block began to roll up. Unfortunately, the agents at the Monroe Hotel could not see it.

"I think we should take down the van now on the street and then move in on the warehouse," Kline said.

"Wait!" Greco said frantically. "What if the van is going to another location? Maybe Tucci misled us and Anazi is waiting somewhere else."

Although clearly irritated at Greco's outburst, Kline paused for a moment to think about the options.

Meanwhile, inside the sedan, Dante said, "Turn into that warehouse."

Tony balked, not knowing if he should follow Dante's instructions or continue driving toward the hotel where he knew the FBI were waiting. But then he felt the barrel of Dante's pearl-handled 9mm handgun press firmly against the back of his skull.

"Turn NOW!"

Tony swerved the sedan up the short driveway and into the warehouse with the van tight on his bumper. The automatic door quickly rolled down with a thud.

The FBI chase car called in. "The subjects just entered the warehouse! The garage door is down! What should we do? Copy?"

"Goddamn it!" Kline shouted. "Stand down! Stand

down!"

They all watched as the unmarked FBI chase car slowly rolled past the warehouse.

"Looks like Tucci *was* telling the truth," Crowley said pointedly to an embarrassed Greco.

"Okay, folks, let's all take a deep breath," said Kline, loosening his necktie. "At least we have them contained, and they still probably don't know we're here."

Greco suggested, "Let's move all our assets in closer and tighten the noose."

"Do it and tell the NYPD to seal off the area," Kline said.

He turned to Ross. "Where are the floorplans for the warehouse?"

With the phone pressed to her ear, she replied, "No luck yet, sir."

Kline pulled Greco aside. "We'd better make some calls to the brass. The Director will have to brief the President and Homeland Security. Plus, the Mayor and Governor need to be updated."

While Kline and Greco huddled in the corner with their phones, Crowley and the other FBI agents watched as armored SWAT vans pulled up to secure the front and both sides of the warehouse.

"I wonder what the hell is going on inside?" asked Bashir.

Crowley speculated, "Well, let's see… We've got an international arms dealer, a bunch of Mafia thugs, a mass murderer and his merry band of jihadi terrorists, and a multi-million-dollar cache of deadly high-tech weapons all confined in one place. What could possibly go wrong?"

70

It was dark and ominous inside the cavernous two-story warehouse. Tony turned on his headlights and slowly led the van through a maze of concrete columns, piles of building debris, and garbage. As they rounded a corner, Volkov emerged from the shadows carrying a black suitcase. He waved them over to an open area under a pool of overhead lighting.

As they slowly emerged from the sedan, Tony slipped the two handguns Dante had given him into the pockets of his overcoat. At the same time, Gino, Al, and Frank exited the van, their guns hidden under their coats.

Volkov placed the briefcase on the ground and raised his arms. "What a great day to make a deal!"

"I see you brought *my* money," Dante said as he and Tony slowly approached.

"Well, if that van is filled with *my* weapons, you just became a very wealthy man," Volkov replied with a hearty laugh.

"Show me," Dante demanded.

Volkov opened the suitcase to reveal row after row of bundled $100 bills. Dante smiled broadly, then nodded over at Gino, who opened the van's doors. Al and Frank dragged out one of the five crates, popped the top, and held up a Stinger launcher and a missile.

"Very nice," Volkov chuckled. "The cartel will be pleased."

Dante spoke to his crew. "Go ahead, boys. Unload it all."

Gino, Al, and Frank began to stack the weapons onto the ground. Dante walked over to the suitcase, grabbed a stack of $100 bills from the bottom, and leafed through it.

Volkov said, "Two million. It's all there."

Dante eyed him carefully. "I have a bonus gift for your clients." Turning back to the van, he said. "Bring over those other toys!"

Frank grabbed the two RPGs, and Al carried the box of compatible grenades. They delivered the weapons to Volkov, and then returned to the van.

"What a nice gesture, Dante!" Volkov said, holding up one of the RPGs and pretending to aim it. "You know, *we* Russians invented the rocket propelled grenade launcher."

"Yeah, but *we* Americans perfected it. Consider this a down payment on our next deal. With any luck, those fuckin' Mexicans will be blowing each other up for years to come."

Just as Dante bent over to pick up the suitcase, Tony saw a few obscure figures lurking back in the shadows. While Volkov continued to play with the RPG launcher, Tony caught Dante's eye and subtly nodded over at the mysterious men.

"Hey, Volkov. Are those your cartel buddies hiding back there?" Dante asked, pointing into the dark.

"Yes, they just wanted to make sure the exchange went smoothly. After all, they just gave you a small fortune."

Dante walked a few steps forward to address the hidden men. "Que pasa, hombres?"

There was no response, but the concealed men began to stir.

Smirking, Dante tried again. "Hola! Donde esta la biblioteca?"

Except for Tony, all the Italians howled with laughter, but there was still only silence from the shadows.

Dante turned to Volkov. "What the fuck? Are they all Mexican mutes?"

He took a few more steps forward to get a better look. All the men wore ski masks.

"Hey, what's with the masks?"

Volkov tried again to placate Dante. "No worries, my friend. It's part of their culture. Now please take all that wonderful cash and go celebrate!"

But it was too late. Dante was pissed. "Wait a fuckin' minute! Why do those wetbacks get to see *our* faces while they hide *theirs*?"

"Yeah, that's bullshit!" Gino yelled, stepping forward with an ominous scowl.

Tony whispered to Dante, "I think we should leave now. This is starting to spin out of control."

Dante glared at Volkov. "Tell them to come out here into the light and show their faces!"

Backing up their infuriated boss, Dante's crew pulled back their coats to reveal their firearms.

There was more muffled movement in the darkness.

After an excruciating long pause, one of the masked men walked out of the dark to the edge of the light. Mustafa Al-Anazi yanked off his ski mask. Speaking in accented English, he declared, "We are not Mexicans. We are holy warriors sent by Allah to destroy your world!"

Volkov dropped the RPG launcher and dashed away.

Two smoke grenades popped and rolled out across the floor into the light. Anazi disappeared into the smoky haze. A moment later, machine gun fire erupted from the shadows, spraying the van next to Dante's men. Gino, Al, and Frank dove for cover, pulled out their weapons and returned fire.

Amid the chaos, Tony removed one of the guns from his pocket as Dante snatched the suitcase stuffed with cash. Tony pushed Dante away from the crossfire, stumbling over to a concrete pillar to seek refuge amid a flurry of bullets.

Men screamed in Arabic as more gunfire ripped into the sedan and van. Al, hiding behind the van, saw two figures circling back around behind him about twenty yards away. He unloaded his semi-automatic handgun at them, and one young man crumbled to the floor.

As Al fumbled with a new ammo clip, AR-15 automatic gunfire flashed from behind a wall farther back in the dark. Several slugs slammed into Al's massive gut. "The Frog's" eyes bulged with disbelief, and he fell face first onto the cement floor in an explosion of blood, bile, and shit.

As Gino and Frank retreated into the warehouse, three insurgents raced in to retrieve the two RPGs and the box of grenades, and then quickly vanished into the swirling mist.

Stumbling around in the smoke and chaos, Gino came across another young driver armed with an AK-47 assault rifle. Without hesitation, he blasted the young man right in the face.

Tucking a shotgun tight against his shoulder, Frank started to hunt for targets too. Thanks to his military training and experiences in war zones, he was calm and confident amid all the shooting. He had killed many men, always enjoying the primal rush of taking a life. He found another driver cowering behind a dumpster and blew him away.

"Let the games begin!" Frank mumbled to himself.

With no one in Dante's crew left to protect the van, six more terrorists emerged from the thick smoke to seize the precious cargo. They ripped open more crates and managed to carry off three Stinger launchers and six missiles.

The battle had begun.

71

The agents in the suite at the Monroe Hotel listened intently to the muted audio feed from Tony's microphone. With the first burst of gunfire, Kline wasted no time unleashing his tactical forces. Speaking into his headset, he yelled, "Gunfire inside the warehouse! All SWAT teams—move in now!"

The back doors of the SWAT vans flew open and heavily armed SWAT units 1, 2 and 3 jumped to the ground, prepared to storm the building.

Crowley turned to Kline. "I'm going down there. We've got to protect Tucci."

Kline nodded his approval and said, "Agent Ross, go as backup. And be safe!"

As Crowley and Ross exited the suite, an FBI sniper appeared in the doorway. With a Texas drawl, he said, "Excuse me, sir, but I can't get on the roof. The only door is rusted shut. Can I work from here?"

Greco looked at Kline incredulously. "His presence puts us all at risk."

"I know, but we don't have another option right now." Kline pointed at the window with the best view of the warehouse below. "Go ahead and set up over there."

Crowley and Ross raced down the hotel corridor and into the stairwell. Agile and well-conditioned, both agents rapidly descended the old, dirty staircase, smashing into walls and leaping over banisters.

315

On the second-floor landing, they surprised a meth addict fixing to shoot up.

"Police! Move!" yelled Crowley.

Panicked, the tweaker dropped his syringe and Crowley stepped on it as he raced by.

"Son of a bitch!" the distraught drug addict screamed.

As she ran by him, Ross shouted, "Just say no, shithead!"

A moment later, Crowley and Ross burst through the hotel's emergency side door and into the sunlight. An NYPD Mobile Command Center was being set up as numerous police cruisers arrived on the scene.

The SWAT commander, Captain Gomez, a muscular ex-military man with a cannonball head and gruff attitude, was running the show. He barked orders into a headset while peering through binoculars as SWAT 1 started to set explosive charges around the warehouse garage door.

Crowley and Ross approached, showing their credentials to the harried commander.

Ross said, "Captain, we're Federal agents. There's an important civilian asset inside the warehouse."

Suddenly, a burst of automatic weapon fire blew out some windows across the front of the warehouse. They all ducked as shards of glass clattered down around them.

Gomez gave them the once over and snorted, "Feds, huh?"

"We need to get him out safely," Crowley said.

"Okay, but put on some vests," Gomez said, motioning at the nearby SWAT van.

More gunfire erupted from inside the building.

Although both agents had their service handguns, Crowley asked, "Can we borrow some extra firepower?"

The Captain shrugged. "Sure. Just don't shoot any of my guys."

Crowley and Ross entered the van and quickly put on bulletproof vests. They slipped their federal IDs into plastic holders and placed the lanyards around their necks.

As Crowley scanned the available weapons on the wall, Ross grabbed a machine gun from a rack and performed an expert weapons check.

"Impressive," Crowley remarked.

"I'll have you know I was the best marksman in my class at Quantico."

"Didn't The Beatles say: 'Happiness is a warm gun'?"

"I doubt they were referring to the Colt M4 Carbine, but hey, it works for me," Ross said as she loaded the intimidating weapon.

Crowley selected a huge 44 Magnum pistol with a short scope.

"That's a big gun, Dirty Harry," Ross teased.

Without missing a beat, Crowley winked, "Size *does* matter."

Crowley checked the cylinder to make sure it was loaded, snapped it shut, and pocketed an extra speed loader. He also grabbed a pair of night vision goggles.

"Let's get some, Agent Starling!"

Side-by-side, they ran low to the ground over to the front of the warehouse, lining up behind SWAT 1 team who were poised to blow and breach the main garage door.

72

In the back of the warehouse, behind a second-floor staircase leading to the roof, Anazi huddled with his five two-man teams and one of the young drivers. Luckily for the terrorists, they had pre-planned to rendezvous in this exact spot if the police ever assaulted the warehouse. He asked his men about the whereabouts of the other four drivers. Before any of them could respond, there was loud gunfire back at the scene of the initial confrontation, followed by the screams of one of their drivers—a wail of unbearable pain.

Anazi sought to calm his comrades. "The great battle is at hand! Our original plans may have been thwarted, but we can still kill many Americans."

An explosion rocked the warehouse as SWAT 3 blew off the side door on the eastern side. "It sounds like the police have joined the fight. Be cautious! They're well-trained and heavily armed."

Anazi pointed at Mahdi and Sakhr from Saudi Arabia, armed with one of the purloined RPGs and several grenades. "You two will remain here. Make sure no one gets past you to the roof."

He handed a machine gun to the last remaining driver, who was shaking with fear. "You will stay here, too. Be brave, my son."

He turned to the other teams: Amal and Hasan from Iraq, Abu Bakr and Kafil from Yemen, and Abbas and Turan from Afghanistan, each equipped with a Stinger launcher and two missiles. Ahmed and Sayid from Libya cradled the other RPG launcher and multiple grenades.

"All you men will go to the roof now. Spread out. There are several safe defensive positions where you can take refuge. Use the Stingers to destroy the largest targets. Also, be prepared for attacks by police helicopters and snipers."

Wasting no time, each Stinger team readied their 32-pound launcher by snapping a Battery Coolant Unit into the handguard, which forced argon gas into the system as well as a chemical energy charge that powered up each twenty-two-pound missile. The RPG launchers were also prepped for the coming assaults.

Anazi pulled out a 9mm handgun and his long knife. "I will stay down here and deliver justice to as many infidels as I can find. Allahu Akbar!"

"Allahu Akbar!" the men replied.

As the four two-man teams ascended the staircase to the roof, the other three jihadis took cover behind the stairwell to await the infidels.

Anazi crept out into the shadows.

73

Dante, still clutching the suitcase, and Tony knelt behind a chest-high concrete wall. A hail of errant gunfire blew chunks of mortar out of the buttress above them, shrouding them in gray dust.

"Let's get the hell out of here!" Dante said.

Tony scanned the smoke-filled warehouse for a possible exit. He gestured towards a faint light in the distance. "Let's go this way."

But before they could move, Tony heard the eerie click of a cocked handgun. Holding a Makarov pistol, Volkov looked down at him.

"Put your gun on the ground," Volkov said coldly.

Tony obeyed, and Volkov kicked it away.

Volkov pointed his pistol at Dante. "Now, hand over the suitcase."

"Fuck you!"

Volkov grabbed Tony by the shirt collar and pressed the gun to his temple.

"Give it to me now, or I'll blow his brains out."

Dante looked up at Volkov and calmly said, "Go ahead. I'm not giving up the money."

Volkov tightened his grip on Tony and glared at Dante. "Okay. Say 'goodbye.'"

Suddenly, there was a massive explosion as SWAT 1 blasted the garage door with plastic explosives. Stunned, Volkov momentarily lost his concentration. Tony pulled the sword from his cane, spun around, and skewered Volkov through the chest.

The big Russian crumpled on top of him with the blood-soaked blade protruding out of his back. Using all his strength, Tony rolled Volkov off and struggled to his feet.

Dante was astonished. "You know I didn't mean what I said, right? I was just trying —"

More gunshots emanated from the area around the blown-out garage door as SWAT 1 entered the warehouse with Crowley and Ross in tow.

Nervously, Dante quickly offered, "Help me get out of here, and I'll give you half the money."

"I don't want it."

In full panic mode, Dante played the guilt card. "Well, at least think about my parents! They'd be heartbroken if something happened to me."

Tony couldn't hide his absolute contempt for Dante. He pulled out the other handgun from his overcoat. For a split second, Dante thought Tony might actually kill him right then and there.

Instead, Tony said, "Let's get moving."

Limping badly without his cane, he led the way.

74

Inside the surveillance suite at the Monroe Hotel, Kline, Greco, Watkins, and Bashir watched the scene below. Hunkered down by a corner window, the FBI sharpshooter followed the action through the scope on his Remington 700 sniper rifle. Whirling over the panoramic scene, a Little Bird two-man helicopter with another sniper swept through the sky like a deadly wasp as more police cruisers and ambulances arrived on the street below.

SWAT 2 lined up outside the side door where Anazi had entered the warehouse the day before. A small blast blew out the door, and the team rapidly filed in. About five seconds later, a giant explosion rocked that corner of the building. Smoke, fire and screams for help poured out the door and fractured windows.

"Jesus! The place is booby trapped!" Kline yelled into his microphone as one smoldering SWAT member staggered out and fell face-first onto the ground. "Attention everyone! Be aware of IEDs and booby traps inside and around the warehouse!"

Watkins crossed himself.

75

Crowley and Ross made their way through the chaotic scene. A short distance in front of them, SWAT 1 encountered Gino hiding behind a stack of wood pallets near the van.

"Drop your weapon!" the team leader yelled as red-laser sighting lights danced across Gino's broad chest.

Forever the hothead, Gino baited them. "Fuck you, pigs!"

"Drop your weapon and put your hands over your head NOW!"

Gino quickly calculated the price of surrendering to save his life. Between the theft of the weapons and a possible murder raps for Raul Garcia and Tommy Mancini, he was looking at decades in the slammer and maybe even the death penalty.

Not worth it, he thought.

As Gino raised his handgun to shoot, a barrage of gunfire sent him down the highway to Hell.

While SWAT secured the area around Gino's bullet-riddled body, Crowley pulled Ross aside. "We'll have a better chance to find Tucci if we split up."

Tossing back her ponytail and clutching the machine gun with both hands, Ross said, "Agreed. I'll stick with these guys and call you if we find him."

"Good luck," Crowley said, veering off into the darkness.

76

Frantic NYPD and FBI field reports poured into the hotel suite. The agents watched as the warehouse stairwell door to the roof suddenly flew open, and three terrorist teams with the Stinger launchers and missiles scattered to separate sheltered locations on the far corners of the building. Hidden, the second RPG team stayed just inside the roof portal to guard their rear.

Speaking into his headset, Kline announced, "Attention! Three two-man teams of terrorists are on the roof with those Stingers! We've got to shut them down NOW! Snipers: Take any shot you've got!"

In addition to the FBI sniper in the room and the one soaring overhead in the helicopter, two other marksmen were positioned on other tall buildings surrounding the warehouse. They all peered through their scopes looking for prey, but the insurgents were too well-hidden for a clear shot.

Down on the roof, the terrorist teams scanned the horizon for the best targets. It was approaching dusk, but visibility was still good.

Abbas and Turan were the first to fire. Across the bay, about two miles away, a group of new high-rise apartment buildings gleamed in the setting sun. "The Scorpion" knew it was well within the range of a Stinger. Kneeling under a metal hood covering a ventilating system, Abbas used the launcher's infrared homing device to lock onto the center high-rise. Turan, knowing the dangers of being caught in the exhaust stream of a Stinger missile launch, knelt down safely beside his grandfather.

After Abbas pulled the trigger, a small ejection motor pushed the five-foot-long missile out a safe distance from the launcher before engaging the missile's two-stage solid-fuel sustainer, which accelerated the deadly projectile with its six-pound warhead to a speed of Mach 2.2. Five seconds later, the missile slammed into the glimmering forty-story luxury residence, creating a huge, deadly fireball.

As cheers erupted from the hunkered-down terrorists on the roof, the police snipers continued to scan for targets, but the insurgents were still difficult to see.

Next, Amal and Hasan launched one of their missiles towards a tall, brick office building about ten blocks to the north. The missile hit near the top of the structure, causing its magnificent clock tower to crumble and crash down onto the busy highway below, crushing many cars and their unfortunate occupants.

77

Frank Salvadore crept through the darkness with his shotgun at the ready. To his right, he spotted Tony and Dante stumbling through the shadows. He ran ahead to ambush them, lying in wait behind the five vans intended to transport the terrorists to the airports and beyond. When Tony and Dante passed by, Frank stepped out and surprised them.

"Frank! Thank God you're here!" Dante said. "We're looking for a way out. Any ideas?"

Frank raised the shotgun. "Yeah. But it'll cost you two million bucks."

Dante was in shock. "What the —?"

"Throw your gun over here, Tony," Frank said, pointing the shotgun at Tony's chest.

Tony complied. Frank picked up the handgun and shoved it under his belt.

Holding the bulging suitcase in front of his chest, Dante surreptitiously removed his pistol from his pocket.

Turning his sights onto Dante, Frank commanded, "Now, give me the money. Nice and easy."

"You're nothin' but a fuckin' punk."

"Yeah, a rich one."

Simultaneously, Dante threw the bulky suitcase at Frank and tried to fire his gun, but Frank pulled the trigger first. The shotgun blast blew off Dante's left arm just below the shoulder and spun him violently backwards against one of the vans.

Tony rushed to Dante's side and tried to stop the gushing blood by cinching his belt around the shredded stump.

Frank picked up the suitcase and took aim at Tony. "Sorry, but it looks like the 'Two Triggers' legend ends here."

Before he could fire, Anazi leapt up behind Frank, yanked his head back, and slit his throat from ear to ear.

As Frank's body slumped to the floor, Anazi pointed his handgun at Tony.

"You Americans are so predictable. Greed is your god. Now, prepare to meet mine."

Suddenly, Crowley's .44 Magnum spewed fire and lead from the shadows about forty yards away. Three bullets slammed into the van near Anazi, shattering the front windshield and blowing off the side mirror.

Ducking down, Anazi grabbed the suitcase and dashed off into the darkness.

Crowley ran up. "You okay, Tucci?"

Drenched in blood, Tony nodded. "Yeah, but Dante needs a medic immediately."

"Hold tight. SWAT will be here soon. I'm going after Anazi."

Crowley raced off in hot pursuit.

Lying limp and half-dead against the van's wheel well, Dante was slipping away fast. Tony cinched the belt tighter around Dante's horrific wound. "Hang in there, Dante. Help is on the way."

"Guess I should've listened to you and my old man," Dante slurred as blood dripped from the corner of his mouth. "It could be the death of me."

Tony wrapped his arms around Dante's shivering body. "Save your strength."

Dante looked up at him with dilated eyes. "Tell... tell my family that I'm sorry... and..."

With a final shudder, Dante bled out.

Stirring from deep inside the warehouse, Tony watched the beams of tactical flashlights slice through the smoke and haze as SWAT crept silently closer.

"Freeze!" yelled the SWAT 1 leader who appeared out of nowhere, pointing his M4 carbine directly at Tony.

"Stand down! He's with us!" cautioned Ross as she moved in with the rest of the team.

"Are you injured, Mr. Tucci?"

"No. I'm okay... Just help me get up."

Ross and some SWAT members pulled him to his feet.

"Where's your cane?" asked Ross.

Tony gestured back into the gloomy warehouse. "I had to use it on Volkov. He's not going anywhere."

As SWAT 1 departed to continue their search of the warehouse, Tony knelt down beside Dante and gently removed the gold crucifix from his neck. Holding the bloody icon in the palm of his hand, Tony dreaded the thought of telling Mario and Carla their eldest child was dead.

Another deafening burst of gunfire echoed from deep within the building.

Ross implored, "Come on, let's get outside!"

And they walked through the smoldering ruins towards the light.

78

In the rear of the warehouse, SWAT 3 members carefully approached the staircase to the roof. Three terrorists with an RPG and machine guns waited to attack them. Sensing danger, the SWAT captain knelt and raised his fist. His men dropped to the ground and switched off their flashlights.

Suddenly, gunfire erupted from behind a barricade of scrap metal next to the stairwell. The captain went down with a lethal gunshot wound in the upper thigh, which severed his femoral artery. As his team fired on the barricade, two SWAT members dragged their leader back to a more secure location, frantically applying pressure to the gruesome wound and yelling for medical support.

As the last young Muslim driver and Mahdi laid down covering fire, Sakhr popped up and launched an RPG at the advancing police. The grenade exploded into a concrete abutment, rocking the entire warehouse and spraying chunks of concrete in a wide arc.

Two deafening flash-bang grenades exploded behind the barricade as SWAT 3 converged on the confused insurgents. Mahdi and Sakhr tried to load another RPG into the launcher, but they were too disoriented by the blasts. Lurching around in the fray, both insurgents were quickly cut down by SWAT gunfire.

With a frantic change of heart, the young Muslim driver threw down his weapon and raised his hands. "I surrender! Please don't shoot!" he yelled. The panic-stricken terrorist was immediately slammed to the floor and cuffed with zip ties.

Sadly, the NYPD medics arrived too late to save the decorated captain.

Just as SWAT 3 prepared to ascend the staircase, SWAT 1 arrived on the scene. After conferring with Captain Gomez, they were instructed to merge ranks and make a joint assault on the terrorists on the roof.

It would be a deadly climb. Ahmed and Sayid waited for them at the top of the stairs, intent on slaughtering every infidel in sight.

79

Crowley tracked Anazi into the deepest recesses of the warehouse. Crouching down behind a rusty old forklift, Crowley watched the terrorist rendezvous with another man who was hiding at the top of a secluded stairway leading to the basement. He didn't know it, but it was Anazi's close associate, Kamel Al-Masud.

As the men disappeared down the staircase, Crowley followed. After he checked the steel door for explosive booby-traps, Crowley entered a pitch-black concrete passage. The moment he put on the night vision goggles, gunfire exploded from farther down the eerie hallway. Bullets ricocheted all around him. One shot grazed his left arm, causing a minor flesh wound.

Crowley dove to the floor as Anazi tried to fire again, but the gun jammed and he threw it away. In response, Crowley fired six thunderous shots from the .44 Magnum pistol and quickly reloaded.

In a mad dash, Anazi and Masud burst through another door, racing deeper into an underground labyrinth of small claustrophobic spaces, dripping pipes, and seeping walls. Behind them, Crowley's footfalls echoed louder and louder.

The two terrorists knew every corner of the warehouse. They opened a sewer hatch and leapt down into knee-deep slime. Trudging along under the street, ancient storm drains drooled down and swarms of rats scurried along the walls. After about thirty stench-filled yards, the terrorists climbed out of the sewer canal and ran to a door secured with a brand-new combination lock, which they had placed there earlier.

Anazi quickly dialed in the numbers and unlocked it. He handed the suitcase to Masud, telling him to go ahead and wait for him—just as Crowley splashed into the sewer.

Leaving the door slightly ajar, Anazi withdrew his long knife and retreated into the dark.

80

The FBI agents in the surveillance suite continued to monitor the chaos around the warehouse. Given the positions of the terrorist teams on the roof, the only place for an aerial assault from SWAT 4 was on the northeastern corner.

A converted black Bell tactical helicopter loaded with eight SWAT members zoomed up a side street, barely a few feet off the ground. Then it rose vertically, hovering over the corner of the warehouse.

Two SWAT members managed to jump out of the helicopter onto the roof before Abu Bakr could fire his missile. The projectile slammed into the engine casing just below the main rotor. The ensuing explosion flung the rotor blade high into the sky as the helicopter's flaming carcass crashed violently to the street below, killing everyone still on board.

Again, excited cheering erupted from the insurgents; however, the backwash from the missile launch knocked Abu Bakr's partner, Kafil, out into the open. The sniper in the smaller, agile FBI helicopter soaring above killed him instantly.

81

Amal and Hasan searched the horizon for more targets. Since the warehouse was close to both La Guardia and JFK Airports, they looked for low-hanging fruit, spotting a commercial jetliner rising in the East. It was only about a mile and a half away, but Amal would have to leave the safety of their brick shelter to take the shot. With no time to spare, the former Saddam soldiers embraced, knowing martyrdom was a heartbeat away.

Hasan laid down cover fire with a machine gun while Amal broke into the open to launch their last missile. Just as he was locking the computerized guidance system onto the exhaust of the airliner, the FBI sniper in the Monroe surveillance suite executed a perfect headshot. Amal dropped dead, and the launcher tumbled to the ground.

"Nice shootin,' Tex!" Kline said with a broad smile, but then yelled angrily into his headset. "People! Why are there still jetliners in the air? Every airport in the vicinity should be shut down!"

Wasting no time, Hasan dropped his gun and dashed toward the launcher, but a volley of SWAT fire punched his ticket to Paradise.

82

A small helicopter from a local TV station suddenly popped up and hovered a few feet above the roofline of the warehouse. A cameraman began to shoot footage of the frenzied scene.

"What the hell?" Kline yelled into his headset. "Get those idiots out of there!"

Waiting inside the small room at the top of the roof stairwell, Ahmed and Sayid could hear the SWAT members climb the steel staircase.

Sayid pointed his AK-47 down the dark passageway and unleashed a long, random burst of gunfire. Bullets bounced off the walls and steps, killing two SWAT members and injuring three others. The law officers returned fire, knocking the gun out of Sayid's hands.

While several SWAT members attended to their injured comrades, the others stormed up to the top of the stairwell.

Ahmed fired the RPG launcher at the hovering TV helicopter. The grenade slammed into the cockpit, blowing apart the pilot and cameraman.

Seconds later, Ahmed and Sayid were dead.

SWAT regrouped and prepared for a final assault against the remaining terrorists on the roof.

83

Perfectly hidden beneath a metal canopy, Abu Bakr had seen the FBI sniper's muzzle flash from the window across the street on the top floor of the Monroe.

Since his partner was dead, he had to reload the Stinger himself in his cramped hiding spot. Once the missile was ready to fire, Abu Bakr peered up at the window through his magnified scope. He could see a group of infidels looking down on the warehouse with their fancy binoculars and cameras.

Taking careful aim through a two-foot-wide gap in the canopy, he pulled the trigger.

The missile soared into the corner of the hotel right below the surveillance suite. The explosion blasted a crater two stories tall in the side of the building, spewing bricks and debris down onto the police staging area on the street.

Smoke billowed out of the rubble and flames flared at the edges of the gaping hole. The bodies of Greco, Watkins, and the sniper were buried under the partially collapsed roof.

Bloody and bruised, Kline and Bashir somehow managed to stumble out of what was left of the demolished suite and into the dark, dusty hallway.

Abu Bakr's celebration was short-lived as SWAT quickly moved in and cut him down.

84

Crowley climbed out of the sewer canal and dropped his night goggles to the ground. He carefully approached the half-open door, gripping the handgun with both hands.

As he reached for the door, Anazi vaulted from the shadows. His knife slashed into Crowley's right shoulder as they crashed to the floor. Anazi repeatedly stabbed at him, slicing Crowley's leg.

Face-to-face, they rolled on the ground, each trying to grab the other's weapon with their free hand. As their eyes locked, Crowley saw his own reflection in Anazi's inert left eye, but the right one burned with an intense hatred.

Inches away, Anazi hissed, "I'm going to cut your head off!"

Despite the searing pain from his knife wounds, Crowley laughed. "Pack your bags for Gitmo, asshole!"

As they continued to wrestle violently, Anazi's shirt ripped open, revealing a suicide vest laden with explosives. Crowley head-butted him, but it only made the terrorist angrier.

Finally, Anazi got the upper hand, straddling Crowley and slowly pushing the knife down toward his throat. Using all his strength, Crowley moved the barrel of his gun closer to Anazi's chest.

Flashing a demonic smile, Anazi said, "Go ahead, shoot me! Send me to Paradise and yourself to Hell."

Crowley pulled the trigger. The explosion from the heavy handgun was deafening, and both men were momentarily stunned. Anazi lost his knife as he lurched backward, blood oozing from a nasty wound to his left shoulder.

Dazed and gasping for breath, Crowley laid on his back beside the sewer trench. The gun slipped from his hand into the muck.

Clutching his wounded shoulder, Anazi stumbled through the door, and bolted it from the other side.

Crowley struggled to his feet and found Anazi's knife. He tried to pry open the door, but the tip of the blade snapped off. Frantically, he tried again, wedging the knife deeper into the frame until the door finally popped open.

The exhausted Federal agent pulled his service handgun from his hip holster and cautiously climbed the staircase, following the blood trail. On the landing at street level, he found Anazi's bloody clothes and an empty backpack.

Crowley pushed the door open, revealing a chaotic street scene filled with police and frightened civilians running everywhere.

Anazi, Masud, and the suitcase stuffed with cash were in the wind.

85

Knowing they were the only survivors of the original five teams, Abbas "The Scorpion" and his grandson crouched in the far corner of the warehouse roof. The Taliban fighters had another missile loaded and ready to launch, but they could see numerous SWAT members slowly inching toward their position.

The end was near...

Abbas sneaked a quick look down at the street, but there were no decent targets. He looked to the skies for any aircraft, but all flights were grounded.

The old warrior shrugged at the hopelessness of the situation. He had been on and off the battlefield for more than forty years, protecting his homeland from foreign invaders—but now *he* was the aggressor in a land far from home.

Abbas knew he would never again see the sun set on the Hindu Kush, enjoy the camaraderie of his fellow freedom fighters, or know his great-grandchildren. Heartbroken, he looked over at Turan, who was clearly terrified as SWAT drew closer.

A short, controlled burst of gunfire rang out. Turan was hit in the foot, and he dropped his handgun.

Abbas hugged his grandson, sharing a fleeting moment of deep affection and respect. Then, Abbas rose from behind their shelter and tried to lock the launcher's sighting system on another high-rise in the distance, but SWAT strafed him with a barrage of bullets.

As he tumbled backwards, he reflexively pulled the trigger launching the last Stinger missile straight up into the dusky sky—the dying flare of another failed jihad.

Turan was captured alive.

86

Tony and Agent Ross slowly hobbled out into the street from the warehouse. Sirens blared, emergency personnel shouted for help, and horns honked with an existential urgency.

They stopped at the bustling triage station where numerous SWAT members and civilians were being treated for every imaginable injury: gunshots, shrapnel wounds, burns, smoke inhalation, and vicious cuts.

Over at the Command Post, Captain Gomez directed paramedics and ambulances towards the warehouse to retrieve the injured, dying, and dead. Amid the still-smoldering wreckage of the helicopters, body bags awaited removal to the morgue. On the perimeter of the three-block radius around the warehouse, NYPD cruisers formed barricades to keep the lookie loos and throngs of news teams at bay.

Covered with soot and dust, Kline and Bashir emerged from the hotel entrance, lucky to be alive after the Stinger missile explosion. As they approached the triage station, Crowley staggered towards them. Blood dripped down his arms from the gunshot and multiple knife wounds.

"Crowley! You okay?" Kline asked.

"Anazi got away," he winced, pushing back the pain. "I was face-to-face with him, but he escaped with some other guy."

341

Bashir supported the tottering Homeland Security agent who was about to pass out from blood loss. Two paramedics ran up to help.

"Anazi is wearing a suicide vest and carrying a black suitcase. Get the word out," Crowley told Kline.

Kline picked up a police radio off a gurney to alert everyone that the international fugitive was on the run.

Seconds later, there was a loud explosion over on the busy street where Anazi had disappeared. A cloud of thick gray smoke rose over the darkening skyline.

Kline listened intently to the chaotic radio reports. An NYPD sergeant verified that two of his officers had confronted a man with a suitcase who fitted Anazi's description. The man was highly agitated and refused their commands to stop and surrender. As they approached, he blew himself up.

The devastating detonation killed the policemen and several civilians, and scattered thousands of $100 bills into the air. First responders were just starting to sift through the carnage as surviving locals scurried around the blast area, grabbing handfuls of bloodstained cash.

Despite the additional death and destruction, Kline was pleased Anazi had apparently checked into the Afterworld. He turned to give the news to Crowley and Bashir when he saw Tony and Agent Ross nearby. Ross was in the process of removing the GPS tracking device from Tony. Kline recoiled at the sight of Tony's blood-drenched clothes.

"Are you injured, Tucci?"

Tony swallowed a small pile of aspirin to suppress the searing pain in his crippled right leg. "That's Dante's blood, not mine."

Ross looked up at the ravaged, imploded corner of the Monroe Hotel, which was still burning. "Where are Watkins and Greco?"

Kline shook his head. "Gone. One of the terrorists fired a Stinger missile right at us. Bashir and I are the only survivors."

He leaned against a police car, gazing at the surreal landscape. "A lot of good people died. But we've secured the stolen weapons, and all the terrorists are dead or in custody."

"And that explosion?" she asked.

"Looks like Anazi blew himself up. Crowley confirmed he was wearing a suicide vest."

"Good riddance!"

Tony's smartphone buzzed and he checked the screen. "I have to take this call. Excuse me."

As he turned away to answer, Kline continued to monitor the frenzied chatter on his police radio.

After whispering into the phone for less than a minute, Tony hung up with a heavy sigh. "That was Carla Conti. Mario just passed away... I have to leave."

"Of course. I'll get someone to drive you," Kline said. "Thanks again for coming forward, Mr. Tucci. Your information made all the difference and helped save countless lives. If there's a hero in this mess, it's you."

"Nonsense. I'm just a chauffeur."

"I promised to protect your identity, and I will."

"Good. Unlike those terrorists, I'd prefer *not* to be a martyr."

They solemnly shook hands.

* * * *

Ross saw Crowley being helped onto a gurney and rushed over to join him. The paramedics had stripped off his bloody shirt and started to dress his numerous wounds.

"That's a lot of blood, cowboy," she said.

In a state of mild shock, Crowley allowed himself a small smile. "Yeah… I might need a transfusion. I'm Type A."

Ross laughed. "Figures."

"What about drinks instead? My treat."

Bashir, still at Crowley's side, tried to insert some levity. "Hey! Am I invited?"

"No," they said in unison.

87

After getting cleaned up at his athletic club and retrieving the limo, Tony picked up Carla and Angela from the hospital and drove them home.

Mario's abrupt passing had devastated everyone, and the mood was very somber.

Tony dreaded the task of telling the grieving women about Dante's death, but he feared they would hear about it secondhand, particularly if the media blasted it across the airwaves.

Once they were gathered in the living room, each holding a stiff drink, Tony broke the news. He spared them the graphic details surrounding Dante's cold-blooded murder, but they suspected it had been terrible.

Despite her mixed feelings about her narcissistic older brother, Angela was upset by his sudden death. Carla wept too; however, after years of brushing up against the flame, she knew Dante's demise was pre-ordained.

Mario's passing was another matter. Everyone had been concerned about his failing health, but the Don was so passionate and bigger than life, he seemed immortal. He had always been there, a strong and powerful presence, and now he was gone.

SATURDAY

88

Sands Point
10:00 a.m.

A profound sadness surrounding the deaths of Mario and Dante hung heavy in the air. The mansion seemed empty, hollowed-out to its core.

The Conti women remained upstairs. Carla, heavily medicated, rested in the master suite while Angela wept and slept in her bedroom. The housekeeping staff went about their chores, maintaining low, hushed profiles.

Sitting alone at the desk in the library, Tony stared at a stack of message slips and notes before him. He was exhausted and still in pain, both physically and emotionally, but he had no choice except to keep going, tackling each and every task.

First and foremost, Tony had to handle all the funeral arrangements. Tony suggested there be two different funerals: a small private service for Dante with the immediate family only, followed by a larger, more opulent service for Mario later in the week; but Carla said she couldn't handle the stress and anxiety of such a long, drawn-out ordeal. She insisted on a joint funeral as soon as possible, preferably on late Monday afternoon.

Tony spent the rest of the morning writing and submitting Mario's obituary to the newspapers, fielding more phone calls from friends and family, and planning the wake with Chef Ciro.

Carla, Angela, and Tony agreed not to disclose anything about Dante's death to anyone until the authorities completed their investigation. Those revelations were going to cause a shit storm and Tony still had to clean up Dante's other messes too.

He got a call from Danny Demarco, the young manager of Inferno. Danny couldn't find Dante and was freaking out about the big opening scheduled for that night. Tony told him Dante was unavailable and "the show must go on." He put Danny completely in charge of Inferno, telling him that if everything went smoothly over the weekend, he would get a nice bonus. Danny was thrilled.

Next, Tony decided to be pro-active regarding Dante's outstanding loans from the mob families in Philly and Boston, who advanced the money to bankroll his nightclub ambitions and insane gambling habits. He called his friend Dominic Romano, asking him to contact those moneylenders, confirming they would all be repaid soon.

Tony suspected that Dante had other unpaid markers on the street and the final tally would probably be much higher, which he would have to deal with as well.

He also spoke with Agent Ross, who said they needed to debrief him about exactly what occurred in the warehouse when all hell broke loose. To protect his privacy, Kline and his team agreed to meet Tony away from FBI Headquarters, because the press was staked out there 24/7 waiting for more news updates. The meeting was set for Sunday afternoon at a secluded hotel in downtown Manhattan.

2:00 p.m.

Wearily, Tony put down his reading glasses and rubbed the bridge of his nose. He turned to the TV in the corner of the library. The news coverage of the thwarted terrorist attack dominated every network and cable channel. As local, state, and federal investigators and forensic teams combed through all the evidence in and around the epic battle scene, the media speculated on every fact and rumor.

Most disturbing was the emerging body count. Besides the dead terrorists, twenty law enforcement officers and more than fifty citizens had been killed. Scores of others had been maimed and wounded. Thanks to Tony's timely visit to FBI headquarters, a much greater tragedy had been averted—but the loss of innocent human life was still staggering.

As more and more information dribbled out about the terrorist attack, pushy news crews hounded the families of the wounded and deceased for interviews and stories. Luckily, Dante's pivotal role in the disaster had not yet come to light, but Tony knew it was only a matter of time before all the awful details came out.

To preserve the reputation of Conti Construction Inc., Tony contacted their PR firm in New York City. For a staggering fee, their crisis management team devised a two-pronged publicity campaign. First, they would use their media contacts to develop stories about how the company had helped build the city and state's transportation infrastructure, creating thousands of well-paying jobs, and for its many charitable contributions to the community. Secondly, they would try to get ahead of the news and leak stories about Dante as the "rogue son" with an out-of-control gambling addiction. By creatively spinning the facts, they planned to portray Dante not as a traitor, but rather as an accidental hero. The revised storyline would assert that Dante valiantly sacrificed himself in the firefight with the terrorists.

It was lipstick on a pig, but the gullible media would probably run with it.

The Conti estate was not yet under siege, but Tony knew the press would be storming the gate soon. Consequently, he gave Enzo Colombo, the affable old guard, a two-week vacation and hired a large security firm to man the front entrance, patrol the property, and if necessary, secure the funeral service to keep the press away.

89

Throughout the day, as Tony handled one crisis after another, he worried about how Paolo Mancini was holding up. When he finally spoke with him on the phone, Paolo was inconsolable.

The FBI had arrived at his home in East Harlem with multiple warrants, questioned him for hours about Tommy, and seized all of his son's online, phone, and other personal records.

Then, after the FBI left, the press descended—pounding on his door and clamoring for a statement about his dead, traitorous son.

Riddled with guilt and anxiety about Tommy's role in the arms theft, Paolo repeatedly broke down on the phone. Once again, Tony offered to visit him, but Paolo discouraged it.

Tony told Paolo to remain inside his house and not answer the door under any circumstance. He also offered to help him with all the funeral arrangements for Tommy.

Tearfully, Paolo thanked Tony for his support and announced he was shutting Mancini's down for the rest of the year—and perhaps, forever.

SUNDAY

90

It was a quiet day at the Conti estate.

Beneath gloomy gray skies, Carla and Tony took a long walk on the beach. They rarely spoke, preferring the natural sights and sounds to comfort them as they sauntered along the water. Tony marveled at Carla's exquisite stoicism and strength after almost two days of incomprehensible sorrow.

After a while, they sat on the sea wall and looked out over The Sound. For a few brief moments, they were at peace until a solitary Canada goose landed near the shoreline. As the big bird flapped its wings in the cold winter breeze, Carla flinched.

"Are you okay?" Tony asked softly.

Watching the large bird walk slowly along the sand, she replied, "Did you know that geese mate for life?"

Carla was implying that she was destined to be a widow forever, but Tony didn't buy it. She was just starting the grieving process and it would take a long time to adjust to life without Mario.

"I think I read somewhere that just because a goose loses their mate doesn't mean they can't find a new partner later in life. Like humans, they are complicated and have their own unique personalities."

Carla shrugged and shifted her gaze out across the bay. "Right now, I only care about my children. By the way, is there any word from the prison authorities about letting Johnnie come to the funeral tomorrow?"

She was referring to her son Giovanni who was serving five years at Big Sandy, a federal penitentiary in Kentucky. He was halfway through his mandated incarceration after Dante got him mixed up in a disastrous drug trafficking scheme.

"I doubt it's going to work out. Our attorneys offered to pay the Justice Department $30,000 to cover all the expenses associated with transporting him to and from prison for the day, but the U.S. Attorney who prosecuted him is raising a big stink."

Tony took a deep breath. "To make matters worse, Johnnie got into a fight with another prisoner last week."

"Oh, my God! Is he okay?"

"Yes, but the man who attacked him was severely injured. Johnnie claims it was self-defense and the matter is being investigated. It could jeopardize his plans for an early parole."

Tony put his hand on her shoulder. "I just heard about it on Friday while we were all at the hospital. There was too much going on to burden you with more bad news."

Wiping away a tear, she said, "You're always looking out for us, Tony."

If she only knew the whole story…

Johnnie's predicament was a lot more serious than Tony let on. He had been jumped by a prominent member of the Aryan Brotherhood while exercising in the prison yard. The skinhead murderer, who was serving life without parole, figured that killing the son of a Mafia don would enhance his reputation within the prison's primitive pecking order. However, he got a rude awakening when Johnnie grabbed the shiv and used it on the bungling assassin, who died a few days later. His neo-Nazi brothers promised revenge and Johnnie was placed in solitary confinement for his own protection.

As small waves lapped against the shoreline and a chilly wind blew in across the water, Carla pulled up her coat collar and quietly wept.

The goose flew south.

91

New York City
3:00 p.m.

Tony drove Angela into the City to see Hal. After dropping her off, he met with Agents Kline and Ross for a few hours to be debriefed about everything he had witnessed leading up to and during the terrorist siege on the previous Friday. They had a long list to cover.

Since the tape recording from Tony's wire was destroyed in the Stinger missile explosion at the Monroe Hotel, the FBI agents needed to reconstruct all the events inside the warehouse. Specifically, they wanted to know how Tony's cane sword came to be embedded in Victor Volkov's chest and the details surrounding Dante's death. More importantly, the Feds sought information about his interaction with Mustafa Al-Anazi and any of the other terrorists.

They informed him that a thorough investigation into all of Dante's affairs would be ongoing, including his new nightclub. Tony told them everything he knew about the operation.

The agents confirmed that Tommy Mancini's death would be ruled a homicide, not an unintentional drug overdose. When the agents searched Tommy's van, they found the handwritten note from Gino with the address of the Conti Construction staging site in Bowery Bay. Further, they matched Tommy's tire prints to tracks found outside the Conti office trailer, as well as evidence from inside his van linking Al "The Frog" Franchetti and Frank Salvadore to the murder.

Knowing that Tommy had been manipulated and murdered by Dante and his henchmen would provide little solace to the grieving Paolo, but it did help to mitigate Tommy's role in the conspiracy. Better to be a drug-addicted pawn than a money-grubbing traitor.

Autopsies had been performed on both Dante and Tommy, and their bodies could be released. Tony arranged for them to be quietly transported to the same funeral home where Mario was being prepared for an open-casket service.

He washed his hands of Gino, Al, and Frank, suggesting the Feds bury them in shallow, unmarked graves worthy of their wretched deeds and wasted lives.

During the course of the meeting, Tony learned that Homeland Security Agent Jake Crowley was in the hospital being treated for infections from wounds he received during his fight with Anazi in the sewer, but would be released soon. Tony passed on his good wishes for a speedy recovery.

Before they parted company, Kline told Tony that a big press conference was scheduled for the next day at noon. At that time, Dante's role in the foiled terrorist plot would be fully revealed to the world; however, as Kline promised, Tony's involvement would remain confidential.

Lastly, Kline returned Tony's cherished cane saying, "Technically, we should confiscate this since it is evidence in our ongoing investigation and contains a concealed weapon; however, given your service to our country, my bosses in Washington made an exception. But please, only use it as a walking stick in the future."

92

Later that evening while relaxing in his cottage, Tony reflected on the past week's events and his lifelong relationship with Mario.

He remembered a conversation he'd had with Mario years earlier when they were discussing the great Roman emperors during a late-night session in the library. At the time, Mario was reading the legendary work *Meditations* by Marcus Aurelius.

He quoted from the text, "Death smiles at us all, all a man can do is smile back."

Tony hoisted a glass of cognac in honor of the late Don. And then, for the first time in many years, he finished the rest of the bottle.

MONDAY

93

Sands Point
Noon

As the entire nation watched, the Secretary of Homeland Security, Attorney General, Director of the FBI, Governor of the State of New York, Mayor of New York City and the NYPD Police Commissioner held a joint televised press conference, presenting all the known details of the foiled terrorist plot.

Shortly after Dante's involvement was announced, the press began to gather outside the front gate of the Conti estate. Fortunately, Tony's PR team and security detail were ready to respond.

Tony fielded another frantic phone call from Danny Demarco at Inferno who was watching the live press conference. As usual, he was freaking out. He couldn't believe Dante was involved in the terrorist attack, but Danny was far more concerned about the rash of visits he'd received in the last 24 hours.

First, the FBI had showed up with a search warrant and seized Dante's laptop and many documents from the office. Later, two NYPD homicide detectives dropped by to question Danny about the suspicious death of the owner of The Palace. And finally, a scary guy named Eddie Giordano burst into the club screaming that Dante owed him some big money and he better be paid fast or "heads would roll."

Tony told the panicked nightclub manager to fully cooperate with the authorities—and he would personally handle the problem with Giordano.

Once he calmed down, Danny confirmed that the opening weekend at Inferno had been a great success. The social media buzz and press reports were very positive, and net profits exceeded $500,000. The cash was stashed in the safe and the credit card transactions were being processed by the bookkeeper. Danny also informed Tony that another shady character, Dino Scarfetti, had given him some envelopes filled with cash, telling him to make sure they were delivered to Gino or Dante. Plus, a woman named Alexandra Dufrane had called twice, requesting a confidential meeting.

Tony knew both Scarfetti and Ms. Dufrane by reputation. He wasn't surprised Dante had let the notorious drug dealer and madam ply their trades at Inferno in exchange for a hefty cut of their illicit profits.

Before they signed off, Tony and Danny set up a time later in the week to have a discussion about the future of the club. Until then, Danny had carte blanche to run things.

Tony got Giordano's cell number from an old contact on the street, and gave him a call. Before he could say a word, the psychotic loan shark started to rant and rave about getting his money back—and even fired up his legendary chainsaw to make the point. Once he heard all the details of Dante's loan, Tony assured him the debt and interest would be repaid in full within a week.

Giordano put the chainsaw away.

Tony added Eddie's loan to the pile of Dante's markers, which pushed his debts to well over $1.5 million dollars.

94

A soft snow fell on a sea of black umbrellas at St. John's Cemetery.

Hundreds of mourners gathered at the Conti family's opulent gravesite for the burials of Mario and Dante, following a funeral mass at the old church in East Harlem. A mountain of flower arrangements and wreaths ringed two polished bronze caskets. Security barriers at the cemetery entrance held back the throngs of reporters who clamored for interviews with the family and friends.

Dressed in black from head to toe, Carla sat front and center. With Tony and Angela by her side, Carla projected a public image of elegance and fortitude in the face of overwhelming grief.

The old family priest, Father Cerruti, quoted from the Bible: "God is our refuge and strength, an ever-present help to those in trouble. Therefore, we will not fear though the earth give way and the mountains fall into the heart of the sea ..."

Carla gripped Tony and Angela's hands as she began to gently sob.

Tony saw Jake Crowley, his arm in a sling, standing alone under a tree far from the crowd.

The priest continued, "... and though you have made me see troubles, many and bitter, you will restore my life again; from the depths of the earth you will bring me up. You will increase my honor and comfort me once again."

Making eye contact with the federal agent, Tony subtly lifted his cane and nodded.

Crowley smiled.

95

Sands Point
7:00 p.m.

The wake was in full swing.

Countless family members and friends milled about the palatial Conti estate, crowding the buffet tables and lining up at the full bars. As a pianist played a Chopin nocturne on the Steinway in the living room, Angela worked the rooms. The tearful hostess greeted guests and encouraged the staff to create a warm and comfortable atmosphere. It was in stark contrast to the throngs of unruly reporters and TV camera crews staked outside the entrance to the compound.

Meanwhile, Carla secluded herself in the library. When she ran out of ice, Tony volunteered to go to the kitchen to replenish it.

As he weaved through the crowd with the refilled silver ice bucket in hand, numerous guests stopped him for fleeting condolences and whispered requests.

Tony noticed a man sitting in a corner reading the *Times*. The front page was covered with photos depicting the epic battle at the warehouse and the collateral damage from the Stinger missile attacks. The headline read:

Unidentified Informant Is Real Hero
in Terrorist Attack

Leonardo Scarpia, the General Manager of Conti Construction, approached Tony. With a weathered face, jack-o-lantern jaw, and calloused hands the size of baseball gloves, he was a formidable figure who looked very uncomfortable in his cheap suit. Leo was a good, honest man who thrived best on the job site, moving dirt and pouring concrete.

"Hello, Leo."

"It's a sad day. Mario was a great man."

Tony could smell bourbon on his breath. "Very true."

"And Dante? Jesus! What a way to go," Leo said, shaking his head.

"So how are things at Conti Construction?"

Leo pulled him into a corner. "Not good. I don't want to speak poorly of the dead, but we both know Dante was never cut out to run the business. A lot of stuff has fallen through the cracks. Important decisions need to be made about contracts, capital investments, labor issues, and more. I can't handle it all by myself."

He tugged at his tight necktie. "I know Mrs. Conti is grieving, but now she owns the company and…"

Tony interrupted. "Can this wait, Leo?"

Leo looked worried. "You need to know something else. The accountant and I just went over the books. It looks like Dante embezzled at least half a million from the company."

Tony glared hard at Leo. "Listen. I don't want Carla to know anything about that—*ever*. She's already dealing with too much… Trust me, I'll figure out a way to replace the money."

"Thanks. That's a load off, but I could really use your help. The ice is melting and…"

"Yes, it is," Tony said, holding up the ice bucket. "Look, Leo, we'll sit down and go over everything in a few days, okay?"

Leo looked very relieved. "Thanks, Tony. I feel better already."

96

As Tony walked through the lobby towards the library, he spotted Father Cerruti sipping tea in a corner by himself.

"Thank you again for the service today, Father. It was very moving."

"I was honored you asked me to do it."

"Tell me, have you received any substantial donations in the last few days for the St. Anthony's project to aid the homeless?"

"No. We had a Board meeting about it right before the funeral service. Donations are seriously lagging. We could really use a big infusion of cash to finally break ground," Cerruti said. "There are so many needy souls to help."

"Be patient, Father. God works in mysterious ways."

97

Walking over to the library door, Tony removed his phone and dialed "The Kid."

"Yo! What's happening, T?" asked Jeremy.

"I can't talk right now. There's a lot going on with the Conti family."

"Yeah, I heard about Dante and those terrorists. Were you in the middle of all that shit?"

"Like you always say, 'If I told ya, I'd have to—'"

"Touché, my man!" laughed Jeremy.

Tony took a deep breath and exhaled. "Nicky Bruno never made that donation to the church—so let's flush him."

"My pleasure. Who gets all his cash and liquidated assets? I can easily access about $5 million."

"After you wash it through the offshore accounts, give an anonymous donation of $2 million to St. Anthony's for that homeless project. Next, I'm going to need another $2 million by the end of the week to cover all of Dante's debts. I think it's only fair that Nicky picks up that tab since he tried to kill his father. And then split the remainder of the funds between the usual nonprofit charities and veteran's groups."

"Nicky is going to go ballistic!"

"Screw him. He had the chance to do the right thing."

"You know, he's gonna come after you, Tony. He's still a very dangerous dude."

"I'll deal with it later."

Condensation was forming on the sides of the slippery ice bucket. "I have to go, Jeremy. Thanks again for all your help."

"We're still 'The White Hats', baby!"

98

"Sorry, it took me so long to get the ice, but there's a lot of people out there," Tony said as he freshened Carla's tumbler of scotch.

Taking a sip from the glass, she said, "God, I hate wakes. Always have."

Looking tired and emotionally wrung out, Carla sat alone in one of the big high-back chairs facing the fireplace, with Buddy at her feet. There was an old photo album spread across her lap. Tony snuck a glance at the open book to see some faded wedding pictures from many years ago.

"Is there anything else I can do for you, Carla?"

"Yes. Please sit with me."

Tony stared down at Mario's empty chair and hesitated.

Carla sensed his reluctance, touching his hand. "It's okay, Tony. Besides, I insist. It will make an old widow happy."

He poured himself a glass of cognac and sat down. "I'm so sorry about Mario and Dante. I wish I could have done more."

"Nonsense. Mario had a good life, and thanks to you, he was blessed with an extra twenty years."

Carla held a rosary and Dante's crucifix in her hands. Before telling Carla about the death of her eldest son on Friday night, Tony had carefully cleaned the blood off the gold cross and chain. Now, it gleamed in the reflected light of the fire.

"And Dante..." she continued, wiping away a solitary tear, "Well, no one could have saved him."

In silence, they watched the flames dance around the large oak logs in the fireplace. Time seemed to stop as they contemplated the past and future.

Finally, Carla downed the rest of her drink and stood. "I really need to go lie down. I've got a splitting headache."

Tony stood too, but she gently pushed him back down into Mario's old chair. "You stay. I'll see you tomorrow."

Tony watched her leave the room.

Buddy nuzzled his head under Tony's hand, wanting to be petted. Tony complied and then turned back to face the fire.

After a while, there was knock at the door. A well-dressed gentleman peeked in. "Excuse me, Mr. Tucci," he stuttered as if in the presence of great power. "A mutual friend said you might be able to help me."

Tony leaned farther back into the chair and said, "Come in."

Epilogue

New York Harbor

In the dead of night, an Algerian cargo ship slowly pulled out of the Port of New York at the mouth of the Hudson River. The busy crew yelled various commands in Arabic as they secured the vessel for the long journey across the Atlantic.

Deep below the deck in a secluded bay, a man in a hammock gently swayed with the motion of the departing ship.

His face was hidden and a crude, bloodstained bandage was taped to his left shoulder.

A Quran, bookmarked with an old photo of a recently deceased friend, lay beside him.

Tortured by a recurring nightmare, the man was unable to sleep. Instead, he stared out a porthole at the glittering New York City skyline in the distance— wondering why Allah had betrayed him.

Cast of Characters

Ali – FBI informant
Jeremy "The Kid" Allen – Computer savant & NSA hacker
Carmine Bertoli – Don of prominent New York family
Nicky & Benny Bruno – Planned the assassination of Mario Conti
Carlos & Mateo – Sinaloa Cartel coyotes
Father Cerruti – Family priest
Clerk – Monroe Hotel, Brooklyn
Enzo Colombo – Gatekeeper of Conti Estate
Conti Family:
>   **Mario Conti** – Godfather
>   **Carla Conti** – Wife of Mario
>   **Dante Conti** – Conti Construction & Inferno Nightclub
>   **Giovanni "Johnnie" Conti** – In prison for drug trafficking
>   **Angela Conti** – Graduate student
>   **Dante's Crew:**
>   **Gino "Juice" Marino** – Capo
>   **Al "The Frog" Franchetti** - Enforcer
>   **Frank Salvadore** – Ex-military weapons/explosives expert
>   **Manny Rizzo** – Ex-con, electrician & security expert

Jake Crowley – Special Agent/Homeland Security Investigations
Danny Demarco – Manager of Inferno
Destiny and Godiva – Call girls
Dr. Hali "Hal" Dia – Surgeon & Angela's boyfriend from Senegal
Alexandra Dufrane – Call girl madam
"White Willie" Duke – Drug King of Harlem
FBI Agents (NYC):
>   **Nuri Al-Bashir** – Brooklyn stake-out
>   **Nicolas Greco** – Chief/Organized Crime Unit
>   **Hank Kline** – Chief/Counterterrorism Unit
>   **Elizabeth Ross** – Assistant to Hank Kline
>   **Steve Watkins** – Brooklyn stake-out

Casey Flynn – Actor (plays chauffeur & Sal, the sexual predator)
Dr. Shelton Fritz – Chief Surgeon at Manhattan Medical Center
Raul Garcia – Owner/The Palace Discothèque
"Chainsaw Eddie" Giordano – Loan shark from New Jersey
Dr. Jorge Gonzalez – University Burn Center in Tucson
Roger Hamid – Director/Homeland Security in Phoenix
High School Bullies – Sheila Burns, Gloria Payne, Pamela Smith
Iraqi Citizens – Truck Driver, Wife & Brother
Jimmy – Nicky Bruno's bodyguard
Clarence Johnson – Former Marine & victim of Omar Karga

Omar Karga – Turkish slumlord
Vincent Leone – Don of prominent New York family
Paolo Mancini – Owner of Mancini's Trattoria in Harlem
Tommy Mancini – National Guard soldier, drug addict
Ciro Manza – Conti Family chef
Jose Medina – Border van burn victim
National Guardsmen – Cpl. Randy Jones & Sgt. Otis Hayes
Nigel Peach – Inferno's interior designer
NYPD:
       Detective Banks – Suicide Investigator
       Captain Gomez – SWAT Commander
       Two Officers – Serve death notice at Mancini's
       SWAT Teams – #1, #2, #3, #4
Ramon – Parking valet
Judge Lewis Randolph – NYC Children's Court jurist
Connie Ricci – Waitress (mother of Gina)
Dominic Romano – Bookie in Philadelphia
Dr. Hunter Rose – Psychiatrist
Sheriff Rex Royal – County Sheriff in Texas
Dino "Dimebag" Scarfetti – Drug dealer
Leonardo Scarpia – GM of Conti Construction
Anne Simon – Tony's ex-wife
Terrorists:
       Mustafa "The Ghost" Al-Anazi – International fugitive
       Kamel Al-Masud – Anazi's key operative
       Abbas "The Scorpion" & Turan – (Afghanistan)
       Abu Bakr & Kafil – (Yemen)
       Ahmed & Sayid – (Libya)
       Amal & Hasan – (Iraq)
       Mahdi & Sakhr – (Saudi Arabia)
       Hashemi – Iranian intelligence officer
Tony "Two Triggers" Tucci – Confidant of Don Mario & Driver
Tucci Family – Fabio & Rosalie Tucci (parents), Sophia (sister)
Victor Volkov – Russian arms dealer
Diego Zapata – Columbian cocaine exporter & Duke's partner

Acknowledgments

Special thanks to: Michael Sutin, Libbie Martin, Jack LeMenager, Dan Haight, Kevin McMurtry, and Jennifer Leonard for their suggestions and editing skills. Also, I am grateful for all my family and friends for their advice and encouragement.

About the Author

John Granville Leonard, a former ad man from San Francisco, lives and writes in Idaho.

Email: jgl3@mac.com